POLLY ❦ BOOK ONE

The Mystery of Bonney's Canyon

I M DAVIS

Polly:
The Mystery of Bonney's Canyon

ISBN-13: 978-0989083928
ISBN-10: 0989083926
LCCN: 2013940026
Global One Productions LLC Tygh Valley, OR

This book is dedicated to my great-grandmother
Polly Hayden O'Neal-Davis. Her stories (myth, fiction, or fact) have given
all of us the wonderment of adventure. Her spirit lives on within all of us.

Acknowledgments

If it had not been for a group of dedicated people inspiring me to tell my stories and to write, this book would not have been finished.

My thanks to Rusty Fisher, who inspired me and gave me encouragement to finish this book. My thanks to my son-in-law, Joe Mochnick, who read many drafts and gave me his wonderful comments and suggestions. My appreciation goes to Alice Hunter, who initially wrote a screenplay about my story of Polly that gave me the idea to write this book.

I could not have written this book without the dedication, support, and love of my wonderful wife, Laila Carolyn.

I would like to acknowledge that I would not have been inspired to write this book without all those wonderful stories that my mother and father told me over the years.

The people portrayed in this book are fictitious. This book is based on myth and stories that have been passed down over the generations in my family. Any resemblance to any person is purely coincidental.

Prologue

TYGH VALLEY, OREGON, 1869

At the foot of a snow-capped mountain, a rough shack nestled comfortably, no bigger than an outhouse, and a single golden light flickered through the front window across the wild landscape. Inside the humble dwelling, fifteen-year-old Polly O'Neal bit back tears and swallowed back pain and nausea as another contraction brought her nearly to unconsciousness.

She was a slip of a girl, as the women in town called her, lanky and bone-thin from malnutrition—a sparrow made of steel.

She'd been in labor for hours, all alone, save for Ada, standing judgmentally in the doorway. Too scornful to help, too obliged to look away, the old woman simply watched and scowled, hardscrabble face affixed with the same sour expression as she had worn when she'd heard Polly's first scream and come to her room.

Polly screamed now, beyond pain, blood trickling down her slender white thighs as the baby's head crowned. Instinctively, she pushed, if only to relieve the intense pressure she felt between her legs, and a great tearing rush spilled from her belly.

She wanted nothing more than to lie back and forget all that had happened, not just the birth, but the baby's conception. Still, even at her young age, Polly understood the fragility of life, and instinct took over once more as she took a deep breath and reached for the fleshy mass nestled between her legs.

Unrecognizable fluids leaked from her body as she took the trembling, quaking, blue-skinned baby in her arms. It was covered in grime and steaming, and she cleared the mucus and afterbirth from the poor child's mouth and nose. Immediately, it cried—no, it screamed. Shrill as it was, Polly was sure she'd never heard such a beautiful noise.

"Here," said the woman in the doorway, moving for the first time in a long spell. An object clattered to a stop next to her ratty, stained mattress. Polly looked down to see a crude penknife.

She didn't bother to thank the woman but reached down with a blood-stained hand, opened the knife, and severed the umbilical cord with crisp precision, the same skillful proficiency she used in her daily chores on the farm—chores, she was sure, would resume later that morning, newborn infant crying and suckling at her teat or not.

Polly felt no different than a cow in that regard but vowed to give this baby the best life had to offer. After all, it could only be better than hers, of that she would be sure.

But Polly's thoughts were suddenly interrupted as the woman advanced and without warning, ripped the child unceremoniously from her arms. Weakened by her traumatic delivery, Polly watching in shock as Ada crossed the room nimbly, leaving with the child, never to return. Polly screamed, and her howls wrenched through the night air, sending insects and rodents scampering away from the cabin and into the night for safe harbor.

As Polly's howls subsided and Ada failed to return, the harsh reality of where she'd gone began to fill her with a quiet, stoic grief. She drifted in and out of consciousness, strange sounds filling her head—doors opening and closing and strange shapes peering in at her, footsteps, the crunch of gravel underfoot, door knocks followed by harsh words, scrambling, a gunshot…finally, a horse galloping away. Was it all her imagination? Was her child safe? Was she even still alive?

As the haze in Polly's mind gradually began to clear, she rose up squinting, the long light of morning replaced with the cold noonday sun filtering through the humble shack's windows. As she struggled to stand, the events of the previous night began to rush back to her, and she made only a single vow: to find her child and bring her home.

Chapter 1

PRESENT DAY

Siobhan Davis stared out the train window, watching the Oregon landscape pass by just beyond the rattling tracks of the Amtrak commuter train. Although the train sped by the green grass and sparse trees at a steady clip, the landscape was so generic and broad it seemed like they were standing still.

The empty stretch of land seemed to go on forever, and to Siobhan, that was exactly how long it felt as if she had been staring at it. She felt tired and greasy from the journey but was unconcerned about her appearance; besides, she was too far gone for such concerns.

On the empty seat next to her sat a new paperback novel, untouched, an expensive magazine she didn't know why she had bought, and her purse, also untouched, except for the half-empty tube of breath mints she'd been nervously chewing ever since leaving the last station.

That was, what? Two towns ago? An hour back? A day? She shook her head, red hair framing her long, slender face. Her green eyes watched the trees blur by, and she imagined how slow going it must have been for the settlers moving west along the Oregon Trail so many years ago.

Siobhan blinked, catching her reflection in the smeared glass. She looked tired and sad but was powerless to alter the grim expression on her thirty-two-year-old face. She needed some sun, and she needed some sleep; she doubted she'd get either where she was headed.

Siobhan sighed, breath fogging the glass. As it cleared, she saw a shadow in the window; someone was standing behind her. She turned, slowly, too numb to be surprised, too weary to be frightened.

An older man, Native American, dressed in faded denim and handmade beads with a kind smile on his wizened face stood casually in the aisle, his gray hair pulled back in a ponytail, hat literally in hand.

She smiled up at him without speaking.

"Is that seat taken, ma'am?"

She shook her head, throat dry from nonuse as she croaked out, "No, no... of course."

She moved her paperback and magazine and stowed her purse under her seat, making room for the man. As she did so, she noticed the dozens of other empty seats in the passenger car.

The man sank wearily into the now-vacant seat and nodded appreciatively. He was tall and thin, his faded flannel shirt hanging off his bony shoulders, his leathery cheeks sunken, but his blue eyes wise and alive.

Again, she smiled. The man smelled clean and old, like fresh soap. His black cowboy hat was battered but looked expensive, and he rested it on his lap, troubling its brim with long, wrinkled fingers. He stared straight ahead, his nose long, his chin strong.

He finally looked over at her, nodding toward the slick, glossy *New Yorker* magazine on Siobhan's lap.

"Manhattan," he grunted, almost reluctantly. "The big city. Do you live there?"

Siobhan looked away, folding her arms unconsciously across her stomach. Under her breath, she mumbled, "Used to."

Turning away from her, as if as an afterthought, the old man grunted, "You're a long way from home."

Siobhan nodded, returning her eyes to the passing landscape, lost in her own thoughts, as if she were alone, as if the man—as well as the other occupants of the train—no longer existed. Outside her window, the countryside was so brilliant and green she had to blink, but she saw only her memories, blurred by the thickness of her tears…

The gel felt cold and sticky on her stomach, the handheld scanner tracing the outline of her swollen belly. The nurse wore expensive perfume, making Siobhan wonder absently, nervously, how much she made. She'd been having those kinds of stray, random thoughts lately.

No one told her that would happen during pregnancy—not the doctors, not the nurses, not the dozens of books he'd bought or downloaded on the subject.

A monitor glowed next to her, a black screen filled by a bright-blue triangle. The triangle was the picture being translated from the scanner on her belly, through a thin black wire, to the monitor. Whenever the young, petite nurse with the fancy perfume guided the scanner, the intense blue triangle on the screen changed.

Siobhan smiled, staring at the screen expectantly. "Hands," the nurse said, equally rapturous as she joined the expectant mother in staring at the screen. "Feet."

Her voice was intimate, conspiratorial, as if they were sorority sisters or both applying for the same job. Daniel stood just off to the side, close enough to be present but subtly apart from the girlishness that Siobhan and the nurse shared.

He was handsome and fit, dressed for work in his trademark gray suit and fitted black dress shirt with matching tie. His hair was prematurely gray at forty-six but distinguished and crisp around his athletic face and chiseled cheeks; he looked a good decade younger.

"You guys ready?" the nurse fairly squealed, her scanner gliding gently over the landscape of Siobhan's distended belly.

Siobhan flicked a glance at Daniel, who bit his lower lip nervously. He nodded at her; she nodded at the nurse.

"It's a girl!" she exclaimed.

Siobhan immediately reached for Daniel's hand, clutching it desperately. The hand was cold, unlike the smile that radiated over his proud, beaming face.

She thought, in that moment, he had never looked so handsome.

They drove home in silence, the sleek black car finding the downtown building on autopilot, both of them lost in thought. Only in the elevator, on the way to their penthouse loft, did Daniel finally smirk.

"If she looks anything like you, I'll have to build a moat around this building to keep the boys away."

Siobhan blinked, lost in thought, lost in time. She looked at the old man next to her, smiling to find him snoozing, his chin on his neck. His hands, veiny and weathered, still clutched the brim of his worn cowboy hat faithfully.

She looked back toward the window, guessing from the shadows cast by the towering trees that more than just a few minutes had passed as she traveled back in time to that glorious day when she'd learned she was going to have a daughter.

She closed her eyes once more, the present growing blurry, the past becoming clear. She dreaded going back there, and yet she couldn't stay away...

Daniel was talking when the elevator opened into the foyer. Harsh words, harsh tones. *Business,* Siobhan thought to herself, trying to occupy her mind with a random maternity magazine from the coffee table in front of the chaise lounge where she sat, head back, hands on her swollen belly.

He stopped at the kitchen counter, where two small bags rested on the barstool. He hung up the phone but didn't turn toward her.

"They were out of Clinique," he said, stuffing a small, blue vial into her makeup case, "so I got the Jergens just for now. The doctor said you shouldn't be in for more than a week, so..."

"Thank you," she started to say, grateful for his last-minute trip to the drugstore on the corner for the lotion she'd just run out of. But he was already gone.

He disappeared, as usual, into his office, his sleek Italian shoes clattering on the hardwood floors. She heard his desk chair squeak as he sat, no doubt to check his email.

She sat back on the sofa, trying—and failing—to get comfortable. She ignored the clock on the wall, knowing she still had a few hours before she was scheduled to check in at City Hospital for her C-section.

She heard Daniel's voice bark a question and almost turned to answer before realizing he was back on his cell, ranting to his business partner.

He walked toward her, stiff heels clattering on the marble tile. Siobhan turned, sliding her feet onto the floor with a smile. He stood above her, tightening his tie with one hand while grunting into his cell phone. "...the Peterson file needs to be copyedited," he was saying, "and I still need to get those attachments from legal before we can finalize Form B. OK, see you in ten..."

Her face dropped. "Daniel?" she asked. He checked his watch, clearly impatient. "Do you have to go? We're due at the hospital soon."

"I'm late already," he said, forcing a smile. "Don't leave this couch until I get back from the office."

She shook her head wearily. He leaned over, patting her hair and kissing her on the lips. His felt cold but lingered, as if desperate to say something his words could not. She tried to remember the last time they'd been intimate and stopped counting at two months.

"The baby," he'd claimed, but she knew—they both knew—it was more than that.

"Please, Daniel," she begged, grabbing his tie as he pulled away from her. "Don't go. It's not every day you become a father."

He gently dislodged the tie from her hands, smoothing it across his thin, flat stomach. Her voice broke as she confessed, "I'm nervous about the C-section."

"Siobhan..." He sighed, impatience oozing through his thin smile. "You'll be fine. Everything will be fine."

She felt bloated, fat, and pathetic, begging her husband to stay, but she couldn't help it. He looked down at her, adding, "We just have to finalize a couple of points on this deal. The office knows I'm going to be out of pocket during your delivery, so we just need to nail this down before I'm free. Listen, why don't you get yourself ready, and I'll be back before you know it."

She looked down at her maternity dress and simple sandals. Didn't he know she was already ready? That she'd been showered, dressed, and waiting since 4:00 a.m.?

"Why am I always your last priority?" she asked, hating the pleading tone in her voice.

"How can you say that?" he asked, looking genuinely shocked. He reached down to kiss her again, but she turned away.

The sun set a little lower, the shadows of the passing trees outside her window now longer, as Siobhan tried to shake off her memories. Her back and neck were sore from sitting so long, and she found her fingers flying to her antique necklace, a gold horseshoe on a chain. She fondled it nervously, an old habit.

The old man sitting next to her noticed her sudden activity. He was awake now and apparently alert. His hat still rested in his lap.

"Nice necklace," he said, nodding appreciatively.

She smiled and explained, "My mother's. Supposed to keep me safe. Doesn't always work…"

His long fingers reached up to clutch the necklace around his own throat. It looked older than hers, a turquoise and garnet Native American charm hanging from a simple leather thong around his neck. It was shaped like a teardrop, matching his wizened face, which looked like it had shed its share of tears. For now, he smiled. "Mine either."

The clock on the wall said 11:48. Their appointment was at noon. With cross-town lunch traffic, even if Daniel drove like a madman, they'd be at least fifteen minutes late. And if the stormy weather held, it might be even later.

She was standing, too anxious to sit any longer. Her calves already hurt; she'd stayed off them too often lately. She paced in front of the floor-to-ceiling window that looked out across the park, peering through the streaks provided by the steady rain that had been falling since morning.

Her fingers played with the good-luck charm around her throat: a simple gold horseshoe hanging from an even simpler gold chain. Daniel had never liked it; he called it "rustic," and so she rarely wore it anymore. But today, she needed it.

The rain continued to pelt the window as she peered outside. It was a slow, steady drizzle, the kind that settled in to stay all day. Down in the street, Siobhan watched a young child in red Wellington boots, playing in the downpour with a sense of abandon.

She smiled despite her anxiety, wondering if one day she'd look down from the window and spot her own daughter doing the same.

A faint buzz on the dining room table beckoned her. She found her sleek cell phone skittering across the table with an incoming text. "On my way," it said, from Daniel's number.

She sighed. It was code for, "I don't have time to come up and help you with your bags."

She grabbed them and walked to the door, pressing the black button to call for the elevator. Inside, she looked at herself in the blurry reflection of the brass doors as they closed.

She tucked a wisp of hair behind her ear and looked away, watching the floors light up as she passed.

"Care for an umbrella, miss?" asked the doorman as she headed toward the street.

"No thanks, Dexter. Mr. Davis will be here any moment."

Dexter tipped his hat and held the door. "Mind the awning, miss," he warned, looking up at the dismal gray sky. "Been leaking all morning."

She smiled and felt the dampness in the air as she stood near the street. Passersby jumbled around her, eager to get lunch before heading back to the office. They wielded their umbrellas like weapons, ignoring Siobhan's delicate condition and jostling her to and fro. She clutched her bags protectively against her stomach.

A few steps away, the little girl Siobhan had watched from upstairs continued to splash in the puddles, bouncing up and down in her bright-red boots.

"They're new," said her mother standing nearby, arms crossed over her chest protectively. "She couldn't wait to try them out."

Siobhan nodded. Just then, the woman noticed the bulge in her maternity dress and smiled.

Water splashed the woman and her daughter as Daniel tactlessly plowed into the curb, flinging open the door for her. "Get in!" he barked, pulling away before Siobhan could apologize to the poor woman.

"You're late," she snapped back as she shoved her bags in the back and quickly began buckling herself in while sliding onto the seat.

"I know," he confessed, jaw muscles working overtime as he fought aggressively through lunch traffic.

In the tense silence that followed, even the scrape of the windshield wipers sounded angry.

As they got closer to downtown, traffic naturally ground to a standstill. Siobhan could feel her blood pressure mounting and knew it wasn't good for the baby.

"Damn!" Daniel cursed as the street became a virtual parking lot. Siobhan closed her eyes, trying to steady her nerves. She opened them again when she felt movement. Daniel had found a gap in the next lane and squeezed himself in, glaring at the other drivers who dared to honk in protest.

"What's wrong?" he asked, almost sounding offended. "I said I'd get you there."

"It's not..." she began, pausing to take a breath so she wouldn't say what she really felt. "It's not...supposed to be like this."

Daniel ignored her, finding another opening in the next lane over and inching through the light just as it turned red. He hit the gas pedal and accelerated through the intersection, barreling toward the exit and down the off ramp.

The rain was coming down harder now. But no, no...that wasn't right. He was just driving too fast.

"Please," she urged, clutching her seat belt protectively. "Slow down, Daniel."

He ignored her, grim-faced as he white-knuckled the steering wheel, the wipers working overtime to battle the sheets of rain that were definitely pouring down harder now.

"Please, will you slow down?"

Daniel made a chuffing noise and rolled his eyes. "I thought you said we were late," he cracked. "It's obviously my fault, so I'm just trying to rectify the situation."

He risked a glance at Siobhan, whose eyes grew big as saucers while pointing out the window at the delivery truck that had just stopped in front of them. He saw it, too late, hitting the brakes and spinning the wheel at the same time.

The car swerved, hitting a puddle and hydroplaning wildly. The wheels kept spinning even as Daniel tried to stop them. Siobhan wanted to close her eyes, to shut out the images, to deny them, even as the driver's side slammed into the back of the truck.

The window shattered, sending an explosion of glass particles through the vehicle. The rain drove down mercilessly, splashing her face and joining her tears, filling her mouth as she screamed. She reached for Daniel, her hands bloody, but feeling no pain.

That was because it wasn't hers.

"Daniel!" she shouted, the sound of sirens rising distant in the background. But she knew, even as her eyes focused, even as she unbuckled her seat belt, even as she clutched his head in her hands, that he was gone.

His eyes stared, unblinking, at the shattered windshield. Blood oozed from his ears, his nose, his broken jaw. Already, his skin felt chilled, as if death was too impatient to wait around before dragging the soul from his limp, broken, and lifeless body.

She heard screeching and winced, as if the past were leaping from her mind and into her real life. But no, it was only the train pulling into the station. She looked up to find the old Indian stumbling away, hat on his head, not bothering to look back.

Was he just in a hurry, Siobhan wondered, or had she said something while buried back in time?

She found the window still foggy from her heavy breathing when she turned back to it. Beyond it, the sun had begun to set on the horizon, a waxing moon already visible in the sky.

The train continued chugging toward an empty station in the middle of nowhere. She looked down into her lap to find the magazine crumpled and sweaty in her hands, the paperback discarded in the seat back in front of her somewhere along the way. She left them both there, sliding her purse over her shoulder and reaching for the carry-on bag beneath the seat in front of her.

While other passengers rushed from their seats, Siobhan dragged her feet, walking to the back of her car to meet the porter and collect her bags. The air was chilly as she stepped from the train. She stacked her two pieces of luggage on the loading dock next to her and waited until the porter took her tip and tipped his hat good night.

She turned, heart stopping as she saw him standing there: Jesse.

He was smoking, leaning against a rail, looking hard as concrete and dull as dirt. His face was etched with the lines earned from his nine lives. He wore denim jeans, a flannel shirt, and a trucker's cap, and smoke curled around, in and out of his flared nostrils.

His eyes flashed a dark brown in the dim twilight as he noticed her, took one last drag, and dropped his cigarette to the loading dock floor, tamping it out under the heel of his weathered cowboy boots.

"Siobhan," he said, voice as gravelly as she remembered it.

"Hi, Jesse," she said, avoiding his penetrating glare.

He seemed at a loss for words. "Well, just look at you."

She looked away, self-conscious, before tucking a lock of hair behind her ear. She cursed herself mentally. It was a bad habit from her childhood.

She said nothing so he cleared his throat, reaching for a bag. "You must be tired."

"I slept most of the way," she lied, clutching the strap of her carry-on tight to her shoulder.

"These your only bags?" he asked, picking them up as if they weighed no more than a tumbleweed. She merely nodded in reply.

They walked for a moment, side by side. He was taller than she was by a few inches; the greasy ball cap made it one or two more. "Truck's over here," he said, aimlessly.

The parking lot was empty now, if it had ever been full. It was a tiny train station, in a tiny town, tucked away from the city or even the bigger towns. The air was heavy with the approaching night, the sun disappearing quickly as streetlamps flickered to life.

He placed the bags gently in the bed of the truck, and she added hers to the pile. He didn't hold the door open for her. She didn't expect him to. The truck started up with a crank and a wheeze, and then they were off, the streets silent if not deserted.

"You hungry?" he asked idly as they approached a small strip of off-market chains that seemed to have sprung up out of nowhere since she'd last been home. "Want to stop somewhere on the way home?"

"That's OK," she demurred, her stomach—her very body—feeling leaden and full. "I'm actually really tired."

Jesse nodded, rolling down the window. She held her arms to her chest as chilly air breezed in. He lit a cigarette and blew the first drag out of the open window.

He stared ahead, and so did she, except for the occasional glance at his profile when he looked in the rearview mirror as they passed through, and then beyond, the town.

His face was weathered and lined from years in the sun. His eyes looked sad, and she wondered if he thought the same about her.

"How are you, Jesse?" she blurted, breaking the silence when he caught her staring at him.

He shrugged noncommittally. "Fine. I guess, nothing much really changes 'round here."

He paused, risking a glance as they turned onto another deserted road. He cleared his throat, looked away, and added, "I'm sorry for your loss. It was good of you to come back. I didn't realize…"

Siobhan shifted uncomfortably in her seat. "Yes," she said, cutting him off. "I know. I was surprised to get your call."

After an awkward silence full of rattling wheels and bad shocks scooting over rutted roads, she finally asked, "How is my father?"

Jesse kept his eyes on the road and answered, soberly, "He's not well. No improvement."

"I see."

She looked out the window, fingers reaching instantly for her necklace. Toying with it, she watched as the battered truck passed battered mailboxes.

"And the ranch?" she asked, still looking out the window. "His precious land?"

"Business is better than ever," he insisted. Then, this: "I was wonderin' what you intend to do with it all. I mean, afterward?"

"Do I look like a farmer, Jesse?" she snapped, voice sounding harsher—and louder—than she'd intended. She instantly felt foolish and bad for Jesse.

He frowned, and she resisted the urge to apologize. "I'll get my father the care he needs and then…"

Her voice trailed away. He drove, and, after a mile or two, she added, more quietly this time, "I don't need six thousand acres on my hands on top of everything else."

Jesse nodded, unable to hide his disappointment. She fumed; it couldn't be helped. He said nothing more, merely reached for the radio and turned the old-fashioned knob. Patsy Cline crackled to life from the preset country station, belting out something about an old photograph and a long-lost lover. She scowled, rolling her eyes.

Before she could unload on him again, he turned down the volume until the crooner was little more than background music for their quiet country drive.

As the song changed, she stared out the window, watching as the faded sign for "Bonney's Canyon" came and went. She sat, dry-mouthed, until Jesse pointed out the window. "Speak of the devil…"

There was nothing to see at the moment but acres and acres of thick forest on the side of the empty, two-lane highway. It was all they'd seen for miles, and if they kept driving, it would be all they'd see for miles upon miles more.

The horizon glowed with the last of the day's sun, a brilliant orange stripe giving way to darkness. Jesse took the familiar turn off the main highway, the incline dipping steeply as the truck went from pavement to brick pavers.

There, in the canyon below, a modern ranch stood where once upon a time a simple shack had been all that existed on the Davis land. It was several stories, with thick beams on the extended porch and a large, circular driveway.

The truck rattled to a stop in front of wide double doors that led to an expansive foyer.

The engine ticked long after Jesse turned it off. They both sat there, in the silence of dusk. At last, he turned to her, breath smelling vaguely of nicotine.

"Welcome home," he said, without a trace of irony.

Chapter 2

Jesse opened the doors with a familiar air and placed her bags inside the front doors, one by one. Siobhan followed him with her carry-on clutched to her side as if it were a security blanket. The foyer was large and expansive, with deep, dark Mexican-tiled floors and a large round table in the middle of the floor. On the table sat an arrangement of dying flowers, a fitting symbol for the air of gloom that seemed to fill the house itself.

There was the stale scent of age trapped in the air. Although it had clearly been masked with air fresheners and the like, Siobhan could sense it in her very cells. She shivered and clutched her arms across her chest defensively.

Inching forward, she frowned with disdain at the dusty hunting trophies mounted along the walls of the grand entrance and, clearly, beyond. The entire ranch house looked as hokey and homey on the inside as it did on the out-side. Stepping from the tiled foyer onto the hardwood floor of the living room, Siobhan heard the echoes of her heels reverberate through the silent house.

She stood, the silence washing over her, weighing on her, stifling her, her face like a mask as she stared at the knickknacks that covered the heavy oak furnishings and lined the walls.

Jesse stood patiently in the foyer, behind her, waiting. She turned and said, "Where is he?"

He looked down a long, dark hallway and then, turning back to her, simply hooked his thumb in the general direction. She looked wistfully up the main staircase, wanting nothing more than to retreat to her room, take a scalding hot shower, and cry herself to sleep.

Instead, she followed him as Jesse stepped into the hallway. Everywhere, it was dark—dark floors, dark walls—with a cracked-open door at the end of the hall the only source of light.

They walked slowly, as if he too dreaded what they'd find at the hall's end. Gradually, the familiar sounds of automated medical equipment began to confront them: the hiss of a ventilator and tubes and dials clicking, thumping, and pumping. Siobhan steeled herself as Jesse waited, just beyond the door.

She greeted him with a droll "Yeah, thanks" face and pushed the door open until she could see into the sprawling room. Like the rest of the house, the room was massive, but all the focus seemed to be around the occupant's bed.

Zachariah sat at the foot of it, frail, withered, in his seventy-eighth year. His hair was wispy and white atop his nearly skeletal head, his once healthy frame eaten away by disease. His face was covered by a blue-and-white-striped pajama top the young nurse was helping slide onto his body. It matched the baggy pajama pants that covered his pale, stick-thin legs.

The pajama top came down, and Siobhan gasped to see the age spots and hollow cheeks that marked Zachariah's face. He looked at her standing there, one foot on the bedroom floor carpet, the other still in the hallway.

His lips moved silently, papery thin, his nostrils quivering as his eyes drank her in. Then the pale lips parted, and he whispered weakly, "Polly?" His voice was soft and frail and yet persistent. "Is that you?"

Somehow, the nurse stood and with finality, with strength, slammed the door shut. Nose inches from the door, Siobhan finally exhaled.

Jesse was still there, standing stoically behind her, and she turned to him. "How long has he been like this?"

Jesse shook his head and turned, motioning for her to follow. She was glad to be leaving the long, dark hallway.

"It comes and goes," he explained. "The confusion between the present, the future, and the past. Try not to worry."

They made their way back to the foyer, standing next to the table with the drying flowers. "He's so frail," she said.

She was having a hard time reconciling the frail, fragile man in the baggy pajamas with her father. Her once handsome, broad-shouldered, tough-as-nails father.

"That's the way it takes them, I believe," Jesse explained, his voice cool and calm in the otherwise silent house. "Makes them weak. Hurts their immune system."

Siobhan shook her head gravely. "But he doesn't even know who I am. He called me 'Polly.'"

Jesse shrugged. "He lives mainly in the past nowadays. I wouldn't take it too personal."

Siobhan felt his rough hand on her shoulder and turned, looking up into his lined, weather-beaten face.

"Try not to worry," he said, in a weak attempt to comfort her.

She barely heard him. "Polly," she mumbled, following him up the stairs as he showed her to her room. "I haven't heard that name since I was a child…"

Chapter 3

OREGON TRAIL, 1866

The wagon wheels crunched over bone-dry earth, filling the hot, dusty air with plumes of wheat-colored sand. Her stockings were thick with it, her shoes coated in it; it filled the crow's feet beside each green-colored eye, the corners of her mouth, and the sides of her nostrils.

The landscape bled beneath the creaking wheels, hot, low, and flat. A high midday sun cast harsh shadows in the dirt, and a bead of sweat trickled down the back of Sarah O'Neal's neck. She let it, glad for the brief respite from the heat it provided.

In the distance, a long train of pioneer wagons rattled its way across the plain. Dust clouds billowed out behind the creaking wheels as Sarah struggled to keep up.

Muscular oxen, their flanks shiny with sweat, pulled their heavy loads inexorably on toward the West, where the land was free and green and cool and ripe.

Sarah's face and neck were sunburned, but so was everyone else's—besides, she had bigger things to worry about at the moment. Nearly thirty, dry as a bone and thin as a sparrow, she clutched her dirty white bonnet to her head and scrambled forward, fighting the dust clouds and ignoring the stench that rose from the nearest team of aching, stumbling oxen.

"Polly!" she cried out, searching the dry, barren landscape for her thirteen-year-old daughter. "Polly?"

Her voice was carried away by the howling wind that turned canyons into dust storms and dirt into screaming, flying projectiles.

"Polly?" she cried, throat sore from calling after the young girl. "Where in tarnation are you?"

Her husband, Patrick, walked a few steps ahead, hand atop his hat, broad shoulders bent into the howling wind. His boots were covered in dirt and dust, and his pants needed a good cleaning, but it had been days since they'd found a water hole and it would have to wait. She sprinted to catch up to him, tugging on his suspenders to get his attention.

"Is that you doing all that hollering back there, Sarah?" His face was square-jawed and corn-fed, at least what you could see of it over his thick, full black beard.

"Yes, I've been screaming!" Sarah exclaimed. "I'm looking for our daughter. Have you seen Polly?"

Patrick shrugged, his favorite mode of expression. "Probably off exploring again," he chuckled. "You know how bored the kids get this time of day. Sarah, honey, she won't be far."

Sarah shook her head, dropping back and nearly stumbling over the tall woman in black behind her. "Ada!" Sarah gasped, looking up into the woman's severe, strained face. "Have you seen my daughter, Polly?"

Ada was scornful and severe, her thin frame covered from head to toe in black mourning dress. A Catholic crucifix hung from around her neck, glinting in the noonday sun.

21

"No," she answered with a sniff, her voice tight and tinged with low-country squalor. "No, ain't see nuthin' all day."

Sarah didn't trust the woman, or her blunt, no-nonsense reaction. "Where's your boy gone?" she asked, shielding her eyes from the sun with her hand.

"Fetching water," Ada said matter-of-factly, avoiding Sarah's eyes.

Sarah squinted into the harsh light, wondering if Polly might have tagged along for the ride.

Chapter 4

Polly hitched up her dowdy pink skirt and climbed fearlessly through the small crack between two boulders. They surrounded her on either side, their shade providing the day's first break from the scorching heat. Polly knew her mother would be mad at her if she found out, but she just couldn't help it.

Following the wagon train all day, turning in to bed each night just after dark, Polly felt like if she didn't break away for just a few minutes, she'd… she'd…burst!

She'd spotted more boulders across the plain, figured the distance by squinting her eyes and licking her thumb, and the minute her mother turned to talk to the woman beside her, she lit out across the flat, dusty land.

She'd looked back once or twice, but fortunately, the dust from the wagon wheels had camouflaged her escape. Now, she'd made it all the way to the rocks and wanted to see what treasure she might find buried beneath.

She knew she had to get back before her mother missed her, but if she could have just a few minutes, ten maybe, tops, she'd at least have one adventure to keep her mind off the rest of the long, monotonous journey.

Just as Polly had hoped, the rocks held more than met the eye, and she almost shrieked with joy to see they revealed the opening to a cave—dark and cool and just waiting to be explored.

Entering the cavern, she found the floor was made of soft, dark sand and a faint light filtered in from above. Polly stepped carefully and made her way further in, hands running along the rugged sides as she proceeded forward with caution. Once her eyes had finally adjusted to the darkness, she gazed up at the large stone walls rising before her. They were worn smooth, and Polly gasped as she realized they were covered with crude Native American carvings of birds, deer, and scenes of hunting and tribal warfare.

She traced them with her fingertips, the stone wall cool and aloof under her dry, trembling fingertips. Suddenly, a noise came from outside and a smattering of dirt fell from the path she'd just wandered down.

"Who's there?" she asked, shielding her eyes to the harsh glint of sun with her hand. There, at the cave entrance, half in shadow, stood Ike. He was a stocky, rough redhead, worn elbows poking through his shirtsleeves, dark stains surrounding his armpits.

He stood perfectly still, staring at Polly.

"Get out of here, Ike," she stammered. "You shouldn't have—" but before she could finish, he swiftly leaped to the ground and covered her mouth with one dry, dirty hand.

She wriggled in his grasp as his other hand quickly dragged her to his side. His eyes were wide, and he smelled of sweat and anger, and she whimpered as he pressed her against the cold stone wall, yanking his hand away from her mouth only to hike up her skirt.

"No," she gasped, gulping in huge gasps of air and panting. "Please don't do this."

His brown eyes grew dark as he yanked a ball of twine from his tattered pocket and used it to frantically tie her hands behind her back. Then he smiled, yanking open the front of her dress as her tears began to fall.

His voice was husky and low. "You're real pretty, Polly. I see the way you smile at me sometimes."

He had sharp rat-like features, and his red hair was greasy and damp, like his skin.

Despite her fear, Polly found her voice. "I never smiled at you."

Ike toyed with the buttons of her blouse until it fell away from her petticoat. She felt embarrassed—and exposed. No boy had ever seen her like this before. Shoot, her own pa had never seen her so undressed! "You've been leading me on for months," he rasped menacingly, licking his thick, leathery lips with a dry tongue. "You give me these urges."

"I never," she gasped, trying to push him away. "Mama told me to be friendly on the trail; that's all!"

He chuckled, piggish eyes never leaving her heaving chest. "We're about to get real friendly, sweetheart!"

Polly's heart was hammering, her pulse pounding in her ears as he caressed her bare arms with his meaty fingers, but she composed herself, trying to reason with the boy.

"Ike, I know you just lost your daddy and you must be missing him something awful, but please—"

Ike's eyes went black, and her words seemed to go straight through him, disappearing into the darkness around them. His caress turned to a hard grip as he yanked her forward, hands clenched around her bony arms. "Don't talk to me about that God-fearing son of a bitch," he spat, spittle flying onto her face. She turned her head as she tried to avoid the intensity of his wide eyes.

"He's better off dead in the ground where he can't hurt anyone no more. I'm in charge now. Don't need to answer to him no more. Don't need to answer to no one…"

His eyes had glazed over halfway through his speech, as if he'd forgotten she was there. He often did that on the trail, stumbling along as if in a haze, one of the living dead. Not that she paid him much mind. For the last few days, he and his mother had been hitching along with them, quietly studying them as they walked or rode or slept or ate. Suddenly, jerked back to reality, he fancied her with a leering smile as the last of her clothes fell to the ground.

He smiled even as she bent into herself, trying to hide her woman's self from his wide, eager eyes. He grunted as he fell to his knees, bending to her trembling, naked body.

His breath was warm and rank against her quivering belly as he choked out, "You won't tell anyone about this, Polly. No one. You hear me?"

It wasn't a question. She squealed, heart hammering, throat dry, forcing her knees together to prevent the inevitable. But he yanked them roughly apart with one hand while unbuckling his belt with the other.

"You'll bring shame on your whole family if they find out." He was breathing hard now, panting as his pants fell to around his ankles. He wasn't talking to her, so much as at her.

She bit her lip and tried to look away as he yanked down his dirty undergarments, yellow and stained as his manhood pressed against her thigh. She screamed, and he covered her mouth with his own, his tongue rough and hard against her teeth as he forced them open and slid inside.

With the taste of him still in her mouth, he pulled away, kissing her neck and her chest with his dry, rough lips. "I'll tell 'em you made me do it," he gasped, fumbling between her legs as he grunted and shoved. "I'll tell 'em it's your fault. Your ma will never forgive you…"

"That's a lie," she croaked, voice tight with emotion.

"Who the hell cares?" He chuckled, rough hands fiddling between her tender white thighs.

She gasped as he plunged himself into her, filling her until she was breathless and backed into the cold cave wall. He was rough and smelly, his body hairy and naked against her own. Her head bounced back against the wall as he filled her, twice, three times, four until he grunted, a spasm jerking his body and he pushed her away.

She cowered and looked away as he dressed and fell to the ground when he yanked the twine from around her hands. Her wrists ached as the circulation rushed back into them, and she lay, curled up in a ball, her tears mixing with his sweat on the dusty cave floor.

She cried until her eyes were dry, and when she looked up, Ike was gone, leaving nothing behind but her naked, bent body and the pile of clothes he'd torn off of her. She dressed with trembling hands, wiping the blood from her thighs with the bottom of her left stocking, which she then buried in her long, black boots.

She stumbled from the cave, struggled up through the boulders and gasped to find her mother standing near the entrance, watching Ike as he retreated across the plain to catch up with the rumbling stagecoaches snaking across the prairie.

Sarah's face was a mask of emotions, blank and composed. She took Polly's hand and yanked her from the cave opening, dragging her across the hot, dusty plain.

"Didn't I warn you?" she hissed as the last wagon in line came into view. "It's dangerous out there, Polly. You'll get hurt if you keep running off like that."

They were almost back now, and Polly could see Ike, a smile on his beady little face, stuffing the back corner of his yellow shirt into his brown britches.

Her mother's voice was even and blunt as she dragged Polly forward, nails digging into her wrist as she stomped across the hard, dusty land. "Men aren't to be trusted out on these plains, to say nothing of boys."

Their wagon was buried in the midst of the others; she knew it by the red lantern that hung from the back frame. It dangled there, day and night, and clanked now as they drew near.

Her mother was breathing heavily now and reached into the back of the wagon for a length of rope.

"No, Momma," Polly gasped as she saw it. But her mother would hear none of it. She grabbed the young girl's hands, barely pausing when she saw the angry red gashes around her wrists where Ike's twine had cut into her during her ordeal. "Please, Momma, no!"

Sarah shook her head decisively, tying Polly to the back of the wagon, knotting the rope angrily, as if irritated by its very existence. Or, Polly thought, angry at hers.

Polly, flushed and ashamed, couldn't meet her mother's gaze.

"I'm sorry, Momma," she stammered. "I promise I won't do it again."

"That's all well and good, Polly," Sarah huffed as she stomped alongside Polly at the back of their wagon. "But talk is cheap, and if you won't tell me where you went, you can't be trusted. You'll just have to be tied to the back of the wagon like the younger children."

Polly's legs were sore, and they itched in between. Her skin was bruised and her heart sad as she began to tear up. "Please, Momma," she sputtered, stumbling along in her dusty boots, "don't do this to me."

Her mother's eyes were filling up, too.

They looked at each other, both crying, both angry and sad and wounded at the same time. "What happened down there, Polly? Tell me."

Polly opened her mouth, only to shut it again as she heard Ike's voice, joshing with his friends as they strode by, ignoring her, without a care in the world. Ike's chuckle died on a burst of wind, but Polly found her eyes cast downward, staring at dust fluffs as they rose from the sand.

"Nothing, Momma," Polly lied, the sound of Ike's voice ringing in her ears, the words he'd said in that cave etched on her heart, the taste of his tongue ready to be spit from her mouth.

Polly watched as her mother stared daggers at Ike's sweaty back. "Hey, boy," Sarah called out, turning to face him.

Ike turned, a slow, snide sneer upon his face. He stared directly at Polly and then said, "Ma'am?"

"The water you were supposed to be fetching, boy? Where is it?"

Ike stared back fiercely at Sarah, but she was not a woman to be bowed easily. Polly offered a little smile of satisfaction as he looked away, shaking his head and muttering to himself as he grabbed a bucket from a nearby wagon and tromped back toward the rocks where he'd taken her virginity—and so much more.

Chapter 5

Polly poked a stick at the dying embers of the campfire. Ever since her run-in with Ike, she'd been angry for no reason, sullen at the oddest times, giddy one minute and downtrodden the next. She had no control over her emotions, it seemed, other than to feel guilt at all times—guilt and shame.

She should have listened to her mother, Polly thought, and stayed with the wagon and not gone running off on some fool's errand. Now she was paying the price.

If only she and her mother, Sarah, could be alone by the fire. But the group they were traveling with was so large, and leave it to Sarah to have taken Ada and her ugly son Ike under her wing.

As usual, after a long day on the trail, Ada cried quietly into her handkerchief as Sarah tried to comfort her.

"There, there," said Polly's mother. "It will all work out; you'll see. It's just this long journey. It seems endless, I know."

Ada sniffed dramatically, blowing her nose into her black handkerchief, which matched her black gloves and black bonnet and the swooping black dress that fell to her dusty black shoes.

"This is no place for a woman without a man," she complained, her voice hoarse and dry from another long day on the trail. "I'll never survive in this world alone."

Sarah placed a comforting arm around Ada's shoulders. Her voice grew serious. "I'm sorry, Ada. Seamus was a good man. He didn't deserve his fate. I'll help you as best I can." Sarah looked over at Polly, who blinked back in the smoke spitting from the rough fire. "Polly and I will both help you, won't we, dear?"

Polly nodded dutifully, though helping Ada or her lecherous son was the last thing she wanted to do. Her skin crawled every time either of them looked at her, and they knew it. Instead, they worked on her mother, taking advantage of her kindness and charity.

Ada ignored the little girl. "It's all right for you, Sarah. You have a husband."

Sarah looked stung by the reproach, and Polly felt bad for her. Here she was trying to help this horrible woman, and all she could do was screech and complain. Polly poked the fire a little harder with her stick, feeling the sting from the flames as it flared before dying back down.

When the smoke cleared, Polly looked up to find Ike standing in the shadows. Startled, she sat up stiffly. *Where had he come from?* she thought. He hadn't been there a second earlier. But that was Ike. He skulked in the shadows and knew more than a thing or two about creeping up on people, especially Polly.

He was chewing on a long weed, the yellow kind that smelled like moldy hay. It didn't seem to bother him, but then, since Ike smelled like a horse stall himself, how could it? His lips were thin and gray and covered with spittle in the flickering firelight.

Stepping from the shadows, he said, "You just need to find yourself a new husband then, Ma."

His voice slithered off his tongue, like a snake crawling from his belly. Polly shivered and looked away, seeing only his rough hands; his long, pale belly; and his dropped trousers in the flickering flames.

Ada looked up sharply at her son, that thin, leathery, weasely face gradually smiling. Ike smiled back, and they both looked at Sarah. Polly didn't like it, not one bit. They were up to something, those two. They always were. How could her mother not see that?

"Polly," Sarah snapped, rising to her feet. Already, Ada and Ike were having a bad influence on her mother, who seemed to be showing off for her guests. "Quit playing with that fire and see to your chores."

Polly groaned aloud and stood, her heels kicking up dust as she gathered the tin plates from their evening meal. Using water from the barrel at the back of their wagon, she rinsed off the plates and tin cups and dried them off before setting them back in the tackle box and shutting it tight.

Sarah turned from the group, embarrassed to be seen knitting her socks for the third night in a row. Not far away, Ada opened a can of peaches for dessert, spreading them out carefully on a plate.

They had settled into a routine of sharing meals, Sarah and Polly and Ada and Ike, and while it had never been fun, now it was downright painful. Polly wished she could tell her mother what Ike had done, but Ike's threat hung angrily in her brain: "I'll hurt your ma and pa something terrible if you ever tell!"

Ike was a seedy, angry, sneaky boy, and though her pa could whip him in a fair fight, Polly would never trust Ike to fight fair. Besides, bullies never picked on the menfolk. It was her mother, Sarah, that Polly really worried about.

Polly sat back down by the fire, drawing Ike's name in the sand and then crossing it out angrily, over and over again, wishing she could do the same with the boy himself. She felt a thump against her head and looked up as the empty peach can that had just struck her fell to the sand at her feet.

She jumped up, not surprised to see Ike standing in front of her with a grin on his face. Polly scowled, rubbing her head. His face was positively beaming, only making her hate him all the more. She bent to grab the can from the ground and toss it in the waste bin with the rest of the night's scraps, but she could barely fit her hand around it.

She soon saw why; the can was bulging. She knew what that meant; the peaches had spoiled, and spoiled canned goods only spelled one thing: botulism.

Ada's jaws were clenched as she watched Polly stand there, the swollen can in both hands. "Ike," she called loudly, though her son was right there by her

31

side, as always. "Bring these peaches over to Sarah so she can have some dessert after a nice, long day on the trail."

"No," Polly protested, keeping her voice down lest her mother hear as she darned her socks. "These peaches are bad. The can is swollen. They'll make someone sick."

Ada waved her black-gloved hand in the air. "Don't be ridiculous, child," she scoffed. "There's nothing wrong with them. Is there, Ike?"

But while Polly had faced off against Ada, shoving the swollen can in her face, Ike had disappeared.

Polly looked around for him frantically, only to find him leaning down toward Sarah, the plate of peaches extended like an offering at church.

Sarah smiled, putting down her socks, and reached for a peach.

"*No!*" Polly shouted, tearing across the prairie dirt and stumbling toward her mother. "Momma, please don't eat them. They're bad."

Polly's voice was shrill, as shrill as Ada's face as she watched from a careful distance.

Sarah turned to stare at her daughter, looking up in disbelief.

"Polly, what *is* the matter with you?" Her mother's voice was low and scolding; she didn't like it when Polly acted up in front of company.

"Momma," Polly gasped, still out of breath from shock and sprinting around the fire. "I saw Ike and Ada take the peaches from a can. It was swollen. Remember how Daddy warned us about botulism? Those peaches could hurt you, Momma, even kill you."

Sarah sat there, mouth wide, eyes skeptical.

"They're trying to hurt you," Polly pleaded.

Ada walked up from behind, passing within inches of Polly and bringing with her a cold wind and a colder heart.

"The child is talking nonsense, Sarah," said the old widow, voice dripping with scorn.

Ada turned toward her son, giving him that same conspiratorial look they had shared before Ike had lobbed the empty can of peaches at Polly's head. "There's nothing wrong with the peaches, is there, Ike?"

Ike turned on his polished charm, using what Polly's father liked to call his "church voice" as he preened, "No, ma'am."

Sarah nodded at the two and then turned her attention back to Polly. Her face was more concerned than angry now, and she asked, "Polly, please tell me what's wrong?"

Polly desperately wanted to but knew she couldn't. Instead, she raised her voice again, turning her back to Ada and Ike. "Don't eat them, Momma. She's lying."

"Polly!" Sarah bleated, her face growing cross and coarse in an instant. "That is a very serious accusation." Sarah looked up at Ada with apologetic eyes.

"I promise you," Polly tried once again, the emotion making her voice crack. "Please don't eat them. They'll make you sick."

Polly tried to push the plate out of Sarah's hands, but Sarah kept a firm grip.

Ada clearly saw an opportunity and, with predatory zeal, zoomed in for the kill. "The child's clearly gone mad, Sarah. For whatever reason, she's taken against us. Been brooding and miserable for days. You have to admit it your own self, Sarah."

Polly fumed. It was almost as if Ada knew why she'd been "brooding and miserable" and was using it to taunt her, right in front of her own mother!

Polly suddenly got an idea and gushed to her mother, "Make her eat them, Momma. If them peaches are fine, then just let Ada eat them first to prove it. You'll see; she won't."

Sarah shook her head, but Ada had already backed up to where she was out of range of the plate still resting in Sarah's hands.

"See, Momma?" Polly gloated, nearly dancing in glee. "See? She won't. She won't eat 'em, and neither will Ike. Because they both know them peaches are bad, Momma."

Ada crossed her thin, bony arms over her equally bony chest. "Why, this is absurd. Don't you have more pride in yourself, raising a daughter who'll sass you—and others—like that?"

Sarah was speechless, looking up at Ada as the woman continued to rail, "This here's the most ridiculous conversation I've ever had in all my born days. I'm a Christian for the love of God. I ain't being badmouthed like this."

Sarah finally stood, taking Polly by the shoulder. "I'd like a word in private with my daughter, please."

Ada clucked a tongue, grabbing Ike by the shoulder as well. "I'm sure you would," she said as she and Ike slunk away, preferring to watch from a distance.

Polly looked up at her mother, her face pinched, her eyes wounded. "Polly," she said quietly, "what's gotten into you? This isn't like you, sweetheart."

Polly shook her head but remained tight-lipped.

"If you tell me what's wrong, honey, I won't eat the peaches. I promise."

Polly's eyes widened with promise. It was on the tip of her tongue, what she couldn't say. She cast a look at Ada and Ike, watching from a distance. They were practically rubbing their hands with glee.

"I...I can't, Momma."

Sarah huffed and crossed her arms over her chest. "Then you leave me no choice."

"No, Momma. Don't do that. Please believe me, Momma. Don't eat them."

"Tell me, Polly." Her mother's voice was part pleading, part distant.

"I can't. Don't make me."

Sarah inched closer, whispering, "Why have you been so upset these past few days?"

Polly stared at the ground, her eyes welling up with tears.

Her mother's voice grew more insistent, more pleading. "What is it, honey?" Then, when Polly wouldn't confess, her mother's voice...changed. It grew colder, less personal. "Well, are you going to tell me or not?"

Polly could only shake her head, literally biting her lip to keep from confessing.

Now Sarah's voice was disappointed and loud, as if for Ada and even Ike's benefit. "I'm sorry, Polly," she said, turning toward the fire and drifting back to the plate of peaches she'd left there. "I thought you trusted me more than that."

Polly was exhausted, shocked, frightened, and frozen. She stood alone, apart from the fire, away from her mother, and started to cry, to weep in great blubbering sobs. "No," she pleaded, reaching out a trembling hand but unable to move her feet. "Please, Momma, don't."

Almost defiantly, Sarah grabbed a peach from the plate and bit into it with relish. It happened so fast, there was nothing else Polly could do. Her mother flinched at the taste. Even in the firelight, Polly could see the peaches were discolored.

"Momma!" Polly said, finding her voice, if not her legs. "No!" she screamed.

But Sarah only reached down, lifted another peach, and slid it into her mouth. Ike and Ada no longer looked at Sarah, but Polly could sense they congratulated each other with their eyes.

Polly fell to her knees, weeping.

Chapter 6

Morning came to the sprawling ranch, but Siobhan had been awake for nearly an hour by the time the sun crested the horizon, throwing golden light on the north face of the house.

She watched it creep through the slats of her room and splash against the far wall until at last it threatened to spill over onto her pillow. Reluctantly, she hauled herself out of bed, wrapping her naked shoulders in the bathrobe she'd had waiting at the edge of the bed.

It felt funny waking up in a different bed from the one she was used to, especially this bed, in this house, now. She tried to rid her mind of the troubling thoughts that had opened her eyes while it was still dark out, but they only stayed trapped in the cobweb that was her mind.

She pulled the robe tighter around her, padding on bare feet to the window and staring out. The ranch proper spanned for endless acres of unbroken land. It looked fallow and dusty in the morning light, and she fleetingly wondered how Jesse, the lone ranch hand, managed it all.

A flash of light caught her eye from below, and she looked down to see her father's nurse wheeling him out into the morning sun. His head was mostly bald, and what remained of his hair was only a fine thatch of off-white bristles. The emaciated look she'd noticed in his room last night was even more pronounced in the harsh light of day, and his thin, frail hands trembled on the armrests of his wheelchair, pale and eerily skeletal.

Her head ached, and she realized she would have to face him sooner or later. She slipped into jeans, a flannel shirt, and comfortable flats and tied her hair back. She smirked to think how quickly she'd adapted to ranch life. Back home, she'd never be caught dead without her makeup on and a power suit, which was her uniform of sorts. Yet here, the jeans and worn shirt looked only too natural.

The house was silent as she drifted down the stairs, the soles of her topsiders whispering along the old-fashioned plush carpet. In the kitchen, she poured herself a mug of coffee, hot and black, and took it with her onto the porch.

Her father sat, wincing against the sun. His nurse sat quietly in the wicker rocker next to him, lost in a thick paperback, which featured a swarthy, muscular man adorned in a kilt and little else on the cover. She looked up as Siobhan stepped on a creaky floorboard and then quickly buried her nose back in her book.

Siobhan sipped her coffee to steady her nerves, a simple pleasure, the pure caffeine like a tonic, instantly shredding through and relieving her throbbing head. If only her emotional problems could be solved so easily.

Her father still hadn't noticed her, or maybe he was purposefully ignoring her. She cleared her throat to get his attention, but he barely flinched.

"Zachariah. It's me—Siobhan."

There was a long moment, followed by a pregnant pause. Siobhan nervously sipped her coffee, tempted to give up and go back in, but ultimately unwilling to back down. Then the chair roused itself to life and, slowly, squeaking all the while, turned itself around.

Her father's face was wizened and severe. He winced with every turn of the wheel that slowly brought them face-to-face. "You came," he said.

"How are you doing?" she asked, putting the cup down on the window ledge beside her. Like everything else on the sprawling ranch, it was wide enough to support the oversized mug and then some.

The look on Zachariah's face was an unspoken answer to her question. He looked pained and fragile, and she was surprised he wasn't already gone.

His voice was angry, accusatory as he wagged a gnarled, skeletal finger in her general direction. "Did you come to pack me off then? Is that it? To let me die alone in some nursing home?"

She had been prepared for his venom but not this much, not this soon. She bit her lip and crossed and then uncrossed her arms. "The doctor said you can't manage anymore," she managed to say evenly. "The ranch is too big. It's just too much."

He made a *harrumph* sound and licked his thin, gray lips. His voice was scratchy, as if the early morning confrontation had already worn him out. "It's my home." He wagged a curved finger over his bony shoulder at the nurse. "I have help."

The nurse seemed to sense it; she looked up and rolled her eyes before returning to the book. She was a large woman, her hefty hands on either side of her book, covered with freckles, like her face. Her hair was auburn blond, leaning more to the strawberry side, cut short no doubt for simplicity over style.

Siobhan looked back down at her father. "This isn't news to you, Dad. The doctor says it's not enough."

He waved his hand aggressively, snorting and turning away from her. "The doctor says…" he mimicked in his thin, reedy voice. "The doctor says…"

His voice trailed away, but his jaw was set.

She sighed. "I didn't come here for a fight, Dad."

He glared at her. "No, you came to pack me off to a nursing home so you can sell everything off behind my back."

The nurse looked up as if debating whether it was appropriate to intervene; she quickly seemed to decide against it and returned to her book. Siobhan shook her head, sighed heavily, and reached for her coffee mug with a wavering hand, eager to take the time to compose herself.

She took a sip, counted to ten, and put the mug back down. Her voice was surprisingly calm when she replied, "You asked me to come."

"I didn't," he spat angrily, hands trembling on the armrests of his wheel-chair. "It was that meddling ranch hand of mine."

"Jesse." She looked away, catching the glint of sunlight on the wire that ran between the fence posts on the perimeter of Zachariah's property line.

When she turned back, her eyes had turned cold and her voice chilly. "Meddling, huh? You don't deserve his friendship or his loyalty one bit."

Zachariah somehow managed to look menacing as he looked back at her, lips thin and voice equally icy. "What do you know, girl? I haven't seen you in over ten years. I'm not dying in a nursing home. Whatever the doctor might tell you."

Now it was Siobhan's turn to flash anger. "They can't look after you here, old man," she taunted. She knew she was treading on thin ice but continued, "What if something were to happen? We're miles away from anywhere, in-cluding the nearest hospital. You know this, yet you refuse to listen to reason. Anyway, you're not dying. You've got years left in you yet."

"Give me a break," he grumbled. "I'm dying, Siobhan. You know it; I know it. Even Ms. Hargraves over there knows it." The nurse shifted uncomfortably and turned the page in her paperback. "Now, all I'm asking is to die in my own home. On my own land."

"Oh, I know," she spat, surprised at the venom that fairly dripped from her tone. "Your precious land."

He looked up at her with a combination or surprise and defiance. "Yes, my land. After all, I've tended it my whole life. With these bare hands." He held them up as if to remind her. "I didn't do that just so you could sell it as soon as I'm dead and gone."

Siobhan heard the tone of his voice and was surprised that anyone so frail could muster up that much anger. His body was like a live wire, trembling with bitterness and scorn. She wondered if that alone was keeping him alive.

And he wasn't through yet! "This land has been in our family for five gen-erations," he growled, throwing himself into a brief fit of coughing.

Siobhan shook her head, feeling the tension building between her shoulder blades. She was amazed; usually, it took her half a day to become that tense.

"I know that, Dad. How could I not, seeing as you never let me forget it."

He seemed to ignore her, mumbling as if to himself, "It has to stay in the family." Siobhan and the nurse, Ms. Hargraves, shared a look over her father's stooped head. He reared up and glared at her.

"If only I could understand why you hate it here so much."

She clucked a tongue and stared back at him. "Well, if only you'd had the son you wanted, right? Then maybe you'd have been a little more inviting. You never let me forget that, either."

His eyes dared her to continue. "No," he sputtered, wiping a gleam of drool off his lips. "If only you'd had a son. If only you hadn't left it too late. Family name is all but dead and gone now anyway."

Siobhan reeled, as if he'd physically punched her in the stomach. She felt the eyes of his nurse on her, the novel she'd been reading suddenly not as interesting as the family drama going on right before her, but she looked away, afraid the woman might spot the tears welling up and threatening to spill over from her rapidly blinking eyes.

Zachariah used the tense silence, and her apparent speechlessness, to twist the dagger even further into her back.

"How is that big-city husband of yours anyway?"

She clenched her fists and fought back the tears she never shed. *This is ridiculous,* she thought to herself. *He doesn't know about the miscarriage. He doesn't know about the accident. He's on a fishing expedition, trying to find your weak spots, and you're handing them to him on a silver platter!*

"You have no idea what you're talking about, old man," she spat between clenched teeth. "You know, it's great to see you, Father. I can't imagine why we don't do this more often."

She stood then and signaled to the nurse. The nurse rose and followed Siobhan down the porch steps and around the corner, where an ancient water pump stood, drops still dripping from the red-painted spout.

"I'm...sorry you had to hear all that—Mrs. Hargraves, is it?"

The nurse took Siobhan's extended hand and pumped it mildly between moist, meaty palms. It felt like sticking her fingers in bread dough.

"It's Ms., actually," the woman corrected.

"Thank you for looking after my father. I hope he's not been too difficult."

Instinctively, they both looked back to the porch, where Zachariah was busy worrying the hem of his tattered blue bathrobe.

"Of course not," said Ms. Hargraves in a brave falsetto. "He's a wonderful man, deep down." The nurse looked furtively at Siobhan, as if maybe she might not believe her. Then she rushed on, "Anyway, I'm pleased to meet you. Polly, isn't it?"

Hearing the name, Siobhan instinctively stumbled a step backward. "N-n-no," she stammered. "My name's Siobhan."

The nurse blushed and rushed to fix her error. "Oh, I'm sorry. I thought I heard him call you Polly last night."

Suddenly, Siobhan remembered and understood. "Yes, you're right; he did. I think he's getting confused. The only 'Polly' I know would have died when my father was just a boy."

Ms. Hargraves nodded. She patted Siobhan's forearm gently, as if suggesting it was naptime and there might be milk and cookies afterward. "Dementia. Sometimes it's like that. They go over and over the past like there's something unresolved."

There was a flutter of apprehension in the nurse's voice as she added, "Is there…something…unresolved in your family's past?"

That made Siobhan snort. It was like asking if there was any tension between her and her father. "Everything is unresolved here. My mother died young. My brother also. I've never known a family be cursed like this one. I used to think there was a reason for it or some kind of explanation; now I think we're just plain unlucky."

Silence followed, and Siobhan noticed the nurse's eyes were downcast and sullen. "I…I'm sorry," she confessed. "I don't know why I just told you all that."

Ms. Hargraves shrugged and said, "It's OK, honey. People tell nurses things they normally wouldn't tell others."

Despite the woman's reassuring tone, she was clearly uneasy. She looked back over her shoulder at the porch. "Well, I'd better go and see to your father."

She stepped away, crossing the dewy lawn in thick white nursing shoes, leaving Siobhan leaning against the pump as if she'd just gone ten rounds with the heavyweight champ.

No wonder she never came home.

Chapter 7

The wagon rumbled steadily along. The landscape blurred on all sides, an endless scene of a dry, dusty trail and long strands of grassy plains. She felt like they were on a loop that never ended, passing the same patch of wildflowers, the same strand of trees, the same dry creek bed over and over again. Polly had long since grown used to the frequent jarring from the wagon's wooden wheels and the uneven, often treacherous ground along the Oregon Trail.

Normally, Polly would have walked with the other children or perhaps stumbled along, pestering her father for a ride on his shoulders or a chaw off his dwindling plug of tobacco.

But for the last few days, Polly had been faithfully tending to her mother. She bent to her now, dipping a kerchief into a pail of sloshing water and wringing it slightly before applying it to Sarah's forehead. Despite the repeated applications of moist cloths and damp water, her mother's fever still raged.

Sarah's eyes fluttered open, looking vaguely unfocused and slightly yellow.

"How long have we been traveling?" Her voice was reedy, thin, almost like a little girl's. Polly had never heard her like that before.

"Father said it's been eighty days now, since we left the prairie."

Sarah nodded, as if she already knew this and then kept nodding a disturbingly long period of time. Just when Polly was going to ask her to stop, Sarah spoke again. "And how long till we get there?"

It was the same every time she came to—the same conversation, the same questions. Polly sighed, trying to be patient. "I don't know, Momma."

Sarah nodded, closing her eyes and managing a slow, weak smile. "You know, my mother always used to say that it don't matter how far you travel in life, because the furthest distance you'll ever travel is from here…"

Sarah placed a forefinger on Polly's head; it was as warm as a fresh biscuit from the camp stove. Then she moved the finger, tracing Polly's nose, her lips, her throat, until she reached the center of her chest. "…to here."

She was quiet for a moment and then chuckled dryly, tempting a cough. "It's a great distance for some."

Polly choked back tears. Her mother wasn't making any sense. For so long, forever, Sarah had been the rock in Polly's life. Father was a man and did man things away from home. She loved him dearly, but Sarah had raised Polly and taught her everything she knew. Now all she did was babble and live in the past.

Sarah opened her eyes, weak though they were, and they seemed to focus on Polly at last. "I've been meaning to give you this," she croaked, lips dry and crackling. She opened her hand and, inside, was a horseshoe necklace. The chain was simple and unadorned, the horseshoe itself rustic and handmade, which made it all the more special.

Polly reached for it, and when she did, Sarah grasped her wrist with remarkable strength. "Your granddaddy swore it was gold that he found out here when he was fur trapping years ago. I never had it valued because it's kept me safe all these years."

With that, she seemed to crumple and let go of Polly's wrist. She took the necklace then and slid it around her neck. It felt solid and warm from her mother's hand.

"Thank you, Momma. I'll look after it until you get better."

Sarah pursed her lips and shook her head, sending rivulets of sweat across the back of the wagon as it rumbled along. "I know you will. You're a woman now, Polly. This trail has been nothing but hardship. I'm proud of you."

Sarah's eyes fluttered open once more, albeit masking a pained expression. "Whatever you must endure, Polly, promise me you'll always have the courage to face life with hope. You must never forget, Polly: there is hope for your future."

Polly nodded, sure that if she spoke, her mother would hear her silent sobs. What was it that her father had told her, before Polly climbed in the back of the wagon to tend to Sarah. "Your mother needs you to be strong," Pa had said. "Whatever you're feeling, keep it inside until you're alone; then you let it out."

Polly did as her father had demanded, nodding pleasantly even as her mother's eyes fluttered closed. Sarah grew still, so still Polly thought she might be asleep…or worse.

Her breathing grew shallow, and, almost to herself, Polly whispered to her mother, "I love you, Momma."

From the depths of Sarah's stillness, she rallied, not bothering to open her eyes as she said, "I love you, too." She paused, frowning, a flicker of pain passing across her face, and then she continued, "I'm so tired, Polly. I must…" Sarah paused, as she struggled to catch her breath. "I must sleep now. I must get my strength back."

She sighed and then coughed, the air rattling in her throat as she struggled to breathe. It sounded dry and painful. It sounded final. Polly cried, not caring if her mother saw, knowing her mother wouldn't, that she couldn't, not through the veil of her own intense pain.

As her mother drifted off into another feverish sleep, Polly wrung out the kerchief once more and applied it to Sarah's head. It was hotter than before, hotter than she'd ever felt it.

Chapter 8

Siobhan looked up from her magazine when the receptionist spoke. "Mr. Cotton will see you now," she said, a little insistently, almost curiously, making Siobhan think this wasn't her first time making the pronouncement.

"Oh, of course," she blustered, standing abruptly and discarding the two-month-old copy of *Fly Fisherman's Monthly*. "Thank you."

The door was open, and she walked right through. A young man, no more than thirty, perhaps only twenty-nine, stood abruptly. He was anxious, eager; she could feel it in the spacious office.

He looked new; it looked new. There was no dust on the generic law books lined just so around the room's several bookshelves, and the diploma looked freshly hung on the wall. A fake plant sat in the middle of a low coffee table in between two leather wingback chairs to the side of the room. It looked comfortable, inviting, and also new.

He indicated the chair directly across his desk instead. "Please," he said, sounding as young—and as eager—as he looked, "take a seat."

"Thank you for seeing me at such short notice."

Mr. Joseph Cotton, Esquire, nodded, and as she looked at his apple cheeks and stubborn cowlick, Siobhan wondered if his secretary ever had a hard time calling him that: "Mister."

He sat as well and cleared his throat. "It's no problem, Mrs. Tanen. What can I do for you?"

She waved a hand subconsciously. "Please, it's Ms. Davis. I took my maiden name after the accident."

The word hung in the air, as awkward as his hastened glance down at his carefully manicured fingernails. Siobhan attempted a smile and an explanation. "Why don't you call me Siobhan?"

He looked back up, smiling. "Thank you, Siobhan. How can I help?"

She cleared her throat, crossed her legs, and dug in. "My father is ill."

Cotton nodded gravely. "Yes, I believe so."

"The doctor wants him to go to a nursing home where he can receive the kind of care he really needs. But he's stubborn. I guess I don't need to tell you that…"

He offered a rare, and genuine, smile. "Indeed not. I know him well."

She smoothed down the hem of her forest-green skirt, struggling for just the right words. "I came here to get his affairs in order. I can't stay here and look after him long term. We don't have that kind of relationship. We can't be in the same room for more than five minutes. We'll end up killing each other. Do you understand?"

By the end there, her voice had risen to just shy of hysterical, bordering on dramatic. She took a breath and promised not to get so emotional again.

Regardless, the lawyer stared evenly at Siobhan, nodding his head.

"You want to find out what your legal rights are?"

She sighed with relief, nodding gratefully. "I understand his physical health will decline quicker than the dementia itself will deteriorate."

The young lawyer nodded noncommittally. She pressed on, eager for a better answer, or at least a better explanation. "When I spoke to him this morning, he seemed lucid, but last night, he didn't even recognize me."

She fought to keep the desperation out of her voice, but it was a losing battle. She cursed herself for not being better prepared, but that was what her father did to her—dashed her control, left her defenseless.

Mr. Cotton both shook and nodded his head at the same time. Leaning forward at his thin waist, he crossed his hands and rested them on his desk blotter. "Your only option is to have your father declared unfit to manage his finances. That would free you to place him in a nursing home and sell the house and the land. Is that what you want?"

Siobhan self-consciously tucked a curl behind her ear. What she wanted was to get out of this place as soon as possible. But she had to do this first, she knew that much.

When he saw it was difficult for her to answer, Mr. Cotton went on, "Ms. Davis—I mean, Siobhan, he's dying."

Her reply, for once, was emotionless. "I know."

He unlaced and then relaced his fingers. Almost sternly, he said, "My advice would be to resolve your difficulties with your father."

She flashed him a look, which he quickly avoided. Busying himself, he cleared his throat and shuffled some papers around the desk.

He seemed to want to avoid silence at all costs. When she didn't answer right away, he said, "Experience tells me…" He stopped himself, midsentence, as if changing his mind. He began again. "Well, anyway, there's no need to get into all that. This was my father's practice for the past fifty years, and he advised your family for all that time. Why don't you think about it? There's no rush."

Siobhan nodded absently. Despite her best intention to remain focused, her attention drifted to the plastic plant on the coffee table to the left.

He spotted her and cleared her throat. When he had her attention, he smiled boyishly. "I just can't keep the real ones alive."

She nodded, as if they were both thinking the same thing.

As if reading from the same script, she kept the thread alive. "They need moist air. Inside, I mean. And nurturing and tender, loving care."

He seemed to wait until she looked back at him to say, "Don't we all?"

She nodded, watching him stand up, feeling his skin against her own as they shook hands. She took the business card and walked down the hall, but her thoughts drifted away as she sat, almost breathlessly, out in the hallway…

It was a fine spring day. Siobhan and Daniel walked down a wide New York street. Brownstones lined either side, neighbors sitting on their stoops, taking advantage of the fresh air. Fresh buds were breaking out on the trees, making her stop every few feet to admire some new color, or varietal.

Almost subconsciously, Siobhan threaded her arm through Daniel's.

They looked like lovers. For now, that's how she felt.

She heard herself say, "Oregon is wonderful at this time of year."

Daniel's voice replied sternly, "You haven't seen your father in ten years."

"I know." She looked at him, but he was waving to another neighbor; Mr. Popularity. Almost to herself, she added, "He was always such a force of nature. It's hard to believe..."

He turned back to her, proving that he'd heard every word. "You said you'd never go back there after how he treated you when your mother died."

"He's dying, Daniel."

Daniel stopped and stared at his wife. She looked at his face, the pain etched there, the anger and resentment, long buried, always simmering under the surface.

She reached out a hand to him but wasn't surprised when he didn't take it.

"I'm sorry, Daniel. I blame myself. If that helps."

His smirk was almost as painful as the words that followed—almost. "I blame you, too."

He turned away from Siobhan, pulling his coat closer to him for warmth. He slowly walked away.

"Daniel," she begged, desperate for him to stay. "Please, don't leave me..."

Once again, she offered a hand, but he only turned his back on it. He stepped off the curb, and she saw only the collar of his jacket, turned high against the cold.

The squeal of brakes woke her from her reverie...

Siobhan sat up in bed, drenched in sweat. The sound of the squealing brakes and the vision of Daniel's collar jolting with the impact were like ghostly sensations on the other side of her eyes. She turned on the light to orient herself, finding the room instead of a quiet city street.

There—the noise again. A squeaking sound, not like brakes, but rubbery, like tires. It was coming from outside—outside her room. She stood, reached for her robe, and stepped out into the hallway.

The hallway was dark, but she could tell it was equally empty. She heard the sound again and inched toward the banister, almost frightened of what she might find.

And with good reason. There, at the bottom of the stairs, lay Zachariah. He was splayed out awkwardly, pale limbs akimbo and not moving at all. The wheelchair was on its side, the rubber wheel squeaking against the wooden railing as it slowed to a stop. He made a miserable moan, soft as a lost kitten's, the only sign that he was still breathing.

He looked lost and so alone; the shock took her breath away. She stood, frozen, staring at the veins on the side of his neck and the way his hands trembled.

Suddenly, she gasped, and thundered down the stairs.

"Zachariah?"

He responded to the sound of her voice, eyes vacant as he stared back at her. They were wide, unseeing, or maybe seeing all.

His voice was choked with emotion as he exploded, "Polly! This is all your doing. It's your fault that it's come to this. You cursed the whole family."

His eyes raved, the veins on either side of his skull pulsing with the effort. He looked haunted, in a word. She seized on it—haunted, yes, haunted by the past.

She reached out a hand, afraid the touch might shock him. It wavered in the air, just shy of his grizzled cheek. "It's me. Siobhan. Father, look! It's me."

"Oh dear!" came a cry from the second floor, and a thundering began on the steps. Ms. Hanagan was there in seconds, her slippered feet shuffling past Siobhan as she deftly reached down and yanked both Siobhan's father and his wheelchair up simultaneously.

He was seated once again, the wheelchair right side up, and the woman barely breathed heavily.

Her father's eyes still wide, he put his feeble hands upon the wheels of his chair, as if to back away. Her hand was still there, reaching out, when at last he focused on it. His voice was brittle and panicked as he cringed. "Don't let her touch me. Keep her away from me."

Siobhan's face flushed with shame as she locked eyes with the nurse. Ms. Hanagan offered an apologetic smile but quickly turned and wheeled him back to his bedroom just the same.

Siobhan stood there, troubling the collar of her bathrobe, the sound of squealing brakes still echoing through her memory.

Chapter 9

Siobhan retreated to the attic. She wasn't rushing anywhere specifically, so much as running away from the downstairs, which seemed to be her father's domestic domain.

The stairs were dusty, as if they hadn't been climbed in years, if not decades. Each of the small, narrow stairs seemed to creak in despair as she crept up them, one by one. The door itself groaned in protest until, at last, she pushed it open and stumbled inside.

She still shook from the encounter as she rested her hand on the attic wall, surveying the distressing scene that greeted her.

The attic looked like a garbage can that had been turned inside out. There were cardboard boxes strewn everywhere, few of them marked, stacked high and low, all of them dusty from years of disuse or neglect. In the corner stood a chipped mannequin, naked save for a man's vest. Strings of Christmas lights, bulbs long broken, snaked from the rafters like long, green cobwebs.

Siobhan knelt in front of an antique trunk. It was large and wooden, with a rounded top like an elongated treasure chest. Its hinges creaked when she opened it, and inside was no treasure, just a faded maroon lining and several old books.

She picked up one, an ornate Bible, and found a satin ribbon, once red, now faded pink, marking a page. She opened it and read the passage that had been marked aloud: "Luke 1:42. Blessed are you among women, and blessed is the fruit of your womb…"

She made a face and snapped the book shut, setting the Bible back in the trunk. "Hypocrite," she murmured, to no one in particular. She dug deeper in the trunk, finding a faded photograph between several historical volumes.

The picture was a moment frozen in time, a small wedding party in a wooden church, clearly from the turn of the century, maybe even earlier. The photograph, though black-and-white, had faded with time, so that it swam in a muted sepia tone. There was a happy couple in the middle, a handsome, burly man and a smaller, wizened, older woman with a shrewd face and beady eyes. They stood so stiffly, they might as well have been figures in a wax museum.

Next to the woman stood a hulking younger man, possibly her son, in an ill-fitting suit he looked eager to slink out of. Next to the groom stood a pretty young girl, thin and hungry-looking, her face pinched and scowling. Siobhan smirked at her open discomfort.

"Someone didn't want to be there," she murmured to herself, feeling the girl's pain as she sat, imprisoned, in a moldy attic. Then she took a closer look at the girl, realizing she recognized her. Could it be?

"Polly?" she asked the empty attic.

No sooner had she uttered the name than a strange, mangled cry filled the attic. Siobhan jumped as the sudden flapping of wings filled the attic. It was a rook, dark and cagey, desperate and caged in the attic for who knew how long. She stood, waving the rook away, as eager for it to escape as it was.

Quickly, Siobhan fumbled for a nearby window, unlatched it, and opened it up wide. The rook flew out at once. It glided up into the sky and circled away.

Siobhan watched it, hand on her chest as her heart continued to pound. She sank back down to her knees, the window now open, fresh air streaming in as well as the morning light.

She looked at the contents of the trunk with new vigor, now able to actually see the titles of the books it contained. One looked more ancient than the rest, more handspun and homemade. She reached for it, pulling out an old leather notebook secured with a red satin band.

She untied it and wiped off the dust to reveal the title: *The Journal of Polly O'Neal*. She smiled to herself, sitting back on the attic steps and opening it to the first page…

Chapter 10

OREGON, 1867

The earth was dry and unforgiving as Polly's father, Patrick, pounded the makeshift headstone into the ground. The sun beat down overhead, as it always did, as if to punish them for taking time off the God almighty Oregon Trail!

Polly shook her head, fists clenched in frustration. This was no sacred or holy place, just a dry patch of land in the shadow of the wagon train that had paused, only briefly, to allow Patrick the time to bury his wife. A patch of dead trees overlooked the random spot, not even hearty enough to provide shade for her mother's eternal peace.

The others stood around, impatient and ill at ease. Polly knelt in prayer until Patrick at last finished hammering and gently helped her up. "I know you're upset, Polly, but we've got to keep going."

Polly shook him off, but Patrick's grip around her arm was as unforgiving as the land beneath her feet. "She's at rest now, girl. We'll reach Oregon soon, and we can start a new life. It's the will of God."

Polly turned and looked up into her father's lined face, tan from months on the trail. "God's will that she died?" she spat.

He flashed her an impatient look and leaned closer to her so the others wouldn't hear. "God's will that we keep going, Polly. Now, stop sassing me and pay your final respects."

Polly finally yanked her arm free as she knelt once more at her mother's side. Around her neck hung the necklace her mother had given her, and she clutched the dangling horseshoe now for good luck. As she stood, at last, she turned to find her father stealing a longing glance at the woman next to him.

Ada. She wore one of Polly's mother's bonnets against the sun, and from beneath its brim, she glared at Polly with a long, triumphant look. Polly stood, fists clenched at her side, helpless as Ada and Patrick turned away, clasping hands as they walked back to the wagons.

Polly's cheeks burned as she turned to the haphazardly hammered and already leaning wooden cross. "I'll get justice for you, Momma."

She made the sign of the cross silently and then turned, only to find Ike standing idly by the back of the waiting wagon, wearing the same triumphant expression as his mother.

Chapter 11

OREGON, 1867

Polly straightened her thin, black dress before opening the church door. It was tiny and new, built entirely of unpainted pine, so fresh she could still smell the sawdust over the white wedding flowers lining the end of each row of freshly varnished pews.

Her father stood in his best suit, not that it was much to look at, at the edge of the first pew, talking to an older priest, who looked not long for this world. Polly took one step and then two, before the door swung closed behind her with a sudden catch.

Patrick whirled, a half-smile frozen on his face until he spotted the color of her dress; then his face froze in a grim mask. The priest openly gasped.

Patrick approached, one finger up as he walked toward Polly with a heavy tread of vengeance. "Just one moment, Father McLeary."

Polly stood, frozen, until Patrick reached her and grasped her by both shoulders, shaking her for emphasis as he spit each word: "Get out of those black clothes. This is a wedding, not a funeral."

Despite her father's firm grip, Polly stood firm. "I'm mourning for my mother." Her father looked dumbfounded, and taking advantage of his speechlessness, she added, "Someone in this family has to."

He raised a hand to strike her, remembered where he was, and instead, struck her with the words, "Don't worry, Polly; you'll have a new mother soon enough."

Polly winced at the thought. Gone was her steely resolve as she crumpled like the thirteen-year-old girl she was, resorting to begging as she pleaded, "You can't marry her, Father. She's a murderer."

Patrick rocked back, finally taking his hands from her shoulders. His mouth moved, lips thin, but no words come out.

She covered the distance between them quickly, her heels clattering on the polished wooden floor of the church. "Why won't you listen to me?"

Finally, Patrick found his voice. "This is the house of God. Why are you spreading these lies? Don't you know God will punish you?"

Polly was beyond reason, tears stinging her eyes at the thought of Ada as her stepmother. "She gave Momma bad food. She killed my momma."

Patrick coughed, avoiding her eyes. "We've been all through this, Polly. It was an accident."

Polly shook her head. "I promise you it wasn't. I can prove it. I still have the can."

Patrick was equally vehement. "That proves nothing. What's wrong with you, child? Are you really so stupid?"

The words no longer stung Polly's frazzled emotions. She had come here to prevent her father's marriage, and she wouldn't leave until the job was finished. She crossed her arms over her chest. "I won't let you marry her."

Patrick's eyes flashed anger and then impatience. He looked back at the ancient priest, so pale and sickly in his own black garb, and then turned to Polly. "Get changed into something else," he hissed.

Polly stood there, resolute, and shook her head, "No."

Patrick's face broke into a hateful grin. "Fine, Polly, then I'll do it for you." Before she could protest, Patrick scooped Polly into his massive arms and, with no less effort than it might require him to carry a sack of flour, tossed her over his shoulder and stomped past the priest into the sacristy.

Along the way, he grunted angrily to the priest, "Father McLeary. Something for my daughter to wear, please?"

The sacristy was small, little more than a spare bedroom in the back of the church. A wooden closet held robes and vestments, now flying left and right beneath her father's hands.

The priest blinked nervously as Patrick searched impatiently through the open closet.

"I'm sorry, Mr. O'Neal," he stammered, wringing his papery old hands, "but those garments are sacred. They're not for the layman's use."

Patrick finally put Polly down and turned toward the priest. His face looked gleeful as he stated, firmly, "Forgive me, Father, but I'm sure you'll make an exception if you want church donations from this family in the future."

The priest withered as Patrick turned to Polly. "Take off that dress."

She harrumphed. "You can't make me."

"Watch me," he said and, with rough hands and overflowing frustration, tore the dress apart. Polly gasped as the buttons sprayed into the air and bounced across the floor. The dress fell unceremoniously around Polly's ankles, revealing her undergarments to the priest.

He averted his eyes, mumbling into the corner, "Mr. O'Neal, please. For the love of God…"

Patrick stared at Polly's neck or, more specifically, at the horseshoe necklace around Polly's neck. With distaste in his voice, he told Polly, "You can take that off as well."

As she opened her mouth to refuse, he clenched the necklace and yanked the chain free from her throat. She shrieked and then stood shivering, half-naked in the church, as Patrick turned on his heel, practically yanking the priest out with him. "Ada will be here any minute, girl. Find something to wear, or find yourself out on the streets."

He slammed the sacristy door, leaving Polly to ponder his offer. She seriously considered it. Leaving Patrick would solve all her problems…for the moment. But she had promised to her mother that she would avenge her death. How could she do that from the streets? Or an orphanage?

Polly bit her lip, dried her tears, and climbed into a thin altar boy's robe. There was a small mirror on the inside door of the wardrobe, and she pinched her cheeks to liven them up, an old trick her mother had taught her. She looked away from her sad blue eyes and found a thin black sash to wrap around her waist.

By the time she heard the door open again, she was as close to smiling as she'd ever come again. Ada stood there, looking in on her. Polly froze as the two locked eyes. Once again, the older woman's gaze was gloating, triumphant, but this time, it only made Polly all the more resolved to show her for what she really was: a killer. If that meant standing silent at her father's wedding, then so be it.

"What took you so long?" Polly asked as she strode past Ada and went straight to her father's side.

Father McLeary, eager to be finished with the proceedings, barely waited until she was situated to begin the ceremony. Polly stood under her father's watchful gaze until Ada cleared her throat, drawing his attention away. Polly shook her head, noticing only a few friends from the wagon train standing in the pews behind them.

She looked toward Ada, groaning as the woman stared piously at the priest, batting her eyes as if she were in a brothel and not a house of worship. Next to his mother, Ike stood uncomfortably in a shirt that looked so stiff and sharp, it must have hurt to wear it.

He caught her eye and licked his lips approvingly until she looked away. Polly gritted her teeth and endured the service. At last, Father McLeary cleared his throat and asked, "If anyone here knows any good reason why this couple should not be joined in holy matrimony, speak now or forever hold your peace…"

Polly looked around, hoping someone from the wagon train might interject, but instead, a long silence fell over the tiny church. Time seemed to drag, stretching moments into minutes and minutes into hours. She thought everyone might hear the heart pounding against her chest, but no one looked at her. No one dared. Finally, she could restrain herself no longer. "She killed my mother."

All around her, the horrified gasps of the wedding guests resounded throughout the church.

Chapter 12

OREGON, 1867

Polly spent the rest of her father's honeymoon chopping wood. That was her punishment, it seemed, for her outburst at the wedding. She cursed Ada's name with every swing of the dull ax blade. It was her idea to send Polly into the barn, and all her father did was point dully at a towering stack of wood, ordering, "Get started, and we'll let you know when you can stop."

That was how he said everything now, Polly noted: "We."

"We'll let you know when to stop," he'd said, not, "I'll tell you when you can stop."

Now, hours later, hands blistered and raw from wielding the splintery ax handle, shoulders sore from the abuse they'd taken, legs barely able to stand, Polly lowered the blade to the floor and leaned against a roughhewn wall, wiping sweat from her brow and trying to catch her breath.

Her eyes were blurry and stung from the sweat, and she blinked them several times, her vision growing more focused each time. She noticed a figure standing in the doorway, a large, bulky shape silhouetted by the flow of a gas lamp on the kitchen table behind him.

At first, relief shuddered through her young body. "Papa?"

Then a steely chuckle, young and squeaky, made the sweat on her brow practically freeze.

The shape moved, just an inch, and the glow from her own lantern, swinging just overhead, illuminated her new stepbrother's face, piggish and warm with threat and anticipation.

"Ike," she spat, much as she'd cursed his mother's name for the last three hours.

Her hand immediately reached for the ax handle, so familiar to her after chopping so much wood it practically leaped into her hands.

He only smirked, shuffling forward in that oddly loping gait of his.

"H-h-how long have you been standing there?" Polly asked, hating the stammer, the uncertainty, the fear in her voice.

"Long enough for me to get worked up and you to get tuckered out," he said in that slow, country drawl.

He held out a hand, cheap gold gleaming in the weak glow of the flickering lantern on the pickle barrel behind her. "What do you think I should do with this?" he asked, dangling the horseshoe necklace in front of Polly's nose.

He was so close now she could smell the soap behind his ears. He was washed and ready for bed, and suddenly, Polly realized it was late at night and her father had never come to stop her.

"It's mine," Polly spat, as angry at her father as she was at Ike and ready to take them both on at once. "Give it back to me."

She reached for it, claws bared, but Ike was as fast as he was loathsome.

His breath was foul as he leaned back in, taunting Polly with the necklace clutched between two fat fingers. "If you want it back, you know what you can do."

Polly allowed a frosty smile to touch her own lips. "Touch me again, and I'll tell Papa."

But Ike only chuckled. "Girl, you think he'd believe you now? After that performance in church? He's gonna work you to the bone. Ain't gonna let you see the light of day. And when he does, Mama will be here to hand you that ax right back."

Polly fumed with the truth behind his boast. As if to rub it in, he parted his thick, rubbery lips and chomped his big, yellow teeth down on the horseshoe pendant Polly's mother had given her. He rolled his eyes and decreed, "T'ain't valuable no-how."

Polly tightened her grip on the ax by her side. Her voice was low and firm as she inched closer to her repugnant stepbrother. "Give me the necklace, or I'll kill you."

Ike brayed laughter and bored his steely eyes into her own. "You ain't got it in you. Good Christian girl like you."

As if to prove it, he snatched the ax handle, wrenching it from her hand and tossing it to the side. Before she could react, his greedy hands were already tearing open her dress. She punched at him, blindly but could barely hold her arms up after an entire afternoon and evening of chopping wood. Her fists landed on him weakly, as soft as mosquito bites. Even her legs were too sore from standing to kick at him effectively. He easily dodged her dusty old boots.

He shoved her against the very wood pile she'd spent all day stacking, the rough bark and splintered wood rough against her bare back. He admired her chest, licking his lips as he said, "Shame what happened to your momma…"

She struck out at him, missing his heaving chest by inches. He grasped her hand and slapped her across the cheek, hard, in reply.

"I hate you!" she spat. "Leave me alone."

He slapped her other cheek, leaving her face raw and her neck sore from the force of his heavy hand. "Shut your mouth, or I'll beat you."

Chapter 13

Siobhan awoke with a start, her cheek pressed hard against the open pages of Polly's journal. She rose and blinked her eyes, finding the ancient ink blurred from her own tears. She gasped to recall what she had read late the night before and could picture Ike putting his rough hands all over that poor, young girl.

Her throat was still sore with emotion as she stumbled into the shower, washing off last night's tears and easing into the hot water as it loosed her tight, awkward limbs.

She dried herself off and dressed, slipping in and out of the downstairs kitchen quickly, if only to avoid her father or even his nurse. She felt increasingly isolated in his house, and it was big enough, and easy enough, to get lost in.

She sauntered onto the back porch, finding it empty, and heard the distinctive whinny of a horse. She followed its sound to the stables, where Jesse was busy saddling up a glorious chestnut-brown steed.

She set down her half-empty coffee cup and approached the animal cautiously. Neither the horse nor Jesse seemed surprised to find her there.

Without glancing at her, Jesse asked, "You want to help? We're driving the cattle up to summer pastures today. Be just like old times."

Siobhan couldn't help but chuckle. "Jesse, it's been twenty years since I've ridden a horse."

He turned to look at her and offered a sly wink that was as lazy as his drawl. "It's like riding a bike. You never forget."

Siobhan stuffed her hands inside the back pockets of her jeans, struggling for a quick excuse. It was too early, and her mind raced to find one.

Pouncing, Jesse said, "Come on. Fresh air will do you good." Before she could answer, he tossed her a fresh bridle and nodded at the nearest horse stall. "You know what to do."

Jesse learned that, in fact, she did. She opened the pen for a horse named Biscuit and, in no time, had her saddled and following him and his horse, Sidewinder, through the pasture on the way off her father's ranch.

The morning sun felt good on her face, and the horse felt slow and easy beneath her. The ranch land was fertile, always had been, covered in lush green acreage that filled the air with the familiar scent of fresh-cut grass. Jesse rode out at a steady clip, graceful on his copper steed, but not so steady that she couldn't keep up easily.

Despite the pleasant ride and company, Siobhan was tense and bothered by what she'd read in the journal the night before. She wondered if she should tell Jesse, if he'd understand why it upset her so. She wondered if her father had read the journal and why it had been buried in that chest up in the attic.

Beside her, Jesse shook his head. She said, "What?"

He chuckled dryly. "I can't remember the last time I've seen anyone so tense on horseback."

She laughed but only reflexively.

They rode for an hour or more, until they came to a stop at a high pasture overlooking the canyon below them. It was something out of a western novel, lush grass dotted by clusters of pastoral trees and littered with a wide array of colorful wildlife in bloom. It was the kind of place you could lie down, where the grass was a thick, verdant carpet and you could rest your head and sleep for days with the clouds and sun passing overhead.

"That's Bonney's Canyon," Jesse told her quietly, almost reverently. "Remember the legend? As the mist rises in the lush canyon, it is said to be a baby searching for its mother."

Siobhan nodded. "Yes, I remember. I was always so scared of the place when I was a child. God knows why. It's beautiful." Biscuit's mane felt soft and yet firm in her hand as she stroked it absently.

They sat in silence, even the horses stood calmly, overlooking Bonney's Canyon.

"Jesse, what do you know about my ancestor, Polly?" She watched his face carefully, wondering if her instinct to ask him had been right. It darkened visibly as he stiffened slightly in his saddle.

"Not much," he began tentatively, avoiding her eyes. "She was a wily old one; that I do know. Lived to be a hundred. She's buried down there in the canyon, matter of fact. Why do you ask?"

Jesse's eyes were curious as he stared back at her. She met them and then looked away again, down into the canyon. "I just…Well, I know nothing about my family history. It's like it's been buried. Don't you think that's odd?"

She heard the creak of saddle leather as Jesse shifted in his saddle again. Morning sounds became background noise as the awkward silence between question and answer grew.

Finally, Jesse cleared his throat. "Maybe you shouldn't dig around in the past. Not now. Leave it alone. It's no use to anyone."

Although his words made sense, clinically, and a few days earlier she would have agreed with them wholeheartedly, Siobhan found herself shaking her head. "It's of use to me, Jesse. Is there anyone who would remember Polly?"

After a long pause, Jesse offered, "There's Estelle."

She felt her heart quicken, certain he was going to say no. Now, feeling like a detective on the case, she had her first clue. "Can I talk to her? Where is she? Who is she?"

Jesse chuckled, holding up a gloved hand to halt her rapid-fire questioning. "She lives in the village. Haven't seen her for some time. I'll ask around. Leave it with me."

With a click of his tongue and a tug of the reins, he signaled his horse to turn slightly and kept walking along the rise above Bonney's Canyon. Untrusting, she raced to catch up.

"Please, Jesse, it's important."

He nodded, tugging the reins once more and signaling to the horse to pick up speed. "I'll do my best."

Galloping at his side, the morning sun in her eyes, Siobhan felt less than reassured.

Chapter 14

The schoolhouse, like most of the town, was new. It was small and un-adorned, with no steeple or paint, but perfectly functional for those towns-people who saw fit to send their kids each day.

The scent of fresh pine benches and long, gleaming desks filled the main school room as afternoon light filtered in through the heavy-paned glass on either side.

The classroom emptied in a scurry of heavy, trampling shoes on the hard-wood floor of the one-room schoolhouse. Polly busied herself, straightening her school books and carefully stacking her schoolwork. She was in no hurry to get home.

Large shoes scuffled at the front of the room as her teacher stood. "How are you settling in, Polly?"

Polly stood as well, unaccustomed to being spoken to directly by her new teacher, Lafayette Davis. He had wavy blond hair and a distinguished, pro-fessorly face. He wore a tan vest over a maroon dress shirt, with pants that matched his vest. He was in his late twenties, perhaps even his early thirties, but his face looked boyish either way. A grave expression masked cheerful green eyes as he twisted a fountain pen between his fingers.

Polly ducked her head, inching past him toward the still-open door. "I…I have to go, Mr. Davis. I have chores waiting for me at home."

Mr. Davis cleared his throat and blocked her way, gently. His voice was neither stern, nor yielding. "That wasn't an answer, Polly."

Polly's gaze dropped to the floor, where she saw that a black beetle had fallen on its back. The beetle struggled to right itself, and for the life of her, Polly had to resist the urge to squash it dead.

At once, fear gripped her heart. Papa had warned her that if her grades slipped, she'd have even more chores to do. "Why do you ask, sir? Is...is... there a problem with my schoolwork?"

Mr. Davis offered a sympathetic smile. "No, not at all. Your schoolwork is excellent. It's just that you seem...withdrawn...is all."

Polly bit her lower lip, unfamiliar with the word. "That and, well, I couldn't help but hear you were fighting in the schoolyard the other day."

Polly shrugged, her face growing hot with shame. "One of the girls was making fun of my clothes."

Mr. Davis studied her. "Is there a reason why you always wear those long sleeves? In this heat?"

The beetle's heavy armor skittered on the wooden floor, and Polly crouched down on her knees and turned it over. It quickly scuttled away. She watched it, wishing her escape could be so easy.

Polly stood back up, dusted her hands off on her long, black skirt and looked her teacher in the eye. "I'm mourning for my mother."

Mr. Davis frowned. "As a child, the church only requires that you mourn for three months. I believe your mother's been dead much longer."

"Mr. Davis, I have to go home. I'll get in trouble if I'm late. Please believe me; I'm fine. Just...let me go." Polly tried to hide the desperation in her voice, in her eyes, in the way she clutched nervously at her high, black collar, but she failed.

Mr. Davis gently put a reassuring hand on her shoulder. "You can trust me, Polly. I'm your friend. If you need me to write a note explaining why I held you up this afternoon, I'll be happy to—"

Just then, the door swung open and in stomped Ike, his freckly face flushed with rage and piggish, yellow eyes starring daggers straight into Polly's skull. She gasped and flinched her way out of her teacher's grasp.

Mr. Davis looked at Ike with obvious derision. "What's the meaning of this? What are you doing in here, Ike?"

Ike looked up at the teacher with equal disdain, snorting. "Come to fetch my sister, sir. Why you keeping her back?"

Her teacher's nostrils flared with the insult. His voice turned at once dark and dangerous. "It's none of your business, boy. This schoolhouse is for girls only. Please take your leave."

Ike ignored him, glowering at Polly as he balled his pink, meaty fists at his side.

She rushed past her teacher, muttering over her shoulder, "I'm sorry, Mr. Davis. I have to go now." With Ike pounding his feet into the dirt outside the tiny schoolhouse, Polly risked a glance back and saw Mr. Davis, standing in the doorway, face fraught with concern.

She turned, eager to catch up with Ike lest he use those fists for something other than cracking his own knuckles at his sides. And yet she knew from experience never to get too close to her stepbrother, either.

Ike turned to her, squinting in the late afternoon sun as he loosed the reins of his chestnut-colored horse, Hazel, from the hitching post outside of the school. "What was that all about, in there, with your teacher?"

"Nothing," Polly said with a forced air of lightness. "Just schoolwork."

Ike eyed her suspiciously as he leaped onto the horse. He adjusted his girth in the saddle, grabbed the reins roughly, and sneered down at her. "Best get yourself home. Ma's got chores for ya." A beaming smile spread on his thick lips.

With a kick of his feet into Hazel's belly, he choked out a "Yaw," and the horse reared up and whinnied its disapproval before settling back down. "Enjoy the walk," he gushed as the horse dashed off, suffering under Ike's weight and manhandling ways.

Polly stood, leaning against the hitching post, enjoying the soft smell of hay in the afternoon light. She knew she should race home, but the thought of Ada giving her another long list of chores that would last until supper turned her stomach. Still, if she dallied anymore, it might get worse.

She took a step but paused. There was a noise, just to her left. She turned, regarding an old, sagging barn that clearly hadn't been used in years. Its front doors were warped, not quite meeting in the middle. The paint was faded to an almost grayish uniformity, holes in the side of the barn big enough for owls to fly in and out.

She took a step closer and stopped; there it was again, the unmistakable sound of a girl sobbing. Polly listened for a long moment and then, against her better judgment, followed the sound into the barn.

The light was soft inside the tiny barn, filtering through cracks in the warped wall beams and the holes in the tin roof. Hay bales, dusty with mold, lay scattered everywhere and, among them, lay a young girl, sobbing.

It was Lizzie, a girl from Polly's class at school. She lay there, head buried in her hands, pigtails sticky with hay.

Polly approached her cautiously, but the sound startled Lizzie, sending her sitting up and scampering back against a hollow, rotted wall. Polly held her hand out and continued inching forward. "It's OK. It's me. What's the matter, Lizzie?"

Lizzie's face was blotchy and red, her cheeks covered with glistening tears. She said nothing, merely shook her head and inched away from Polly and closer to the wall.

Polly kept walking, eyes tightening along with her chest as she put two and two together. "Was Ike here?"

At the mention of the boy's name, Lizzie looked up sharply, eyes wide, still crying. She paused, uncertain, and then nodded, looking back down at the ground.

This time, it was Polly's turn to ball her fists at her side...

Chapter 15

Mr. Davis greeted the Saturday morning with an early ride out to the O'Neal ranch. He'd been trying to find the time all week, ever since he'd spoken to Polly about her mourning clothes, but paperwork and parent conferences had kept him at bay.

The morning was warm and fragrant with the smell of freshly mown grass as he approached the ranch, a new but humble affair on the outskirts of town. He slowed his horse to a stop and dismounted, tying the old black mare up to the gleaming new front porch. Like most of the houses in town, the O'Neals' was new—and humble.

Before he'd even looped the last inch of reins around the post, the door opened and a harsh, severe-looking woman clomped onto the porch in stiff black shoes.

She wiped her hands on an old cloth and shook the teacher's hand. "Mrs. O'Neal, it's nice to meet you. I'm Polly's teacher, Mr. Davis."

"Yes, sir," she said, accent stiff and formal as she turned and led him into a small foyer that quickly led into a tidy but grim kitchen. The curtains were closed against the beautiful morning, the trappings sparse and as severe as the woman offering him a seat at the damp breakfast table.

He sat, she sat, making no move to offer him coffee or, preferably, tea. "I apologize for arriving unannounced, Mrs. O'Neal."

"You can call me Ada," she said with an expression that clearly hoped he'd do anything but. "What can I help you with?"

"Well, ma'am, I came to talk to you about Polly."

Immediately, Ada's mouth curled up into a thin line.

Her expression went from placid to perturbed in the blink of an eye, and her stiff accent turned guttural and frank. "Girl in trouble?"

Mr. Davis shrugged. "A couple of fights lately in the schoolyard, that's all. She's a spirited girl. It's not serious."

The woman's scornful expression reminded him of her son Ike's, especially when she blinked and almost spat, "So why you here then?"

He was accustomed to the rough trade that crossed the Oregon Trail only to set up homesteads on the fertile land. They worked with their hands, barely read, and were mostly uneducated. From time to time, as was clearly the case with Ada and her son, Ike, they were also contemptuous, bitter, cruel, and coarse.

He set his jaw and, as pleasantly but as firmly as he could, said, "Actually, I'm new at the school and I'm making my way around all the parents to introduce myself."

Clearly, Ada was no fool. She stood, dramatically, her severe black dress skirting the floor as she approached the stove. Without asking, she poured steaming-hot coffee into two mugs and brought them back to the table. When she sat this time, she wore a thin smile on her even thinner lips.

He took the mug, but it was much too hot. She sipped it without wincing and fixed him with her eyes, which were as dark as her dress. "You the girl's teacher, Mr. Davis, or some kind of social worker?"

Davis recognized the question for what it was: a challenge. He hoped to meet it in his reply: "I'm someone who sees Polly's potential."

Ada's chuckle was forced and humorless. "She's a girl. Ain't no potential to speak of, is there?"

Davis felt his stomach lurch and, unable to speak for a moment, could only listen as Polly's stepmother continued, "Women are of no consequence here, on the new frontier. Girl is lucky she gets any kind of schooling, you ask me. When I was her age, I was put to work."

Davis cleared his throat. "Fortunately, times are changing. It's called progress, Mrs. O'Neal."

Ada O'Neal clicked her tongue and rolled her eyes, looking from Mr. Davis to the slit between the joyless curtains that covered the kitchen window. "Don't see no progress from where I'm standing."

"Your daughter is exceptionally bright."

Ada's head snapped back, eyes like slits and tongue like venom. "She's not my blood."

Suddenly, it all made sense. This woman was a mother in name only. She cared little for her stepdaughter, or even less than little. He straightened and leaned in a little closer. "May I ask what happened to her mother?"

Ada looked away. "Got sick on the trail. Didn't make the journey," she said, momentarily avoiding his sympathetic gaze. Then, turning to meet his eyes with a thin, sick smile, she said, "Only the strongest survive, Mr. Davis. It's the law of nature."

"Yes, I made the trip myself just last year," he returned.

This seemed to disappoint her, and she quickly changed the subject. "You seem rather interested in the girl."

Her tone implied threat, and the arched eyebrow noted a most unwelcome curiosity. In the pit of his stomach, Davis not only knew he couldn't trust this woman, but he feared her. He could only imagine how poor little Polly felt.

"As I say, she's an exceptional student."

Ada made a loud "harrumph" and sipped her coffee.

Davis noted the stillness in the house and looked around. "Where is Polly, Mrs. O'Neal?"

She turned that thin, crowing smile back on him and with a satisfied expression told him, "Out working in the fields where she belongs."

Davis almost shivered with the sudden chill in the air. He looked down at his untouched coffee and promptly stood, extending a hand. She ignored it and remained sitting.

He wiped it on his linen jacket. "It was a pleasure to meet you, Mrs. O'Neal."

She nodded but did not return the forced sentiment. At last, she stood and reluctantly led him to the front door. In the foyer, there was a small, thin wooden table. In the center of it, in a cracked milk jug no longer fit for any use other than a planter, sat a cluster of vibrant daffodils, clearly the only source of light and beauty in the whole, grim house.

Ada saw him looking and pounced. "Beautiful, aren't they?" she asked, opening the door. When he agreed with a nod, she added, "My son. He's a thoughtful boy. Turning into a fine man, if I say so myself."

Davis nodded absently before exiting the house. He turned to say, "Goodbye," only to find the door had already shut in his face.

Chapter 16

Polly gathered up the last of her books, relieved that Mr. Davis was occupied with one of the other girls so he couldn't ask her any more probing questions. Lizzie had left minutes earlier, and Polly struggled to catch up.

The ground was soft beneath her feet, the breeze cool on her cheeks. Lizzie disappeared over a hill, heading toward the humble house she shared with her family.

She wore a tight blue dress, and her blond hair was in pigtails that bounced with each step. She trod through a vibrant field of wildflowers but barely looked down as her feet trampled the pretty yellow and purple petals.

"Lizzie!"

Lizzie paused just outside the family barn, her face buried in the midafternoon shadows cast by the roof.

She turned, glaring, almost stopping Polly in her tracks.

"Leave me alone," she said, holding her books across her chest defensively. Still, she remained just outside the big red barn door and hesitated to slam it in Polly's face.

Polly approached cautiously. "Lizzie, please, just hear me out."

"No," Lizzie said, turning toward the barn. Desperate, Polly grabbed her arm and yanked her around. The books in her hands fell to the ground, but neither girl stooped to pick them up.

"Why should I?" Lizzie asked, chin trembling and voice choked with emotion.

"You have to tell your father about Ike and what happened in the barn that day."

Lizzie looked nervously around her to make sure no one was watching. Leaning in, she said with a pleading tone, "I can't, Polly."

Polly shook her head, signifying that "can't" wasn't an option. "He has to be brought to justice."

Lizzie shook her head just as resolutely. "You don't understand, Polly. It would kill my father if he knew what that boy done to me."

"But if you don't tell, he'll just keep doing it. Think about all the others. He's must be stopped."

Lizzie stopped whimpering long enough to give Polly a shrewd, knowing glance. "So why don't *you* tell on him?"

"Because they won't believe me. He's my stepbrother. They'll think I'm making trouble."

Lizzie only frowned again, pleading with her school friend. "Polly, I'm not like you. You're smart. You'll be OK. My father wants me married. He's already set his sights on a husband. I'm only fourteen years old."

Polly looked at her friend shrewdly. "Then let's get Ike some other way, Lizzie," she answered. "We can set a trap for him if we're clever."

Lizzie cast Polly a withering glance. "Whether we trap him or I tell on him, can't you see the problem? I'm spoilt goods. He's taken my honor. I've brought shame on my family. It would kill my father. I just can't do it, Polly."

Polly's heart broke to hear the emotion in her friend's voice as she continued, "Leave me alone, will you? I wish I'd never met you and your horrible brother. Damn the pair of you. Stay away from me, Polly O'Neal!"

She turned quickly and disappeared into the barn, heavy shoes clattering on the hay-covered floor. The door was still open, and Polly started to follow but thought better of it. What good would it do? It was clear that if Ike was ever going to come to justice, it would have to be at her own hands.

Chapter 17

Of all his chores on the new ranch, Patrick never quite minded chopping wood. In fact, secretly, he hated it when Ada suggested they let Polly do the work as some type of punishment. He actually preferred doing it himself—the feeling of power; the smooth, repetitive motions as the ax rose and fell; and the satisfaction as the firewood finally splintered and the bit split the timber in half.

The long, hot afternoon was almost over, and the evening weighed heavily in the sky. Patrick paused and wiped sweat from his brow as he stood among the piles of split wood, the scent of freshly chopped fir hovering lazily in the evening air. His pants were dirty from the long day's chores, and his suspender straps hung loosely at his knees. The sleeves of his sweat-stained undershirt were rolled up, the chest open to the second button. He pressed a warm and calloused right hand massaging his sore left shoulder and heard the light footsteps of his new wife, Ada.

He smiled dutifully as she offered him a tin cup brimming with cool water. He drank it greedily, enjoying the fresh splash the water made as it overflowed his parched lips and dotted his sweaty chest.

Ada waited patiently until he'd drained the cup dry and then accepted it into her small, frail hands. Taking the cup from Patrick, she said ominously, "A visitor came by the house today."

"Who?" His question was perfunctory; he merely wanted to get back to his chores before sundown so he could eat and hit the hay; it had been another long day.

She shrugged and then scowled. It was her favorite expression. "Some meddling teacher from the school."

"What did he want?"

Ada's expression warned that it wasn't a social visit. "The girl's in trouble again, Patrick. Causing fights. Brawling in the schoolyard. They don't know what to do with her. Say they're at their wits' end."

Patrick shook his head, admiring the glow of the setting sun as it graced the horizon of his sprawling property. It was a bittersweet feeling, to be so proud of what he'd accomplished and so disappointed in his daughter.

"But I had such high hopes for her here. A new start, a fresh start..."

His voice trailed off, and Ada quickly silenced it. "They want us to pull her out of school, or they'll expel her."

Patrick looked up with a start. Expulsion? Polly? It hardly seemed conceivable, and yet in his mixed-up, topsy-turvy world, nothing really seemed real anymore. He had to admit, the girl had been lost since her mother passed. Still...expulsion?

He sighed heavily, leaning on the handle of his ax as if he were carrying the weight of the world on his shoulders.

His voice ached as he voiced his frustrations to his new wife. "Doesn't make any sense, Ada. Girl loves learning. She's always been that way. Like her mother."

Ada's eyes grew pinched and far away. Her voice crept into a lecturing tone, one Patrick quickly tired of. "Maybe so, Patrick, but she needs discipline if she's to get anywhere in this life."

Patrick nodded as he stared out at the horizon, watching the day slip away as swiftly, as easily, as his past. Where had his old life gone? Buried, it would seem, in the ground with his first wife, Sarah. If only she were still alive, he fretted, she would know what to do. Or, better yet, there'd be nothing to do because Polly would still be the happy, radiant, smart girl she'd been before Sarah died.

84

He'd hoped that Ada would be a good influence on the girl, but so far that hadn't come to pass. With the ever-growing list of duties of the farm pressing tighter and tighter on his chest, not to mention his time, he hardly had three hours of sleep per night, let alone the time to tend to poor Polly. Ada's voice was shrill, as if sensing he needed to be jerked from his reverie.

"School's no use to her anyway, dear. She can learn more about housekeeping from me. She'll be of marrying age soon. Time she learned to cook and sew and care for a man in the proper way."

Patrick watched his wife's mouth move, heard the words she was saying, but it all gave him pause. Sarah had always wanted Polly to finish her schooling, to get as much education as she could, for as long as she could, so she could have a life away from the farm, if that was what she wanted.

As far as Patrick could remember, that was what she'd wanted. Not a life away from her parents, necessarily, but a life of her own, a journey to call hers and hers alone.

He looked up at Ada, her arms crossed severely over her chest, lips pinched tightly. He wasn't up to an argument, not tonight. He still had the barn to clean, the hay to bale, and he'd had nothing but cold biscuits and jerky for lunch.

"Whatever you think is best, Ada. I'm up to my eyes in it here already."

Even as he bent over, sore at the back, to retrieve his ax, Patrick knew he'd given away much more than a mere decision about Polly's schooling. And yet, as Ada kissed him and shuffled away in her long, black gown, it seemed he had bigger fish to fry.

The night grew dark, and he lit the hurricane lamp with a hiss and a flicker to finish his chores. He drank water from the pump when his day was finally done, splashing water down his neck and under his arms to clean up for supper.

Breaking the quiet silence of the evening, he heard banging in the kitchen as he stood, just outside the screen door.

"I hate you!" Polly was shouting at Ada as she stood before the kitchen table, fists clenched. "You did this on purpose!"

Ada shook her head. "You did this, dear. If you hadn't acted so poorly, the school wouldn't have felt the need to expel you."

"They didn't!" Polly exploded, looking every which way for relief. Patrick knew she'd spot him and inched back into the darkness. Her eyes found only an empty porch as she began to cry, stomping up the stairs without another word.

In the wake of her outburst, Patrick could have sworn he heard Ada chuckling to herself as she dished up the stew that was their nightly dinner. He sighed, stomping his feet on the porch and walking into the kitchen.

"What in tarnation?" he asked, putting his hat on the rack by the door.

She didn't bother to look up from where she was placing biscuits on the table. "Don't you worry yourself none, Patrick. You asked me to take care of it. It's done taken care of."

He sat heavily, gulping sweet iced tea from a jelly jar until at last his thirst was slaked. Ada sat down across from him and sighed. "I don't know how I'm going to put up with her ill manners in this house all day long."

"She never used to be this way," Patrick grumbled around a mouthful of stew. It was too salty, as usual, but that was what the sweet tea was for. "Maybe…maybe I should talk to her, bring her up some dinner."

"You'll do no such thing! Punishment is punishment, Patrick. She'll go hungry and like it," Ada demanded. "Maybe she'll learn something tonight."

Patrick nodded. She was probably right. She was a woman, after all. A mother in her own right and Ike had turned out all right. Hadn't he?

Chapter 18

Siobhan tried to continue reading Polly's journal but realized the light in her room was almost gone, and her face was coming dangerously close to the carefully scripted print. She'd only just sat down to read a few pages, or so it seemed, and that had been midafternoon!

Now she flicked on a lamp and, peering out the window, saw Zachariah sitting on the porch. From above, he seemed as frail and out of place as a Halloween decoration left out too long in the sun. His limbs were tiny and weak, his hair sparsely covering his liver-spotted scalp. She knew he liked to sit there in the evenings, his nurse nearby but not close enough to be a bother, keeping watch over the property.

What's more, she knew he liked to do it alone.

But tonight, she needed answers, and unfortunately, the old man was the only one able to give them to her. She grabbed a sweater from the foot of the bed, wrapped it around her shoulders, slipped her feet into her leather driving shoes, and crept down the steps.

She stood at the screen door silently, waiting for some sound of acknowledgment, a grunt or a sigh, but none came. She watched his lanky frame in silhouette, his cowboy hat slung low over his forehead, slippered feet resting gently on the pads of his wheelchair, a cup of coffee cooling in his lap.

The nurse sat in a wicker rocker, reading another giant romance novel by the weak porch light. She looked up, saw Siobhan, and faintly nodded before returning to her book.

Siobhan cleared her throat gently, and the old man barely stirred.

"Last night on the stairs..." she began softly, so as not to jar him. "You thought I was Polly."

Casting his gaze out from under the brim of his cowboy hat, Zachariah merely grunted. He raised the coffee to his lips and sipped it slowly, as if stalling for time. She noticed his hands trembling but wasn't sure if that was just palsy or a reaction to her question.

Siobhan pressed on. "Polly's my ancestor. But I don't know anything about her."

At last, Zachariah cleared his throat and turned to face her. By then, Siobhan had slunk through the screen door and stood, leaning against its other side.

"Why the sudden interest, girl?" he spat, sneering at her. "You don't want to know anything about her. She's a curse, and curses are best left in the past."

His voice was curt and sour, as if he'd just bitten into a coffee ground. He was normally close to comatose; she wanted to know why the sudden ire. "Why? What did she do?"

His eyes were dark beneath the brim of his hat, or maybe it was just a shadow cast by the weak porch light. Either way, she took an involuntary step back. "Why do you think this family has suffered so much bad luck? I won't have Polly's name mentioned in this house again."

Then she found herself taking two steps forward. She could barely conceal the fury in her voice.

"I'm not a child, Zachariah," she snapped. "You know, I can't believe how selfish you are! You won't even tell me about my own family. Why? What's wrong with you? You're dying, aren't you? You never let anyone forget it."

He waved a liver-spotted hand. "You don't understand."

"What don't I understand?"

He cast his gaze past the porch to his sprawling ranch. "We're a product of the past."

She was sitting on the porch railing now, arms folded, staring back at him. "What are you talking about?"

The nurse creaked in her chair, and when Siobhan shot her a look, she noticed the romance novel now folded over her lap. Her voice was firm. "You're upsetting my patient."

"Well, he's upsetting me," Siobhan spat. "Besides, this is a private conversation."

The nurse sat back, as if she'd been slapped, and quickly hid in the pages of her novel. Siobhan instantly felt bad, but they both had it coming.

She turned back to face Zachariah. It was as if he'd been waiting for her full attention to croak, "Polly was a murderer."

She stopped cold, head swimming. The nurse looked up, sliding the paperback in the oversized pocket of her colorfully patterned work smock. "I think…I think that's enough for today, Mr. Zachariah, sir," she stammered, turning the man away from the porch and backing him into the house.

Siobhan stepped from the porch, heart hammering. The moon was full, the lawn wide, and she just…started running. It came upon her like a flash, the sudden inspiration to put one foot in front of the other, faster and faster. She bolted down the steps and onto the lawn and just. Kept. Going. Sprinting, fast, and far away from the porch. She ran until her legs gave out, and she sat, splayed, panting, beneath a giant tree, the distant light from the ranch house just a pale star on the grassy plain,

She pulled her knees to her chest, gasping for air, too shocked to cry, too numb to worry about anyone seeing her theatrics. As she caught her breath, she wished, wished for all the world that she'd brought the diary with her…

Chapter 19

Polly stood dusting the mantelpiece absently, arms sore from the morning chores she'd already done. Up before dawn, she'd beaten her own father to muck out the stalls, replace the hay, milk their cow "Bessie," and feed the pigs in their disgusting trough.

Now, exhausted before breakfast, she noticed a gleam of light as she stared out the window. She squinted to see it better, noting it was the light reflecting off the buckle on her teacher Mr. Lafayette's horse.

She gasped and gave the mantelpiece one last wave of her rag before reaching down to a wicker basket by the fireplace. To Ada, who was in the kitchen whipping up buck cakes for breakfast, she called out a frantic, "I'm off to fetch eggs."

She dropped the basket on the way out of the door and used both free hands to sprint down to the end of the lane before Mr. Davis could ride into view.

She was panting by the time she reached him, grabbing his horse's reins and staring up into the man's thick glasses.

"What are you doing here?" she hissed angrily.

He was taken aback by her tone and, flustered, answered, "You haven't been at school in weeks. I came to see what is wrong."

Polly clenched her fists and glared up at the man. "Wrong? I'll tell you what is wrong. You came and saw Ada, didn't you?"

Lafayette's eyes softened as he peered down at her. "You're angry with me."

She softened a bit, too, remembering how hard he'd tried to help her. Her voice was clipped. "You don't know who you're dealing with. She's evil." Even as she said the words, Polly glanced over her shoulder to make sure the stick-thin woman wasn't stomping down the lane in her black dress.

She felt a gentle hand on her shoulder. "Polly, I want to help you."

She looked back up at her teacher and shrugged off his hand, backing away. "Then get out of here, now."

He set his jaw and crossed his arms over his chest, the brim of his weathered gray hat casting shadows over his face. "I'm not going until you tell me what is wrong."

"Ugggh," she grumbled, biting her lip and stamping her feet. She turned once more, casting a worried glance back in the direction of the ranch.

His voice was calmer now, quieter. "I'm your friend, Polly."

Polly tried, and failed, to keep the naked desperation out of her voice. "Please, sir, if you're my friend, you have to go before she sees you. You're only making things worse for me right now."

She turned to him, naked fear in her eyes, stubborn persistence in his. Polly sighed, wriggling with uncertainty and paranoia. She knew, she just knew, Ada would be stomping down from the ranch at any second.

Finally, he leaned down in his saddle, leather creaking with each inch. "Meet me at the barn tonight, Polly. The ruined barn at the edge of Bonney's Canyon. We can talk then."

Ugh, he was making things worse, not better! "How will I get out after dark?"

Lafayette was persistent. "Just find a way to meet me there, OK? I'll wait for you. Come when you can. We'll work this out, I promise."

Polly shook her head even as she agreed, anything just to get him to go, to leave her father's property. "I'll try. Now, please go."

Lafayette turned to go and gave a backward glance. Their eyes met one last time. His gaze told her that he regretted leaving, and Polly only hoped he didn't see the look of desperation in her eyes as well.

She turned, hearing the sound of his horse's departing hooves in the rich dirt.

Chapter 20

Later that night, Polly held her boots in one hand while fluffing up a pillow under her blanket with the other. It didn't look terrible but in full light, not exactly believable. She blew out the candle next to her bed, and with the low light of the moon casting shadows from her tiny window across the room, it was an improvement.

She crept over to the door and hid in the corner so that, when it opened, she would be behind it. She waited, clutching her boots to her chest as if they might somehow protect her, until she heard her father's heavy footsteps out in the hall.

She sighed with relief; at least it wasn't Ada coming to check on her. The door opened slightly, and she held her breath. Her father, busy and impatient, cast a cursory glance inside Polly's bedroom and finding nothing out of sorts, shut the door behind him.

Polly breathed a sigh of relief and slipped into her boots, treading carefully across the floor until she reached the window. After quietly lifting the latch, she opened it quickly, slid out, and climbed down the tree just outside. The minute Polly's boots hit the ground, she raced down the lane and away from the ranch.

It wasn't far to Bonney's Canyon, but Polly walked carefully in the moonlight, none too eager to sprain an ankle tripping over a rock or old stump she couldn't see. The moon was half-full, but the night was cloudy, and her progress was slow.

She found the stream by sound first, the gurgling leading her slightly east until she saw the splash of water against slimy, slippery rocks and followed it down. The barn lay at the bottom of the stream, dilapidated and forlorn in the half-moonlight. A great oak tree stood beside it, towering and majestic, as if protecting the rotten beams and grassy foundation of the tired old barn at its feet.

Inside, a lantern flickered quietly and Lafayette looked up, relieved, when at last she walked inside the sagging doorway.

He stood abruptly from a broken chair. "Here. I brought you these." Polly looked down to his hands, which contained a pile of thick exercise books. She leaned closer to see the titles in the flickering lamplight: *Human Anatomy for Primary Students, Nursing for the Young Lady in Training.* Her heart swelled to think he'd remembered her interests, and she reached out, uncharacteristically, to hug him.

The books fell, and he leaned down, awkwardly, to grab them for her. "Thank you," she said when he handed them back, hoping he understood she meant it was for more than just the books.

He stood, straightened his jacket, and cleared his throat. "Polly, I'm sorry Ada took you out of school. It was my fault for coming to your house that day."

"No, it wasn't. You just gave her the idea. She wasn't smart enough to think of it for herself."

Polly offered a little smile at her own joke, but her teacher wasn't amused. "Will you tell me what is going on at home?"

"She wants to make my life a misery, and there's nothing I can do about it."

Lafayette nodded. "And the boy?"

Polly bit her lip and looked away. Lafayette sat back down on his seat, waiting patiently. A scratch of wood on wood shocked Polly out of her silence as she looked down to see that he had pulled another chair across from him. Heavily, she sank into it.

"Will you tell me about Ike?"

Polly bit her lip so as not to speak and resolutely shook her head. Lafayette sat back and nodded, taking off his hat and fiddling with its brim in his lap. "What do you want to be when you grow up, Polly?"

"Be? When I grow up?" Lafayette nodded; Polly shrugged, her voice low. She'd gotten so resigned to Ada's life view for herself that she no longer dared to dream of any other kind. "I'll work on my father's farm. Then get married."

"But what do you want to do?" her teacher persisted.

"Don't you see, Mr. Davis? It doesn't really matter what I want because women are worthless."

He sat forward, eyes shining in the lamplight. "That's not true, Polly. This land is crying out for skilled workers. Education is the future of this country."

Polly sat back and huffed. "Tell my stepmother that."

"I'm not interested in your stepmother, Polly. I'm interested in what you want to do with your life."

Polly sighed. "I'd be a nurse or a midwife. Help people, I guess. I like helping people…" Her voice trailed away, as she realized her ambitions were little more than a pipe dream at this point.

Lafayette's voice was firm, as it was in class when making a point. "You can't help people unless you help yourself. Haven't you heard of the saying, charity begins at home? Polly, if you tell me what is wrong, then I can help you."

Polly stared back at him numbly. This man didn't want to know what went on at home, not really. And even if he did, she couldn't tell him, not all of it.

He grunted and sat back, hanging his hat off one knee like her father often did. "You must get back. Take the books, Polly, and study when you can. Hide them if you must. We'll meet here again, OK?"

Polly nodded, but she had other business before she got back. "Please, sir, will you keep an eye on Lizzie? Don't ask me why. Just keep an eye on her. She's not as strong as me."

Lafayette sat back, looking surprised. "Of course, I will, Polly. I take care of all my students; that's why I'm here."

Polly nodded, a weight off her shoulders. She looked down at the books in her lap and then stood abruptly and hugged him quickly before heading for the door.

Chapter 21

Polly woke with a start, raising her head from her *History of Nursing* book, which she had used as a pillow. The lamp next to her bed still flickered, but she knew by the pale blue seam on the horizon that another morning had dawned.

She quickly checked to make sure her bedroom door was still closed and hurriedly hid the book with the others, beneath her mattress, where she was sure no one would look. After all, only Polly was ever given the chore of making anyone's bed!

With the books out of sight, Polly breathed a sigh of relief and blew out her lamp in the same gasp. She quickly dressed for the day and raced downstairs to begin her chores. She started in the kitchen, throwing out yesterday's coffee— but not without taking a sip or two for herself to start the day—and putting a fresh pot on to brew.

She bit a wedge off of a piece of stale biscuit from a tin she kept above the oven and took a swallow of fresh milk from the ice box to wash it down. When the dishes from last night were done and the breakfast table was set, she stole from the kitchen, still in the dark, and set out for the barn.

Polly bent herself to her chores all morning long, just as she did every day. She missed the rush of running to school and meeting friends like Lizzie behind the schoolhouse, whispering and gossiping until the schoolmaster Lafayette called them in with a knowing wink.

She missed turning in her assignments and the rush of pride it gave her to get them back with an "A" or even a "B+" in red wax pen at the top. She missed the hush of the classroom as Mr. Lafayette walked around the room, reading aloud from one of their story primers, his voice booming when necessary or soft and hushed if the story called for it.

Most of all, she missed getting off the farm for a few hours every day, traipsing through the woods on the way home, getting into adventures, even trouble. Now she worked so hard, so long, and so often, there was little time for either anymore.

Noon came before she knew it, the dull growling in her stomach a reminder of how quickly the morning had flown by. Polly stole into the kitchen when Ada wasn't looking and grabbed a wedge of thick bacon off of Ike's plate. She took pleasure that he wasn't there to try to stop her but ate it with a frown, wondering where he might be. With Ike, no news was ever good news; it just meant he was up to something sneakier than usual.

She found out what it was later that night when, exhausted and dirty, she slumped back into the kitchen. The room was silent, which was odd since the whole family, pitiful as it was, had gathered around the kitchen table.

She reached for a biscuit with dirty hands, not caring if Ada smacked her hand with the worn wooden serving spoon as she often did. When no one said a word, her attention was slowly drawn to the middle of the dinner table, food forgotten and getting cold. Her heart went to her stomach as her eyes fell on the stack of books carefully placed in the middle of the table. Polly's books.

Her face burned as she turned to Ike, sitting proudly across from the kitchen door. "I found 'em in your room, Polly," he said with a cruel smile, nodding toward the pile in the center of the table.

"What were you doing in my room, Ike?" Polly demanded.

"That's not the point," said her father, his face a stone mask.

"Why not? I'm not allowed to go into his room, Papa! Why is he allowed to go into mine?"

"I asked him to," Ada interrupted, avoiding Polly's eyes, proving her words a lie. "I...I wanted him to see if you had any laundry. While looking around, he spotted a lump under your mattress. Thinking it might be some dirty clothes you didn't want me to find, he found...these...instead."

Polly clenched her fists at her side, knowing the woman was lying, knowing Ike went snooping specifically looking for something to incriminate her but powerless to dispute it. Polly knew from experience that even if she raised the roof with her protests, Papa would only listen to Ada.

"Where did they come from, Polly?" Her father's voice sounded guarded, and he kept flicking glances at Ada as if he were reading off of a script.

"I...I kept them from when you took me out of school," she said back to Ada.

Ada's nostrils flared. "Liar!" she hissed. "I know they're from that meddling teacher who keeps sniffing around here. I've a good mind to go straight to the school board about this, tell them what—"

"No!" Polly begged, falling to her knees with the thought of her schoolmaster getting into trouble. "It was my fault, I promise. I asked him for the books. I begged him for them. Don't...it wasn't...don't say anything, please."

Ike and Ada smiled to each other. "Be that as it may..." her stepmother said, rising from the table and taking the stack of books with her. As she spoke, she fed each book into the fire, one by one, Polly's dreams of an educated future far away from the farm burning like cinders with each smoky page. "It was his responsibility to listen to your family's wishes. I think young master Lafayette will be looking for another job, in another town, by the time I'm through with him..."

The last thing Polly saw before she stormed up the stairs was Ike's face, sneering back at her from the dinner table.

Chapter 22

Siobhan knelt in front of an old gravestone, clearing away old flowers and overgrown weeds with her bare hands. Carved into the marble, roughly with little fanfare, was a simple name and set of dates:

POLLY O'NEAL (1853–1953)

Siobhan rocked back on her heels, resting gently in the cold, bare earth as she sat alone in the weed-strewn cemetery. It felt so final, finding Polly's grave in the small, unmarked graveyard nestled in Bonney's Canyon.

The grave looked so cold and unadorned; she was sure no one had been to visit in years, possibly decades. How could one so strong, with so much potential, live a life so uncelebrated by the end? It gave Siobhan pause to wonder who might visit her own grave, years from now.

The crunching of leaves alerted her to someone else in the graveyard, which was not only surprising but shocking. The place looked as if it hadn't been visited in years. She stood, spotting a small, frail woman leaning against the small, rusty gate at the cemetery's mouth.

She was old and terribly thin. Siobhan rushed over, only then spotting the long white cane the woman clutched in two gnarled hands. Dark glasses covered her eyes and half her small, withered face.

"Who is it?" asked the woman in a soft, tremulous voice, nonetheless tinged with alarm. "I...there's never anyone here to come when I visit. Who's there?"

Siobhan spoke gently, so as not to shock or surprise. "My name's Siobhan. I'm from the Davis ranch."

The woman nodded and then offered a thin-lipped smile around large, coffee-stained teeth. "I'm Estelle," she said. "I live in the village. You're one of Polly's descendants, aren't you?"

Siobhan nodded out of instinct and then realized the blind woman was waiting for an answer. "Yes. I heard about you too. I wanted to talk to you about Polly."

"Can I look at you?" Estelle asked shyly after a long pause.

"Of course."

Estelle held out a hand, gently applying her fingertips, cold and calloused, against Siobhan's face. She took her time, and to make it easier, Siobhan crouched down considering the old woman's slight stature. Gently, Estelle traced her fingertips across Siobhan's features, as if trying to figure out the answer to a problem.

"You look just like her," Estelle said, hands still clasped on either side of her face.

Siobhan stiffened; Estelle removed her hands. "What is it, dear?"

Siobhan stood back up, leaning against the waist-high fence that circled the neglected graveyard. "My father said that, too. Did you know Polly?"

Estelle nodded, leaning against her cane. She wore a heavy tweed jacket and tiny khaki pants. "I knew her when I was a little girl. She was my friend. My mother died when I was young, and Polly used to look out for me. She had a difficult life. She endured a lot. She needs your help now, Siobhan."

Siobhan felt her jaw go slack. "I-I-I don't understand. How can she need my help now?"

Estelle dug into the pocket of her jacket and found something. She gently placed it into Siobhan's hand. Siobhan slowly opened her hand, finding a posy of fresh lavender resting gently in her palm.

Estelle smiled. "Polly always loved lavender."

Though Estelle said no more about it, Siobhan suddenly understood; it was Polly that the old woman had been coming to visit, Polly for whom the lavender was intended. She walked away, a few gentle paces over dead leaves and twisting ivy, placing the small bundle of lavender at the base of Polly's headstone.

She stood and turned back to Estelle. "What happened to Polly?"

Estelle merely offered a wry smile. "Just keep looking. You'll find the answers that you seek. Polly will help you, too. She'll help you understand…"

Siobhan stood next to Polly's grave, slightly mystified. Estelle offered another wry smile. "I don't even have to feel your face to see you're confused, Siobhan."

Siobhan nodded, aware that Estelle couldn't see her. She took a step forward, and Estelle spread out her hands. "You're in the right spot, dear. Bonney's Canyon is the key to understanding Polly."

Siobhan nodded. "Bonney's Canyon is where Polly used to meet her teacher. What happened to them?"

Estelle offered a curious expression. "Just keep looking, Siobhan. I have to go now."

Then the old woman turned and, using her cane, gently began walking away. Noting the sudden silence, Siobhan asked, "Estelle? Where have the birds gone? I can't hear them anymore."

From over her shoulder, Estelle counseled, "The rooks are here. When they leave, the birds will come back."

Siobhan followed restlessly, as if the morning's spell might be broken if she lost sight of the old woman. "And when will that be?"

Estelle paused. "The rooks always leave their nest at the first sign of death."

Siobhan nodded and looked up into the treetops, finding them darkened with shadows and eerily still. When she looked back to ask Estelle again, the old woman was gone. She felt an odd shiver and crossed her hands protectively across her chest. The morning hadn't felt quite so cold before the old woman's visit.

Chapter 23

The saloon was rowdy with sweaty cowboys drinking, playing cards, and gambling, some of them sitting with painted ladies on their knees. The rough-hewn floor was covered with sawdust and wet with beer foam, and there was a spittoon full to overflowing every few steps.

Ada stood just inside the swinging doors, dressed all in black, the shawl over her head like a hood as she let her eyes adjust to the dim, flickering oil lamps that provided the saloon's only light.

The cowboys ogled her openly, but she ignored their catcalls and narrowed her eyes, searching the darkened room intently, as she did most everything else.

She spotted Ike leaning casually against the bar, eyes glassy and no wiser to her appearance than he was to his mounting bar tab. He hoisted another sloppy shot of rum to his lips but never tasted it. Ada waited until the greasy glass was halfway to his mouth before grabbing his ear and yanking him away, the glass spilling its amber liquid onto the pitted bar.

"Ma?" Ike gasped, far more interested in staring at his spilled shot than facing Ada's wrath.

Ada continued yanking as Ike finally let go of the brass bar rail. "That's quite enough, young man."

The cowboys roared with laughter, patting Ike on the back as his mother dragged him through the crowd and out the saloon door. He was dead weight, but she'd brought the trail cart, low and long and sagging beneath him as she hoisted Ike in the back.

He sat up, scratching his head, face flushed with alcohol, tongue thick with rum. "Ma? What is it?"

Ada stared back at Ike, face like stone, mouth set into a grim, tight slash. When at last she spoke, her tone was as sharp as steel. "You need to be more careful, son," she hissed. "There's only so much I can protect you from."

Ike sat there, mouth open, eyes closed, limbs slack, already passed out.

Ada clucked her tongue and pushed him over, waiting until he'd slumped into a ball to slam the cart's gate shut. Without another word, she mounted the stiff box in front, lashed out at the single dray horse, and headed for home, Ike snoring with every mile.

Chapter 24

Polly paced anxiously, fretting in the dilapidated barn deep in Bonney's Canyon. Every minute that passed meant one more opportunity for Ada to rise from her slumber, slip into Polly's room, and find her missing.

She hadn't wanted to meet with her teacher so soon, but what choice did she have? Polly was especially desperate for news of her best friend Lizzie. She'd gone missing the day before, and no one had seen her since.

Now Lafayette was late, which made her even more nervous because her former teacher was always—but there, what was that? The crack of a stray twig, the creak of the barn door, and there he was, face flushed by the long ride in from town, eyes downcast.

He spoke quickly, putting Polly at ease. "They found Lizzie."

"Oh thank God," she sputtered, collapsing onto a moldy hay bale. "I'm so relieved. So she's OK. What happened?"

But his words, which brought Polly such relief, didn't match Lafayette's face. He said nothing, eyes sad and watery as he stared down at his muddy shoes.

She waited for him to speak, but his silence spoke volumes. Suddenly, a horrified look washed over Polly's face. "No!" she shouted, springing to her feet. "No, it can't be. Tell me, tell me I'm wrong. Tell me…tell me you're wrong!"

She paced wildly, not sure what to do or where to go. Lafayette grabbed her firmly by the shoulders and forced her to look at him. "She's dead. Suffocated."

His voice sounded hoarse, distant, but his eyes told the truth. She slumped back down onto the hay bales, struggling to take in the news, desperate to make sense of it all.

Lafayette stood before her. "Listen to me, Polly. We don't have much time." He began pacing, talking with his hands. "I...I want to get you away from that woman." Polly looked up. He didn't have to say the name for her to know he was talking about Ada. "I want you to come with me right now. It's not...not safe where you are."

Polly shook her head instinctively. It was out of the question, ridiculous for him to even suggest it. Didn't he know what it was like under Papa's roof, Ada and her black shawl and iron fist, her beady eyes and Ike's thundering feet pounding everywhere?

The very thought made her panic and, yet, gave her hope. She found herself repeating the offer, almost soundlessly: "Come...with...you?"

He paused, looking down at her, eyes wide. "You're in danger, Polly. I can feel it. Come with me, and we'll get away from this place."

She was still shaking her head, even as she allowed her heart to hope, to dream. "Where...where will we go?"

Now it was Lafayette's turn to shake his head. "It doesn't matter, Polly. I'll look after you. It will be a challenge, but I can't leave you with that monster."

Polly crossed her arms over her chest, resolved to her fate. "I can't come with you. That would just be running away. And I have to make sure Ike gets what's coming to him."

He paused, staring down at her, eyes softening. "Ike, how...how did you know he was the last person to see Lizzie?"

Her head jerked up, eyes wide. "He was? I...I didn't know that, but it only figures."

"Why do you say that?"

Polly's eyes grew small, her voice lowering to match. "Ada and Ike, they killed my mother. And then he..." Her voice trailed away. "Shamed me," she finally confessed.

Lafayette reached out a comforting hand and then thought better of it. He stood, firm, face set with more resolve than ever. "Polly, whatever happened, it makes no difference to my feelings for you."

A voice from the darkness stunned them both into silence: "And what feelings are those?"

Ada stood, framed in the doorway, a triumphant look on her face. Polly gasped, stomach turning, palms instantly sweating. Her former teacher looked equally surprised as both turned to face the sudden—and most unwelcome—intruder.

Lafayette would not be deterred as he turned to Ada, taking a defensive position as Polly rose to join him. "I'm taking Polly with me."

Ada inched slightly into the barn, moonlight from a broken window casting shadows against her pallid skin and haunted cheeks. "How many times do I have to tell you, Professor? She ain't my blood. Take her if'n you want her. Ain't of no consequence to me. But I'll have to explain it to her father. So it'll cost you."

Her dark eyes shone with greed as Polly inched closer to Lafayette.

"What are you talking about?" he barked.

She nodded her head at Polly for emphasis, a twisted smile crossing her hard, wicked face. "A Catholic school teacher like you in love with a minor? Girl's only fourteen years old. What would your precious church say?"

Polly looked up at her teacher, finding him at a loss for words for the first time in his life. Color rose to his cheeks, but that didn't stop Ada. In fact, it only egged her on. "Don't matter where you run," she hissed, taking another step closer. "Your reputation will follow you. I'll make sure of it."

Lafayette tried to sputter out a response, but Polly cut him short. "I'll come home, Ada, just leave him out of it. You can do what you like to me, but please leave him alone."

Lafayette stood his ground, suddenly finding his voice. "No, Polly. I won't be blackmailed by this woman."

Ada's triumphant smile never faltered as she gloated. "There's examinations they can do you know. See if she's still a virgin."

Polly dropped her eyes to the floor, her cheeks aflame. Lafayette shifted from foot to foot even as Ada drew ever nearer. "Face it, Mr. Davis. You ain't got no choice in this here matter." She shook her head. "Taking the honor of an underage girl. That's a prison offense."

Lafayette finally snapped, wagging a finger back in Ada's tight face. "You evil woman. You talk about honor! What about your son?"

Ada only shrugged, her eyes never leaving Lafayette's. "Don't know what you're talking about. Ike ain't done nothin'. He's a good boy."

Polly rushed between them. It was clear Lafayette was outmatched, and the more he said, the worse it would be for her in the end. "I'll come back with you, Ada. Just leave Mr. Davis out of it."

Ada looked through her and stared cruelly at Lafayette. "I'll do that all right, but mark my words, you two won't be seeing each other no more."

Polly turned to Lafayette, tugging on his jacket to get his attention. He offered a weak smile in return as he looked down at her. "It's better this way. Forget about me, Mr. Davis."

He reached out to squeeze her shoulder, turning toward Ada. Puffing out his chest, he took two quick steps until he was standing before her. For the first time, Ada flinched and shrank back.

Lafayette's voice thundered off the old barn walls as he quoted from her own good book: "Cease from anger, and forsake wrath for evildoers shall be cut off, but those that wait upon the Lord, they shall inherit the earth."

Recovering herself, Ada chuckled dryly. "I'm not afraid of your unforgiving God. He ain't never shown me no mercy anyhow."

At last, Ada turned her cold glare toward Polly. "Come on then, girl."

Without another word, Ada pushed Polly out the door. As she was ushered out the door, Polly turned and saw Lafayette staring after her, fists clenched at his sides, lips moving silently, begging her forgiveness.

Chapter 25

Polly lay on her bed, curled into a tight ball, bruised and sore from Ada's vicious beating. Her tears were long since dry, and now, instead of sniffling, she listened intently to the heated discussion her father and stepmother were having in the kitchen below.

The voices were muffled, but the ranch house was full of small gaps and cracks where, if one knew to look out for them, one could still make out everything that was being said in one room or another.

Polly could hear her father's big boots pacing on the pine slats of the kitchen floor, his heavy, muscular body working up and down the room as he argued with her stepmother. "I won't hear of it, Ada. She's my daughter. I will not abandon her."

The words gave Polly reason to unfurl from her bed like a slowly creeping flag, and she crept toward her door. As her father spoke, she used his deep voice to mask the sound of her bedroom door opening.

Moving carefully from her room, she stepped cautiously and quietly, to avoid the squeaky spots in the hallway floor. Gently crouching, she listened from the top of the stairs, her father's voice clearer now, but no less upset. If she leaned forward just a bit, she could see his dirty work boots pacing the clean pine floor. Ada, hidden from view, seemed no less dangerous as her bitter words filled the kitchen.

"She's nothing but trouble, Patrick. She won't be happy until she destroys us. God knows I've tried to be a mother to her."

Her father stopped pacing momentarily, disappearing from view. Probably to hug or comfort Ada, Polly thought with a sour face. Soon, his voice returned, calmer now, softer, almost soothing.

"I know, Ada. But we need to give it more time. Be patient. She's grieving. Can't you see it?" he asked. "I thought you, being a mother yourself, would understand."

Ada's voice was firm and, like her posture, unyielding. "No, Patrick. She's got to go."

Polly held her breath, waiting for her father's reply. Every second that ticked by on the old grandfather clock in the hall broke her heart just a little bit more. He should have fought for her, begged for her, demanded on her behalf. Instead, his long, stony silence only revealed how little he thought of his own daughter.

She was about to stand, to crumple back onto her bed and find fresh tears to cry when the silence was abruptly broken by the loudest banging she had ever heard as someone pounded on the front door. She quickly scrambled up and out of sight, using the pounding as cover for her furtive footsteps.

Kneeling at the top of the stairs, just out of sight, she watched as her father strode to the door, Ada still clinging to his shoulder, tall, thin, and rigid in her tight black dress.

"Who can that be at this hour?" Patrick demanded, yanking open the door.

Polly had to cover her mouth to hide a gasp. There, on the front stoop, stood two burly men. One was short and stocky, with a shiny tin badge reading "Deputy" over his left pocket. The other man was tall and imposing; he wore a sheriff's badge on his chest that glinted in the light that came from the oil lamp burning in the hallway.

Next to him, his deputy tipped his hat. They looked back at Patrick as Ada stood, just off to the side, quietly, coldly calculating.

There was a slight pause as Polly watched her father straighten, staring back at his guests speechless. As long as she'd been alive, he'd never had any dealings with the law.

The sheriff took one step forward. "You the head of this household? Mr. Patrick O'Neal?"

Polly's father cleared his throat. She could tell from the sound of his voice he was nervous but trying hard to hide it. "Yes, sir, I am. What business brings you here at this hour, Sheriff?"

The sheriff jutted out his jaw and announced, "We're looking for your boy, Ike. He's under arrest."

Ada gasped. Polly watched, with some satisfaction, as she clung to the doorjamb for support.

Patrick ignored her, moving closer to the sheriff. "Under arrest? What in God's name has he done?"

"A young woman by the name of Lizzie Macintyre was found suffocated earlier today." The sheriff took off his hat and held it in his hands before continuing. "Her father found a letter in her bedroom. She implicated this young man, Ike."

Polly watched as Patrick shook his head, stealing a glance at Ada. Finding her clinging to the wall at his side, he squeezed her shoulder. She shrugged it off vehemently and stood next to him, looking up into the sheriff's weathered face. "No, there must be some mistake, Sheriff. My boy didn't do it. Girl could have been crazy in love with him for all you know. What legal bearing can you give to a note?"

The sheriff looked uncomfortably from Ada to Patrick and back to Ada again. "With all due respect, ma'am. There's no mistake. Other witnesses have come forward."

Ada stood in shock, her mouth opening and closing silently, like a fish gasping for air. Polly was watching her, no longer gleeful, when there came a sound behind her. A window slid open in Ike's bedroom, followed by the scuffling of feet. Polly ran to his room, swinging open the door just in time to see her stepbrother leaping from his second-floor window.

He landed with a thud that she was sure could be heard from the front of the house. Polly ran back to the stairs just as the sheriff turned to his deputy. "That's him. He's trying to get away. Get after him!"

Without pause, the deputy bolted from the porch, coiled and fast despite his massive size. Polly stumbled down the steps, still clad in the clothes she'd worn to her clandestine meeting with Lafayette earlier that night.

At the sound of her boots clomping down the steps, her father turned. "Polly—"

Then he turned as Ada slunk through the doorway, wiry and already defensive, following the sheriff around to the side of the house. Polly followed, her father at her side.

From the back of the house, just down the trail to the barn, came the unmistakable sounds of a scuffle—grunting and punching, whining and moaning.

From down the rise, the deputy dragged Ike beside him, the young boy's face red and puffy from the effort, his eye puffy from a recent punch. Ike pleaded desperately with his mother, tears springing forth as he blathered, "I didn't do it, Ma. I'm innocent."

The deputy cuffed the boy on the head as Ada protested. The sheriff ignored them both. "Quiet, boy. We already got a list of convictions as long as your arm after all your petty thieving. The court will decide who's innocent."

Patrick tried to collect himself. Ada wept in his arms.

"We're taking him to the county jail. He'll be sentenced in the morning," said the sheriff.

The two men each took one of Ike's arms and led him, sobbing, toward the coach parked in front of the cabin. Polly stood on the porch, watching as they tossed Ike in the back of the rough wooden coach and locked it tight.

Ada followed, breaking away from Patrick, howling into the night. Polly's father walked toward the coach just as the sheriff and his deputy rose onto the front seat.

He turned, just in time to see Polly turning to go into the house. His voice was quiet, almost soft. "Polly?"

Polly vaulted up the stairs, suddenly and violently sick. She barely had time to climb the steps and sprint into her room before vomiting into the chamber pot beneath her bed.

Sweat covered her body, trickling down her neck and covering her forehead and beneath her arms. She stood on wobbly knees, kicking the chamber pot back beneath her bed. Staring out her bedroom window, she watched as the sheriff's coach rode quickly away, the horses pounding back out into the night.

The glass was cool as she leaned her forehead against it, rubbing her swollen belly.

Chapter 26

The range was long, and Siobhan had ridden for acres and acres before she heard the telltale sound of clicking and chirping as the different ranch hands herded the two hundred head of cattle in their own, distinct way.

She paused at the crest of a slow, rolling hill, staring down into the small valley where Jesse and his cowboys circled the steer in what looked, to her at first, like controlled chaos.

But after a few minutes, she could see a pattern developing, the way some cowboys kept the herd moving forward while others corralled stragglers, keeping them in line.

It seemed so simple and yet so very complex. She smiled to think that cowboys had been herding cattle this way for centuries. Finally, her excitement overtook her admiration, and she gently tapped the side of her horse, plunging forward down into the small valley until the ground grew smooth under the horse's hooves.

She steered clear of the cowboys and their work, but as Jesse came around the revolving circle, she waved him over. His face lit up to see her, perhaps simply because she was a break from the dull monotony of moving a hundred thousand pounds of beef from one side of the valley to the other.

"Siobhan," he said, almost out of breath from the dash across the valley. "It's great to see you out here, looking so…happy."

"I am," she gushed, breathless herself, but for different reasons. "Jesse, you'll never guess what just happened."

He looked skeptical but pleased. "Go on surprise me. Where did you get to?"

"I went down to Polly's gravestone. I remembered where it was. I saw Estelle. We talked about Polly."

Jesse's face literally fell. One minute, he had been happy and hopeful, sitting on his horse looking like the Marlboro Man, the next, it was as if death had touched his shoulder. "Siobhan, that…that can't be."

The sudden change upset her. "What's wrong, Jesse?"

She heard the sound of creaking leather as he shifted in his saddle.

"Estelle died last night."

Siobhan sat back in her saddle, wounded by his words. In the distance, the cowboys were whistling and hollering for his return. "I…I'm sorry, Siobhan."

With a click and a tug on the reins, he wheeled his horse around and sped off toward the herd. She watched him go, the sound of his clicking and the horse's hooves growing distant as the herd drifted away across the valley.

Up a gentle incline, the cowboys led the herd toward a summer pasture, ripe with the rich field grass that kept the cows big and hearty until they had worn out their welcome and would be moved yet again.

She watched them march, heart pounding, breath shallow, until she noticed a young cowboy who had paused at the foot of the incline. He was facing her, as was his horse. She inched closer, watching him until he took off his hat and placed it against his chest, the way cowboys will at a rodeo when they play the national anthem.

He silently mouthed the word "Hello," and she gasped.

"Mitch?" she asked, just as silently. As Siobhan reeled, Mitch put his hat back on and guided his horse up the gentle slope to catch up with Jesse and the rest of the ranch hands.

Siobhan turned, shell-shocked. The horse loped slowly back to the ranch as if on autopilot—first, Jesse with the news that Estelle had passed away the day earlier, and now here was Mitch. With the ranch coming into view, Siobhan couldn't help but feel that she'd seen two ghosts that day…

Chapter 27

SIX MONTHS LATER

Polly knelt by her bed, shifting until she found a comfortable position. It was early still, and she had much to do, despite her delicate condition. As always, now more than ever it seemed, she greeted the day with her morning prayers.

Bowing her head reverently onto the freshly made bed, she quietly whispered so she wouldn't wake her father: "Hail Mary, full of grace. Our Lord is with thee..."

Polly smiled bittersweetly, remembering fondly how she and her mother would often recite the prayer together before bed. Now Polly was so tired after her daily chores, she barely had time to pull back the covers before falling fast asleep, never mind praying.

"Blessed art thou among women, and blessed is the fruit of thy womb, Jesus. Holy Mary, Mother of God..."

Over her whispering, Polly heard the sounds of stirring from the thin walls that separated her bedroom from her father's. As the iron bed slowly creaked, Ada's shrill voice hissed urgently, in midconversation: "...told you she is evil, Patrick. What's more, she has brought shame to this household."

Polly leaned back from the bed, struggling to rise. She favored her swollen belly, which seemed to grow by the day. Even now, the tiny child inside squirmed with the movement, making her smile and then frown at almost the same time.

Fear gripped her as she sat on the narrow bed in the darkened bedroom. She had had little choice but to admit her pregnancy, especially with Ada always snooping around, "grading" how well she did her chores and noticing how, each day it seemed, she was wearing looser and looser clothing.

At first, Polly was sickened by the thought of bearing Ike's child. It seemed so monstrous, so incredibly sinful, but as the weeks dragged on and she came to terms with both her changing body and the innocent being that was growing inside, she gradually fell in love with her own child.

She sat down on the bed gently, close to the wall. Ada's voice was growing even shriller as she continued, "I'll take care of the baby like I said I would."

Polly clenched her pillow tightly, eyes growing wide. Her father's voice was deep but quiet as he asked, "What do you mean by that?"

Ada's reply was chillingly calm. "I mean I'll do what's best. For my family. For our family."

Polly rose quietly, using the nightstand to steady herself. On quiet feet, she left her room and crept down the stairs. Beneath the sink was a bucket she used daily, containing all the cleaning supplies she'd need to keep the tiny ranch house spic and span, from top to bottom.

She bent carefully, grabbing the bucket and inching into the living room. It was sparsely furnished, a few chairs and small tables, a woven throw rug that needed batting each week.

Polly left the kitchen behind, knowing that Ada preferred she cleaned it after breakfast was prepared and lunch and dinner as well. For now, she approached the mantel to dust its odd gathering of sad little knickknacks: a porcelain cross Ada had picked up somewhere, a framed picture of Ike that always made Polly wince, a small tin box full of spare buttons and pins.

As she dusted and polished, lost in thought, the pressure from her swollen belly already making her back sore, her legs tired, she noted a fresh newspaper clipping sitting next to Ike's framed photo.

Polly picked it up and stared at it, her eyes taking in a recent photo of Ike. It looked like it was taken in prison; his hair was cropped short, his eye blackened, probably after a run-in with some guard or other inmate. Even bruised, battered, and behind bars, his eyes looked smug and satisfied, as if he was in control and just where he wanted to be.

In bold type above his picture, the headline screamed: "Outlaw Breaks Free from Portland Jail." Next to it, a smaller but more chilling subheadline read: "Whereabouts Still Unknown."

As Polly put it back, a floorboard creaked behind her. She jumped at the noise, turning, and clutching her dust rag to her chest in fear and surprise. "Papa." She sighed, breathing a sigh of relief as Patrick stood, chiseled face buried in shadows from the flickering gas lamp on the coffee table.

The last six months had not been kind to Patrick. He'd lost weight, and combined with a bad case of insomnia, he looked haggard and gaunt. His thick, lustrous hair now hung limply, and Polly noticed his shirt was sticking out of his stiff work pants.

She pointed to the clipping. "Why is this here, Papa? It's so...shameful."

He followed her eyes and studied the clipping carefully. When he turned back to Polly, his eyes were sad and tired. "Ada can't read. I lied and told her it sounded like Ike was doing well. To protect her."

Polly let out an instinctive huff. Choking back tears, she croaked, "You didn't do a very good job of protecting me." As he stood, impassively, she added beneath her breath, "Or Momma."

Patrick's jaw clenched before he turned and left the room without a word. In the kitchen, he set to making the coffee, and she heard the kitchen chair scrape across the floorboards as he sat, waiting for it to brew.

As she turned, finishing dusting the last knickknack, a searing pain flared through her lower belly. She bit her lip and whispered to herself, "The baby..."

Chapter 28

Somehow, Polly managed to slip through the back door and hobbled down to the barn without alerting Patrick to her absence. Along the way, her water broke, splashing across her stockings and shoes, gushing onto the dewy earth as dawn still lurked just below the horizon.

She limped carefully into the barn, crouching in a dark, quiet corner where they stored the towering hay bales, hoping none of the still-sleeping animals would rouse her father. She lay there, whimpering and in pain but powerless to stop the force of nature that gushed between her legs.

The pressure, the pain, was intense. As her pain neared its worst, she feared she might bite off her tongue to keep from screaming. She found a stick and wedged it between her teeth, biting down as, at last, the baby rushed forth, spilling into the folds of her dress, sticky and quivering.

Still in searing pain, she gasped, spitting the stick from her mouth and grabbing a pocketknife from her pocket. As at last her little blue baby, a gurgling girl, gasped, she cut the umbilical cord and wrapped her in an old horse blanket from a nearby hay bale.

Sweat dripped down her forehead as she cried with relief, hugging the child to her chest and creeping up to lean against a hay bale, rocking her gently as she coughed and sputtered and cried gently in her arms.

One chubby pink arm slipped through the blanket. Polly smiled, moving her hand to replace it when the child grasped her fingers, weakly but instinctively. She cried openly, weeping from the pain and the shame and the shock and the sheer joy of motherhood.

Her voice was hoarse with emotion or perhaps simply exhaustion. "I'm going to call you Bonney, beautiful girl." She reached down, kissing the baby's head. Her skin was so warm and soft, covered in a soft smattering of hair so fine it could be thread on a loom.

The baby gurgled and cooed once more, halfway between waking and sleep, eyes struggling to stay open as Polly held her close. A shadow filled the door of the stall, and Polly gasped as she looked up to find Ada standing there, dressed as ever for a funeral, hands on her hips and wizened face scrunched up even further as she scowled down at the new mother.

"Keep away from me," Polly warned, inching back as far as she could go against the leaning hay bales.

Ada just stood, eyeing the squirming child. "Give it to me," she said, voice black as coal.

Polly held the child closer. "No. You can't have her."

Ada reached, and in her condition, Polly was no match for her wiry stepmother. Like a whirlwind, Ada filled the tiny horse stall and in seconds, yanked the crying child from her mother's arms.

Polly wailed, struggling to her feet as Ada turned and stomped across the barn. Polly stumbled, trying to follow, only to find her father there to catch her when she fell, just outside the stall door.

"Papa," she gasped, crying, beating his chest helplessly even as he lifted her and carried her back inside the house and up to her room. "Please, Papa, stop her!"

"Shhh, shhh now," he cooed gently, laying her in bed as effortlessly as a bag of cotton. "Rest now. Your stepmother knows what's best. She only wants a proper home for the child."

"What could be more proper than growing up with her mother?" Polly croaked, tears streaming down her cheeks. Her father's face was pale and slight, worn from the constant strain of Ada's browbeating and running the farm. He seemed, if anything, weaker than his daughter, who had just given birth.

Polly sobbed, as much for her father's cluelessness as for her child's predicament. He left the room, heavy on his work boots, shutting the door behind him. Polly felt faint, eyes flickering closed as her body seemed to sink into the bed. She blinked them open, not knowing if she'd dozed for a moment or for hours. Forcing herself, she rose heavily from the bed. Her skirt was ruined and damp, bloody and sticky as it brushed across her legs.

She walked to the window. Leaning on the sill, she threw it open, looking across the property until she saw Ada standing by the stand of trees that bordered their property. In the eerie blue light just before dawn, half-illuminated by the setting moon and the rising sun, Polly saw Ada bent to a task.

She only realized what it was when she saw the glint of a shovel as she tossed it aside. Then, without remorse, Ada grabbed tiny Bonney by one leg and tossed her into the shallow grave, the same way she often flung a doomed chicken onto the chopping block before she lopped off its head.

As Polly slumped to her knees while choking on a silent scream, Ada quickly covered the child in soft, dark soil.

Polly collapsed to the floor, pulling her knees to her chest as she lapsed into unconsciousness. She woke with a start to the sound of raised voices and Ada pounding her dirty boots on the front stoop.

Her father's voice sounded shocked as it drifted upstairs. "What...what have you done?"

Ada's voice was high and harsh in response. "What have I done? Don't you dare look at me that way, Patrick O'Neal. You were part of this, too."

Polly rose to her knees, using the bedpost as a guide, waiting for her father's reply. Either she missed it, or there was none, for the next voice she heard was Ada's as well: "What's wrong with you? She brought shame to this house. I rectified the situation. Don't blame me. It's her fault."

"But, Ada," her father finally sputtered, boots stomping across the floorboards as he followed his wife. "The child. You said you'd find it a good home... You said there were deserving parents waiting for it..."

"I said what I did, and I did what I said," Ada sneered, sounding so close she could only be at the foot of the stairs. Polly winced as her steps clamored upward. "Are you not a man? You could have stopped me if you wanted to, dear, but in the end, you knew I was right. I've always been right about her."

Their bedroom door slammed, and Polly winced. Downstairs, the house filled with silence. A few moments later, gravel crunched beneath her father's feet as he stomped toward the barn and once inside, slammed the massive door behind him.

Polly rose at last, silently slipping from her shoes. She walked out her bedroom door, half-conscious, drifting down the stairs as if in a dream. The light outside was still an eerie half-black, half-blue as the sun began its slow, inevitable rise.

She walked across gravel and dirt, pinecones and pebbles, until at last, she knelt at the foot of her poor child's grave. There was no headstone, only a soft mound of freshly dug earth. There, cast aside, was the same red blanket, still warm, with which Polly had swaddled the crying babe less than an hour before.

Polly stood, grabbed a fallen branch, and used it to dig into the soft, new earth. At last, she saw pale skin, bluish gray, the child already cold. Dropping the stick, Polly dug the rest of the grave by hand, until at last her child, her Bonney, was free of the dark, cold earth and once again swaddled in the warm, red blanket.

As if in a trance, Polly rose, clutching poor Bonney to her chest. She drifted along a familiar path, past the barn where her father worked, or sulked, or sometimes both. As she walked, she passed the stream that bordered their property and continued down into the quiet canyon finding the silent, dilapidated barn where she had so often met with her teacher, Lafayette.

A lone oak tree stood, just beyond the barn, nestled in a clearing. As if it were calling out her name, Polly approached the base of the tree and kneeling, laid the silent child at her feet. Finding a rock about the size of her fist, she began digging into the stubborn earth. The sun began to rise in earnest, warming the back of her neck, already soaked in sweat from her toil.

When at last the grave was deep enough, Polly dropped the rock and took one last look at Bonney. Her face was silent, neither smiling, nor frowning but completely expressionless, eyes closed forever in peace. Polly wept silently as she covered the babe once more in the red blanket before gently lowering her into the grave.

Quickly, she refilled it, packing the earth tightly, stamping it down. A cluster of wildflowers sat to one side, teeming yellow black-eyed Susans and white daisies and other valley flowers of purple and pink. She gathered a small cluster and laid them in the middle of the small plot of freshly moved earth.

She said a silent prayer, her second "Hail Mary" of the morning, before rising to one knee. In her pocket, she felt the heft of her folding knife. She spied the tree and in childish letters carved out the name: "Bonney."

Looking down upon the grave, smiling softly at the spray of wildflowers gently covering it, Polly whispered a solemn pledge: "I promise you I will never leave you. This land belongs to you now."

Closing her eyes and bowing her head, Polly made the sign of the cross. While far from at peace, Polly walked home her head held high. She had done the best she could, for her child, for herself. Now she had to—

A shotgun blast tore through the daybreak sky, echoing through the canyon as if a great battle were being waged. Polly instinctively broke into a run, sprinting back toward the cabin, knowing the only battleground in six miles was the one she'd just left...

Chapter 29

The closer Polly got to the ranch, the faster she ran. Her lungs were on fire, legs still weak from giving birth, pale arms pumping as her ruined skirt clung to her stumbling legs.

She reached the barn, finding the door open, the stalls empty. "Papa?" she cried out, listening for an answer but knowing she would find none. The cows eyed her and mooed plaintively, and the old gray mare stamped one foot, agitated. She must have heard the shot, too.

Polly stumbled from the barn, exhausted and limping now, breath ragged as she finally reached the small tract house. There, the door stood open, the house silent. Polly paused at the bottom of the front stoop.

"Papa?" she asked again, taking one tentative step. Even from outside, the smell of fresh gunpowder, and worse, was instantly recognizable. "Papa?"

Her voice broke as she stumbled up the steps, racing through the door and stopping cold.

Ada lay at the foot of the steps, head twisted unnaturally, eyes open and cold, as if staring out the door. Her skin looked pale and waxy. Even from the doorway, Polly could see angry bruises around her throat where it looked as if Patrick had choked her. She'd wished Ada dead so many times, seeing it in real life left her with a surreal, pulse-pounding feeling. The sight of her dead body was both grotesque and surprising.

Polly turned toward the kitchen, gasping at the sight of her father, slumped over the kitchen table. His shotgun lay on its side, blood splattered, his left hand still clinging to the barrel.

"Papa!" Polly raced to him, propping him up only to see his chest blown open, rib cage shattered, blood and guts everywhere.

She let him fall back to the table, dropping to the floor. This couldn't be happening. He was all she had, and now...now, he was gone—her father and her daughter, both in the same day.

She sat, her father's hand in hers, growing colder with each passing moment. Suddenly, the cock crowed, rousing her, stirring her to action. She stood, using the table for support.

She grabbed her father's hand and, grunting, using the last of her energy, dragged him from his chair. He was dead weight, and enough of it, as she dragged him from the house, down the steps, and out to the small stand of trees where she had buried Bonney. She struggled, grunting, sweating, already strained from her intense labor and now the shock of her father's death.

Polly finally let her father's hands go and reached for the shovel. She gripped it, intensely, as a sudden wave of nausea passed through her, or perhaps it was simply exhaustion. Or shock. She could barely believe this was happening, let alone that she was the one left behind to clean up her father's mess.

She rested on Ada's shovel for a moment, the sun inching higher and then began digging. When the grave was long and deep enough, she used the blade of the shovel like a wedge and rolled her father's body into it. Thankfully, he landed face first.

She fought back tears to finish filling in his grave before kneeling and saying her third "Hail Mary" of the morning. After trying to stand, she sat instead, gulping in huge gasps of air, trying to catch her breath, dry her tears, and focus her eyes all at the same time.

She rested she knew not how long. A minute? An hour? Two? She only knew the sun was in her eyes when she awoke, looking up at a pale-blue sky.

She felt better. At least, physically. She stood, using the shovel for support. She dragged it behind her for a while, the metal spade clanging against the gravel path to the barn.

She dropped it along the way, having no more use for it. Inside the barn was a small can of petrol. Her father used it now and again to start brush fires as he cleared the land or to clean his tools with once a week.

She grabbed it, finding it mostly full, and dragged it from the barn. It was rusty and dented and even more so after she dragged it up the steps and into the house.

She dragged it upstairs, stepping cautiously over Ada's twisted body as it hit each stair with a sloshing, "Clunk, clunk, clunk." In her room, Polly looked around for anything to take. There was little beyond a small satchel, a few clothes, and her comb.

In her father's room, she found even less. She ignored the giant Bible on the nightstand and Ada's cheap jewelry and closet full of black clothes. Her father had socked away a few crisp bills beneath his drawers, and she shoved them to the bottom of her sack and then turned from the room without looking back.

At the top of the stairs, she twisted the cap off the gas can and tipped it over, watching as it tumbled from step to step, sloshing its slick, oily contents to the base of the steps and across the knotted, wooden floorboards. The gas can landed next to Ada, the last of its contents gurgling out into a pool that stretched all the way from the living room and into the kitchen.

Careful to step over the puddles on the way down, Polly grabbed a long matchstick from the hearth and struck it using the flint rock on the side. It flickered to life and fanned hypnotically as she walked through the house, past Ada, past the doorway.

At last, she knelt, the match half-burnt now, and dipped it to the nearest puddle of gas. There was a brief moment where time seemed to stand still, and the breeze through the open door threatened to blow the match out. She watched it waver, tendrils of smoke oozing from the flickering flame.

Then it ignited with a violent flare, surprising Polly with its sudden fury and immense heat. She shielded her face from the blast, inching across the porch as the fire flickered and grew, devouring the wooden house her father had built by hand.

It mattered little now, the man who built it being dead and gone. And by his own hand, no less! As Polly stumbled back down the steps, clutching her small denim satchel, it suddenly struck her that her life as she knew it was burning inside that house. She found, surprisingly, that she didn't mind in the least. She turned, the flame crackling behind her, causing a fierce wind at her back. Walking down the lane, she paused once when she reached the road and smiled as she watched the house Ada had cherished so much become engulfed and burst into flame.

She was in no hurry. It would be an hour or more before anyone close enough to do anything could see the smoke rising from the ranch stead. And another hour before the small local fire crew traveled out from the nearest town. They would be too late.

She rested against a tree, watching as the flames licked the kitchen curtains, as the windows exploded, as the sides burst their seams like bubbling boils and smoke poured from the eaves of the roof and out the upstairs windows. It burned quickly, hot and dry like a stick of seasoned kindling until at last the roof cracked, crunched, and fell in on itself.

Only then did Polly turn, avoiding the main road where they'd be looking for her, to head down past the barn, and off across the fields. Where to, she knew not, but as long as the ranch was at her back, she was heading in the right direction.

Chapter 30

Siobhan heard a loud clap and sat up in bed, clutching the diary to her chest. The room had grown dark save for the small reading lamp by her bed and, for a moment, she felt disoriented and lost in her own room. Then, as her eyes adjusted and a sliver of moonlight slipped through the curtains, the familiar room came into focus, and she realized the crackling fire and roar of Polly's life was only written on the pages of her slim leather volume.

She rubbed her eyes and slid the diary onto her nightstand before stumbling into the bathroom.

The water burst from the spigot as she washed her face, urging herself to awaken fully. Siobhan's face was almost flushed, having just experienced the fire along with Polly through her journal. The water felt good on her hot skin, even if she was only imagining it through Polly's ancient words.

Her eyes were puffy from crying, lost in Polly's world of pain, heartache, and betrayal once again. As Siobhan reached for a washcloth, she could feel the water heating up, steam rising as she rubbed her face vigorously to bring herself back to life.

As she fumbled to hang the washcloth back up, the sound of crying filled her ears—not just any crying, a baby's cries. She turned toward the bathroom door, gently illuminated by the nightlight in the corner, but instinctively, as the cries grew louder, she knew they were coming from behind her.

Her heart stammered, and her hands shook as she turned back toward the mirror, now covered with steam, as the child's cries grew louder and louder. It was a sad sound, fraught with emotion and desperation; despite the reality of her situation, where she was, alone in her room, Siobhan wiped the steam away from the bathroom mirror.

She gasped, stumbling backward for there, in the mirror, was a harsh woman dressed all in black, clutching a newborn wrapped in a rough red horse blanket. The woman peered out from the mirror, all hard edges and curves. Ada! She smiled, clutching the babe to her breast so that its cries were muffled. Above the child's struggling cries, Ada opened her mouth and cackled and cackled and cackled...

Siobhan blinked her eyes shut, hoping the vision would disappear. When she opened them again, she saw only her face in the mirror, blurry and pale from crying, eyes wide from shock, chin trembling. "Pull yourself together," she hissed, fists clenched as she leaned against the sink, peering into the mirror as the child's cries faded.

She hung her head, muttering to herself, "Leave me alone. Leave me alone..."

But as the cries faded away, leaving her in silence, she grew angry and disoriented. "Leave me alone!" she shouted, staring back into the mirror. Instinctively, she raised one curled fist and slammed it, hard, into the mirror.

The shattering glass crumbled into the sink with an awful clatter. She saw blood and looked down, staring at her bloody fist. As tears splashed her bloody fingers, she sobbed, "Leave...me...alone."

Chapter 31

Standing beneath the old, gnarled oak, Polly pulled her arms across her chest against the night's chill. In her haste to flee the ranch, she'd packed little in the way of warm clothes and now clung merely to a thin shawl. The schoolhouse seemed vacant, until at last, the little room at the back began to glow with warm light as an oil lamp flickered to life.

Polly had no idea where she was going to go when she left the ranch, the flames licking the windowsills and the immense heat at her back. She walked aimlessly, not bothering to eat or drink until she found herself, just past dusk, standing behind the tiny schoolhouse.

She knocked, timidly at first, barely aware her hands were shaking. When there was no answer, she knocked again, louder this time, and heard boots scrape against the wooden floor on the other side of the door.

"Yes?" came the familiar sound of her headmaster's voice as Lafayette peered cautiously through the half-open door.

His eyes grew big as he recognized Polly, standing helpless and alone. He threw open the door and yanked her inside. "Polly!" he gasped, slamming the door behind him. "What is it? What's wrong?"

He pulled out a chair, and she collapsed into it, suddenly realizing how tired she was from her daylong sojourn. "Bonney," was all she could squeak.

Lafayette paced, hastily tucking his shirt into his pants. She realized absently she'd interrupted his early evening rituals. "I'm sorry," she croaked, too tired for tears. "I didn't mean to...I had nowhere else to go."

He shook his head. "Nonsense, Polly. You're no imposition, and, whatever is chasing you, you're safe now. This is a safe place."

Polly arched one eyebrow, which was about all the energy she had. She knew, even if Lafayette didn't, that nowhere in the county was safe for her. Not anymore.

"I...I have to leave in the morning."

He paused in his pacing, rolling up his sleeves. "But...I haven't seen you in six months."

She shook her head, desperate to tell him why. "Please understand. I promise I'll come back."

Shaking his head, Lafayette resumed pacing the tiny room at the back of the schoolhouse where he lived. "But where will you go?"

"I don't know. I just...I know I have to go away."

He paused in front of her, looking down with worn eyes. "Why, Polly? Why is it so important for you to leave now, right now? Tell me the truth."

Polly knew she couldn't do that, not entirely. Instead, her hands still trembling, she pulled out one last souvenir she had saved from the ranch. He took it from her. He carefully unfolded the newspaper clipping and read the headline out loud, "Outlaw Breaks Free from Portland Jail."

"This is the last I heard of Ike."

He handed back the clipping, and instinctively, she folded it before slipping it inside her pocket. "You're going to find him?" he asked, incredulously, running his hand through his hair. She nodded. "That would be madness, Polly," he exploded. "He's an armed criminal. You're a...well, you're a child."

At last, Polly stood, albeit on wobbly legs. "I'm not a child," she insisted, voice hoarse from crying off and on all day. "I'm nearly fifteen years old. I have to find my stepbrother and bring him to justice."

Lafayette leaned against the far wall, as if afraid of her sudden ire. "Justice is not your concern. Can't you leave it to the law? They'll find him. A man like that will never come to any good."

Polly turned away, facing the crooked mirror hanging over Lafayette's dresser. She looked a fright, hair scraggly, face lined with dirt and tear streaks, eyes wild and insistent. As much to herself as him, she explained, "He destroyed my family."

Lafayette nodded. "I know that, Polly. We both know that," he hesitated, "but…what will you do when you find him? Kill him?"

Polly only turned and met her former teacher's gaze with a cold stare. He shook his head with a look of astonishment. "I can't believe what I am hearing. I can't, Polly. Can't you see? I can't let you do this. I won't!"

She strode closer, hands against her chest as she begged him, "Please don't ask me to choose. You're my only friend."

"Friend?" His voice sounded hurt to match the look in his eyes. Polly staggered back, overwhelmed by the power of his emotional response, the way his body sagged in the flickering lamplight. "Can't you see, Polly? I love you. Ada could see it. A man like me in love with a minor. She knew, Polly. It shocked me that it was so obvious."

Lafayette had inched forward and soon stood in front of her. Gently, he took her hands in his. Polly trembled, overwhelmed and uncertain. She'd come to Lafayette in friendship, hoping for earnest, adult advice. Now she struggled with how to respond.

"I've watched you grow from a child into a woman. And I understand how much you've suffered, but I could never support this kind of plan. I'm a Christian. I believe in God and righteous action, not revenge. If you do this, I can't be there for you. You have to choose."

Her voice was an emotional squeak in response. "Please, Lafayette. He murdered my family."

But Lafayette was firm. "You have to make a choice. An act of violence will change you forever. I'm trying to save you from that, don't you see?"

Polly shook her head. "Please, I don't want to lose you."

His voice was firm, his grasp insistent. "Then stay here. Sleep on it, and see how you feel in the morning."

She turned away at the implication. "Not like that," he explained, grabbing a horse blanket from the wardrobe. "As friends. I'll sleep here, on the floor."

She sagged onto the bed, knowing she couldn't complete her mission without at least a good night's sleep. "I won't change my mind."

"We'll see about that." He winked, slipping off his boots.

He settled onto the blanket, lying back on his hands. She knew he was as stubborn as she was and lay back as well. Her eyes grew heavy as she relaxed her weight onto his soft, single bed.

"Please," she whispered as his breathing grew heavy. "Please give me your blessing."

"I'm sorry, Polly," he croaked, sounding more like a whisper. "I can't."

He turned away, rolling over and soon snoring. She wanted to get up, to leave, and yet sleep pulled her down. She awoke hours later, the sky dark, the lamp still flickering on the nightstand.

Lafayette snored heavily, coiled in the blanket, turned toward the far wall. She smelled his hair tonic on his pillow and smiled, but only for a moment. Then she crept out of bed, careful to avoid his sleeping body as she grabbed her knapsack and stole through the door.

It was close to dawn, as revealed by the blue-black sky that hovered around the horizon. She stumbled into the outhouse behind the school, fondly remembering the times she had hidden there while others looked all over creation for her during recess.

Now she merely stuck to her business, preparing for the long journey ahead. Outside, the sky was clear and growing bluer by the moment. She crept through town, silently, glad instinct had woken her before anyone else was up. She didn't want to explain why she was there or looked the way she did or where Ada and her pa were. She wanted only to walk, to be free of the town, and walk she did.

She itched to turn back and look at the schoolhouse, the oil lamp still flickering in the window, and yet she walked on. The past would only weigh her down, and, soon enough, Lafayette, like the ranch and her poor papa's grave, was receding into the distance as Polly set out alone once again.

Chapter 32

Siobhan sat at the corner of the bar alone, nursing a bottle of beer that had long since grown warm. Sawdust and peanut shells covered the floor at her feet and country music, tinny and sad, played on the jukebox.

For the third time that evening, the bar stool next to her scraped across the floor, and for the third time that evening, she turned, ready to make the same worn excuse about her boyfriend being in the bathroom. Instead, familiar eyes met hers, and she smiled.

"Mitch. I thought it was you I saw out on the range yesterday."

Mitch slid onto the vacant bar stool and inched his beer onto the bar. "Siobhan Davis. How long's it been?"

She didn't reply but merely lifted her bottle toward his. He smirked, slow and soft, and clinked hers against his own. As he took a long swallow, he surveyed her carefully with his deep green eyes.

"You haven't changed at all," he lied, setting his bottle down and smiling.

Siobhan chuckled. "You've changed beyond recognition."

He shook his head good-naturedly and glanced at her bandaged hand. "What happened there?"

She shrugged, dragging her wrist out of sight. "An accident. Burned myself on the kitchen stove."

Mitch arched one dark eyebrow. "Since when did you cook?"

At last, she laughed. "I learned. I've learned a lot of things in the past fifteen years."

Mitch ignored the hint of steel in her voice and nodded at the jukebox. "Well, one thing you never needed to learn was how to dance. So come on, Ms. Davis. Let's dance for old time's sake."

Siobhan's first instinct was to resist, but she was too tired to be stubborn. Reluctantly, she let Mitch drag her off her bar stool and take her by the hand onto the dance floor.

Only when they turned to face each other amid the other half-dozen or so couples lazily shuffling in their matching cowboy boots did she recognize the song as "Crazy," by Patsy Cline.

Perfect, she thought as Mitch took her good hand in one of his and grabbed her hip with the other.

"What's that?" he asked, closing his eyes as they found their rhythm.

"Don't you just hate country music? It depresses the shit out of me."

He chuckled, suddenly staring back at her. "I think it's hilarious."

She sighed. "You would."

He chuckled dryly and pressed his hand tighter against her hip, nudging her forward. She resisted only momentarily before yielding, inching closer as they revolved in short, quiet circles.

As always, Mitch was never one to take an inch without reaching for a mile. As his hand slid down her backside, she stiffened and then deftly ducked out of his grip. Tossing an apologetic grin over her shoulder, she sped from the dance floor.

Her bar stool beckoned, but instead, she walked past it, grabbing her purse on the way and heading straight for the door. The cool night air struck her like a slap, and she paused, slumping down onto a split cedar bench just under the flickering "Cactus Juice Saloon" sign.

In seconds, the door opened and Mitch's boots fell heavy on the plank flooring of the bar's wide porch.

He whistled coyly, hitching his cowboy hat up on his head. "You want to tell me what happened back there?" he asked, slumping down on the bench next to her.

Siobhan stared at the endless rows of pickup trucks filling the gravel parking lot of the local watering hole. "I'm sorry," she said, voice cracking with emotion she'd never intended to show. "I...I was in an accident recently. I lost everything. My husband. My baby. It's too soon. I had no idea I'd see you here."

Mitch inched closer but was careful to give Siobhan her distance. His voice was soft and kind. "It's OK, Siobhan. Look, I'm not here to make life more difficult for you. I'm just trying to be a friend."

She eyed him skeptically. "We were never really friends though, were we?"

When he didn't reply, Siobhan found the words tumbling forth. "My father. He doesn't even know who I am. Never mind what happened. Still the same old tyrant. Worse, if anything. He's either mean and difficult or just plain crazy. I don't know what to do with him."

Gently, Mitch reached out and took Siobhan's good hand. She noticed and, feeling his familiar warmth, plunged ahead, "I keep having these dreams, terrible dreams. Hallucinations. I think I'm the one who's going mad, not him."

At last, she grew breathless, and her voice trailed off. She turned to him, finding him patiently watching her, a concerned smile on his face. "Do you believe in ghosts?" she asked.

Mitch shook his head. "Siobhan, you're grieving. It's your mind playing tricks on you. I can see how much you've been through. It's written all over your face."

She waited for him to continue and, realizing this, he did. "Ghosts do not exist, and yet they are with us all the time. It will be even worse if..."

His voice trailed away, his eyes following it to the row of trucks lined up in front of them.

"What?" she pressed.

"You have to make your peace with your father. Are you going to wait until he's dead to forgive him?"

Siobhan stared out into the black night. "I lost my baby, Mitch. I lost my husband. And the only person who understands how I feel is also dead. What if I'm next? What if all this is a warning?"

The denim of his tight jeans rasped against the cedar bench as he inched closer, slinging a long arm around her shoulder. Instinctively, with no regrets, she leaned her head on his chest. A small smile, bittersweet and sad, inched across her face. He still wore Old Spice. "What are you talking about, woman? What kind of warning?"

"The dreams I have," she explained. "They're all about my ancestor, Polly. I found her journals. My father never told me anything about her until now. And she suffered so much."

"Maybe he had a reason, Siobhan. Maybe he was trying to protect you. The past is the past. Your father's sick. Real sick. Give him a chance. Try and make it right..."

His voice was so soft and soothing, his chest so broad and warm. She nuzzled there, quietly, lost in thoughts of the now, the past, the future, all of it comingling in each steady rise of his chest, each whiff of familiar Old Spice cologne.

He sighed, contentedly, and she wondered if he felt the same.

Chapter 33

Polly walked through the morning but soon found the paths leading out of town too well populated for her liking. Just before noon, she found a dark, thick wood and slipped inside, grateful for the cool and quiet shade and the dense cover of trees towering high.

She was tired and thirsty, and the sound of a gurgling brook was like music to her ears. She drank heavily and, smelling the road and the fire and the flames and even the last of Lafayette's cologne upon her skin, slipped off her shoes. Too exhausted to disrobe, she left her clothes on as she sank under the cold, shallow water.

She washed herself, disrobing layer by layer—her blue cotton skirt, her petticoat, her high-waisted white shirt, and corset. She left her bloomers on and used the sand from the creek bed to wash the grit and grime off her skin. When she was done, she hung the clothes from a tree to dry and dressed in the other outfit she'd so hastily packed from home.

She combed her long, Irish red hair with her fingers and tied it up out of her face with a thin strip of fresh tree bark from a young sapling. Her stomach growled, and she inched along the riverbed until she found a stretch of fresh blackberries ripe for the picking. She gorged herself on the sweet, ripe berries, the fleshy fruit swirling around her taste buds, the sugar reviving her spirits and filling her dry, dusty cells. She used her fresh denim skirt to carry nearly a pint back to the campsite for later.

She sat, dozing in the sun, full and clean and exhausted. She'd slept little at Lafayette's, afraid he might wake first and prevent her escape. She slept now, heavy and often, until at last the sun began to fade and she sat on the trunk of a fallen tree, tasting the last of the berries as she gathered her crisply dried clothes and repacked them in her pack.

She slung it over her back, tying the straps across her chest and clinging to them as she emerged from the tall stand of trees just as the sun set. She walked, continuing her journey out of town and away from her sordid past.

By Polly's way of figuring, her best bet of finding Ike was at Fort Dalles. It was the land end of the Oregon Trail, and once the travelers had salvaged what they could, they broke down their wagons and wheels and sideboards and turned them into rafts.

The voyage then turned dangerous as the pioneers entered the frigid and treacherous Columbia River, trying to float downriver so they could continue their journey to Oregon City. Polly's pa had told her that approximately 20 percent of the pioneers never even made it to Oregon City but were drowned in the turbulent river. Those who survived the treacherous trip still had a long way to go before reaching their final destination in the frontiers of the West.

Still, if Ike were going to flee, he'd have to do so from Fort Dalles; otherwise, the law would never stop looking for him on this side of the Columbia River.

The thought of the long trip both excited and scared Polly. She was no fool; she knew the dangers of staying home, of living with a woman like Ada, and even a snake like Ike paled in comparison to what awaited a young girl alone on the Oregon Trail.

There were scoundrels and cutthroats at every turn and renegade Indians to boot. And even if she could somehow avoid the dangers from two-legged animals, there were plenty of the four-legged kind and other critters to be on the lookout for—from bears and mountain lions to snakes and scorpions and all manner of God's creatures in between.

And, of course, she no longer had Pa to look out for her, to say nothing of Ma. Polly was by herself in this world, absolutely and completely alone.

She would need supplies eventually and was glad she'd pocketed the money her father had socked away. She thought of him now as she walked through high grass on the side of the main road out of town. Town was far behind her now but never quite far enough.

Her uncle James had a farm a day or two's journey by horse, which could mean three or four, maybe five days for her—more if she could only travel by night. Still, if she could find a general store on the way, a trading post, or even a generous stranger's farm where she could resupply with hard tack or salt pork, she could get to family and tell Uncle James what had become of his brother.

Polly settled onto an old horse trail the cowboys used when they needed to scoot out of town in a hurry, usually on the run from the law or a gambling debt or woman scorned. It made her smile, if only for a moment, to think she was an outlaw now, too. The farther she got from the ranch, the better she'd feel, but Polly knew there would be no smiling for much of the trip.

She had no trouble walking and made good time. The endless days of chores under Ada's watchful eye had hardened her, making her fit, lean, and tireless. At the ranch, she had often gone entire days without eating, if only to avoid hearing Ada cluck over every scrap of food she put into her mouth and how it cost her father dearly.

As the night wore on and her legs loosened, she listened to the prairie sounds on either side of her even pace. Animals scattered in her path, and she wondered which ones they were, how many, and how big. Polly spotted the occasional coyote lurking in the shadows behind the tree line, and in the mountain ranges that rose majestically out of the landscape, wolves howled mournfully.

She walked without fear, knowing that anything loud enough to be of danger, like a man on foot or on horseback, would make himself known soon enough to give her plenty of time to hide. In the meantime, she walked and walked and walked.

Just before dawn, she came across an old, dilapidated homestead that looked abandoned. Polly only spotted it in the first place because she was traveling off the beaten path, looking for a place to bed down for the day and stay out of sight.

The path that led toward it was so overgrown she had to high-step over the weeds just to spot the hitching post out front. The front door was locked, but the window was broken and she climbed in by stepping onto an overturned crate on the porch.

The cabin was small and cluttered, an overturned chair here, a half-empty satchel there. Cobwebs clung to the ceiling and between open doors. She stomped her feet and kicked her heel against the wall, hoping to scare any critters who might have taken up lodging there.

Relieved, she heard a few tiny feet scamper but nothing bigger. She found a lantern with a little oil left inside and lit it with a pack of moldy matches she found in the tiny kitchen. She was hot and thirsty from the road and pumped the handle by the kitchen sink. Nothing happened at first, until finally black water churned into the dry sink followed by a clear gush of fresh water from the underground well.

She drank greedily and washed her face and the back of her neck. She found little else in the kitchen but a few bent forks and dirty dishes. Then she spied a half-empty wooden crate that had been left behind; inside was a tin of sardines and two jars of peaches someone had canned and forgotten to bring along.

She gorged that night, righting the chair and sitting at a proper table, filling her belly and falling asleep, arms on the table, head in her arms.

Polly woke when the moon was still high, face sticky from the syrupy peaches and a rat nibbling at the last of the sardines in the tin. She batted the shiny metal can away and watched the rat scurry as she rose from the table, still sleepy, wondering where she was. She saw the tiny cabin, the sun setting outside as she blinked her eyes. She frowned and choked back a tear. For just a moment, she thought she was back home and safe, and that Pa would be standing behind her, ready to put her to bed...

Chapter 34

The trading post was shabby and isolated, just the way Polly wanted it. Tattered furs hung drying from rusty metal hooks and a sad mule stood, belly sagging and dirty, tied to a hitching post with a fraying rope.

Inside the open door, it smelled like tobacco and cinnamon and a harsh woman behind the counter eyed her suspiciously.

"Hep ya?" she asked in a thin, reedy voice that immediately set Polly's mind to thinking about Ada.

"Just looking," Polly said, though there was little to look at beyond barrels of dried beans and sacks of flour. Cured ham hocks hung behind the counter, and she bought half a pound along with a few bricks of hard tack; it was all her pack would carry, and she wanted Pa's money to last. She'd long since devoured the peaches but kept the jar, filling it with water whenever she passed a fresh creek or stream.

The woman wrapped the cured ham in wax paper and the biscuits in a square of burlap that she tied with a knot. She took Polly's money and gave her coins for change. Polly thanked her, but as she turned, the woman grabbed her arm.

"You alone?" the woman asked, voice high and tight.

Polly shook her head, ready with a story. "My pa's camping out yonder. He ate some bad berries and is too ill to come in himself. He gave me this money here to buy him some proper food."

She nodded skeptically, releasing her arm. "Reason I ask is, a couple just come in here squawking about Injuns raiding local farms for horses and whiskey."

Polly gave a start. Despite her grim appearance and Ada-sounding voice, she was concerned for her safety. "Thank you kindly," Polly said, a slight tremor to her voice. "I...I'll be sure to tell my pa."

Her pack was heavy as she left the trading post, her eyes a little wider. Night was an hour away, but she was far enough away from home to walk a little taller now, a little braver. She knew the post was near her uncle's plot of land; she'd heard her father speak of it more than once. A day or two at most, and she'd be among family once more.

She crossed the trail and slid into the woods, just off the road, keeping it in view but safely at a distance. Walking parallel to the trail kept her close enough to the path to follow it but also close enough to the brush and shrubs should prying eyes get too curious. The sky grew dark, and she heard the sound of a creek, gurgling, gushing gently to her right. She followed it, moving forward, ever forward, but also sideways, flanking the creek.

Reaching it, she stopped, and drank her fill while nibbling on a strip of ham and crunching on the tough, dry biscuit. She ate slowly, not wanting to fill her stomach too fast after a day without eating anything. The meat tasted tart and firm on her tongue, the salt reviving her senses, filling her bones after the long journey.

She packed up her food, filled her jar, and hoisted her heavy pack. The night was young, and if she hoofed it the whole while, she might reach her uncle's farm by daybreak, maybe earlier.

She followed the creek, knowing his farm wouldn't be too far off. The way was slow for the rocks and trees that dotted her path, but she was grateful for the cover they provided as the forest echoed with its natural creaks and groans.

She walked for hours, until the moon was high with the witching hour, and a foul smell started to rise as she followed the muddy riverbank. She found its source a quarter mile on as the carcasses of dead animals littered the shores.

Gutted and skinned, the beasts had most likely been killed for their hides—raccoons for caps, deer and coyotes, and the odd horse or dog.

She thought of the skins hanging from the trading post roof and knew that trappers must work fast and heavy in the area, perhaps even Indians.

As the moon continued to rise and her legs grew steadily tired, she heard the sound of horses galloping at her back. She had been inching away from the creek, away from the smell of the animals' bodies when she turned to see torchlights blazing and, in their flickering glow, the painted faces of redskins.

She gasped, clinging to a tree as the hooves galloped closer and closer. Falling to her knees, Polly peeked from behind the tree as they approached. She could hear them now, their voices triumphant. Male voices, older, strong, and vibrant, a dozen of them, maybe more, and twice that many horses as they thundered into the night.

Polly wedged her pack and its last precious contents under a rotted tree trunk that, to her dismay, wasn't big enough to hide her as well. Squirming around and around in the rich, black mud that covered the creek bed, she coated herself from head to toe, blacking her face with thick mud despite the foul smell from the riverbank.

At last, she lay in stealth, mired in mud, just beyond a string of trees as the Indians approached, slower now to accommodate the riverbed. She was in a gulley, her back flush with the land as the horses passed so close she could feel the ground move as they walked.

They had slowed now, inching forward as the first of their horses splashed across the shallow creek. Even mired in mud, she could smell their sweat and the whiskey they drank. One of them dropped an empty bottle that rolled, stopping just shy of her head.

Polly thanked God that it contained not another drop, or they might have come looking for it! Instead, they proceeded on, crossing the stream—ten, fifteen, eighteen men and twice that many horses. They set up camp across the shore, nearly causing Polly's heart to skip a beat.

The "camp" stretched forever, it seemed, with no less than three fires and an improvised horse pen. To her astonishment, unless her eyes deceived her, and how could they with the raging fires, there were cows as well. Six, eight, nearly a dozen.

She squinted through the mud noticing a brand on each shank; they were stolen! The Indians had just returned from a raid, and with a local rancher's horses and cows in a makeshift pen, they passed around bottles of whiskey, celebrating the evening's spoils.

They were fearsome warriors, clad in leather buckskin pants and little else, the fine sheen of sweat covering their naked torsos, dotted with smears of war paint and ancient symbols. Their hair was long and black as the night. Some wore headbands but none of the fearsome headdresses she'd been taught about by Lafayette in school.

They rode their horses and danced around the fires, clinging to one another, fighting each other playfully, telling stories to one another in their native tongue, and whooping and hollering for all the world to hear.

The creek was narrow, and Polly felt she could have hit them with a pebble from its crooked shore. She wriggled forward carefully, using her elbows for traction and moving very, very slowly.

It was a game of inches, and her life was at stake. God only knew what eighteen drunken brutes might do upon finding a teenage girl wriggling in the mud, and she oozed forward, elbow by elbow. In the back of her mind, she knew her life depended on it.

Polly cut her hands on sharp pebbles, and her eyes stung with sweat and the stink of rotting flesh. She was cold and damp and froze every so often when an Indian would venture away from the fire, to the banks of the creek, sometimes merely feet from her, to relieve himself in the running water with a celebratory whoop.

Each time one approached, she would pause, and not move another inch until the Indian's back was at last turned, revealing once again, a stolen whiskey bottle in his hand, head held high to the moon in celebration.

She crawled for what seemed like miles only to cover a few feet, her eyes watering from the stench of death in the water, bones stiff and frozen, arms sore from not being able to move the rest of her body. She dragged herself along, endlessly, until at last her head shoved against something large and hairy.

She started, at first seeing only dewy black fur and wondered if she would have to choose between being eaten by a bear or savaged by a group of drunken men, but a quick glance revealed the long, leathery flap of a beaver's tail!

She inched forward, hoping to nudge the beaver free so she wouldn't have to go around it, but it never budged.

Suddenly, from the opposite shore, there came a war cry and the splashing of water. Polly winced and risked a glance, only to see the Indians had seen the beaver and were pelting it with pebbles from the creek bed.

One hit her in the back, another in the leg, and she bit her tongue to keep from crying. A couple of the warriors tossed empty whiskey bottles, falling short and dashing in the creek bed.

Annoyed at the disturbance, the beaver made a high, slight whine and waddled away, rocks and bottles pelting after it as the Indians stood on the shore, clapping each other on their backs and hollering at their hunting prowess.

Inches away, covered in mud and daring herself not to breathe, Polly lay motionless. If any one of them were to give chase, trample the opposite shore after the fleeing beaver, they would surely discover her, and yet they were content to give chase from afar, watching until the beaver was out of sight and then returning to their revels.

Polly was too frightened to move after that. She lay frozen, the mud drying on her back, in her hair, bugs crawling across her clenched fists as she tried desperately not to whimper into the dirt.

The braves were tireless, dancing, drinking, and partying for hours. She watched them as the night wore on, too exhausted to stay awake, too frightened to sleep, trapped between life and death.

After hours of revelry, the flames burned down, and slowly, they began to fall, quite literally, around the dampening fires. They landed in clusters, passing out from the endless bottles of whiskey that lay, dry and scattered, like bones across the opposite shore.

At last, snores rose from the ground as the men lay where their bodies fell, drunk and exhausted. Her eyes scanned the shore until the last man slumped, whiskey bottle in hand, against the trunk of a tree. She could see the firelight dancing in his open eyes and watch his lids rise and fall, rise and fall, as if dead set on making her wait as long as possible.

At last, they shut, hard and firm, his lips going slack as he, too, began to snore the sleep of the drunk and half-dead. She waited still, until the sounds and the sleep were so deep no one would rouse from their slumber. And even then, she would not risk it. She saw a pebble, one the braves had thrown at the beaver, and tossed it into the water.

It splashed, loud and hollow, and no one moved, no one flexed, or picked up a spear or ran to impale her with a knife made of bone. She found another and tossed it, watching as a horse whinnied, swatting its tail, then little more.

Only then did she rise, mud cracking and falling off of her in untidy flat sheets that crackled when they hit the riverbed. She inched quickly behind the nearest tree, watching, waiting, for the faintest sign of life.

From one tree to the next, tree by tree, she ran, until she could no longer see the fires behind her, until she could no longer hear the snores. Not risking returning for her pack, she ran along the riverbed, muscles sore from lying still in the mud for hours. She passed skinned corpses rotting in her path and merely stepped over them, desperate to be far and away by sunrise.

Eventually, the smell of rot and fear and drying bones was no more, and as the sun rose, she tumbled upon a split-beam fence and the rich, green field of a tended farm.

Smoke rose from a chimney, and she stumbled, ever forward, collapsing next to the woodshed. She could walk no further, and besides, she knew on a frigid morning like this, the first place a family member would come would be to collect wood.

Chapter 35

"Lord, child," came a voice, distant to Polly even though she could feel the hot breath of its speaker on her cheek. "What did you get yourself into?"

Polly felt arms lifting her up off the ground and squinted as her eyes struggled to open. She was hungry and dehydrated, gasping for air as a man's face swam into her field of vision.

"Pa?" she asked, seeing his face in front of her eyes as tears trickled down her cheeks. "Pa?"

There was a dry chuckle. "Polly?"

Polly blinked, and the face grew more defined. It wasn't her father but his younger brother, James O'Neal. "Uncle James?" she gasped, wrapping her sore arms around his broad shoulders.

The next few hours passed in a blur. She cried through most of them. James and his wife, Tilly, fed her, filled her with strong coffee from a blue tin cup, bathed her, and put her into bed.

Polly was sitting there, propped up on goose-down pillows when her uncle walked in, shutting the door behind him. There was a humble wooden chair in the corner, and he dragged it over to her bed. She was already tearing up when he sat down and reached for her hand.

"Now, Polly, are you ready to tell me why you're here, so far from home?" Her uncle looked like a younger version of her father, even though they were fairly close in age. Or, Polly thought, maybe it was being married to a woman who didn't harp on you every five seconds about this or that. Ada had worn Polly's father down so badly, he'd looked ten years older than his age by the end. Tilly seemed happy and content, a loving, kind wife. Maybe that was why James looked so much younger.

Polly dried her tears on the sleeves of her borrowed nightgown and began. "I have no home, Uncle James. Everyone I know is dead. Momma was poisoned, Ada fell down the stairs, and Papa shot himself."

James shook his head, struggling to conceive of all her accumulated losses. "You poor thing," he said, clasping her hand. "I wish, I wish we'd known, but your father, when he wrote to us, never told us any of that."

She shook her head. "He wouldn't, Uncle James. I don't think he even knew the evil he married until it was too late. He was in love—or thought he was."

They sat quietly, both grieving in their own ways and for very different reasons. "We're glad you're here, Polly. You can stay as long as you like."

She shook her head. "You've already been so kind to me, Uncle James," she croaked, voice tight with emotion. "But I'll be moving on when I'm rested up."

Her uncle looked at her with those same soft eyes as her father's. If it hadn't been broken already, it surely would have cracked her heart in two. "Where will you go?" he asked, but Polly could tell he was slightly relieved.

The farm was small but humble, the house tidy but poor. They were clearly struggling. She saw it in the humble portions they served her, the faded clothes hanging on the line, and the nervous way they awaited her answer. However nice they'd been, or would be, they didn't need, as Ada often called Polly, "another mouth to feed."

"I'm sure one of these little towns up yonder will need a good schoolmarm," she lied. "I can read and write, which is better than half of these frontier schoolmasters can muster."

He smiled, seeming pleased with the lie. She had seen the look in Lafayette's eyes, the desperation in his voice, when she had confessed her true intentions about hunting down Ike. She didn't want to go through the same thing with her uncle.

There was a knock at the door, and he stood, sliding the chair back in the corner as he went. Tilly came in bearing another tray of food. Polly protested, but once she smelled the ham steak and fresh biscuits, the jam and fresh-whipped butter, she could hardly help herself.

She slept again, off and on. Day turned to night and night to day and finally night again. She rose to use the outhouse and found her uncle snoring through the open bedroom door, his wife lying on her side, dead to the world.

She crept from the house, feet bare but reveling in the dewy grass. After she used the outhouse, she felt wide awake. The sky was cloudless and black, with a million stars peppering the darkness. A full moon bathed the humble farm in brightness as she made her way back to the tiny farmhouse.

Smoke curled from the chimney, and she heard a horse whinny to her left. She paused and turned from the house, creeping toward a humble stable that housed a few cows, some chickens, and two horses. One slept, leaning against the stable door, but the other stared at her bleakly with his big black eyes.

The horse was white, Polly could tell, but in the moonlight, his lustrous coat gave off a slight blue tint. Her father had always had horses, on and off the trail, but none so beautiful—so magical—as this one!

She approached him cautiously, gently reaching out a hand to caress his soft white mane. He let her, and she found a bag of oats, open by a bench across from his stall. She fed him from her hands, his giant tongue scratching her empty hand when the oats were all gone.

He neighed and nuzzled her, and she sat on the bench across from him, watching the horse watching her. "What are you thinking?" she asked the beautiful horse with the big black eyes. "What's in that big noggin of yours?"

The horse nodded, as if he really understood. She chuckled and felt a warm glow just sitting there. In all this time, on the road, lurking in the shadows, hiding from the Indians, collapsing on her uncle's farm, she'd felt alone.

Now, she felt somewhat at peace. Maybe it was just the soft bed she'd spent so much time in lately at her uncle's, or the good food prepared by his wife, or simply the quiet companionship of a noble beast, but she smiled and sagged against the wall.

She didn't sleep that night, yet still, when the cock crowed at dawn, she felt rested and revived. She heard soft footsteps and smiled as her uncle crept into the stalls, hair bumpy from sleep and still fiddling with his suspenders.

"Polly, goodness!" he gasped, surprised to see her. "Have you been out here all night?"

She smirked. "I was just talking to your horse here."

He scratched one of his unruly brown curls. "You mean old Blue?" Just then, the white horse snorted and Uncle James smiled.

Polly nodded. "What a perfect name. All last night, as the moon shone done, this horse radiated an almost unearthly blue."

"You're right to admire him, Polly," James said, patting Blue's unruly mane. "This horse has quite a history."

Just then, Tilly came around the corner, a relieved look on her face.

"Oh, Polly," she said, wringing her hands. "Thank goodness I found you. I thought you'd run off."

James nodded toward her. "She's about to, Tilly. Can we rustle her up some supplies for the road and maybe a more suitable traveling outfit?"

"You're leaving so soon, child? Wherever will you go? And…however will you get there?"

"She's got her heart set on teaching," James said, patting Blue's haunches as he led him from the stall. "And, apparently, her heart's set on Blue here as well."

"Blue?" Tilly asked and then shook her head. "But, James?"

Uncle James gave her a stern look, and Tilly turned to Polly and forced a smile. "Polly, come with me, and we'll get you good and ready for your travels."

While Uncle James saddled Blue, Polly went inside and washed up. When she turned from the chipped porcelain basin in the guest room, she found a leather pack bursting at the seams with fresh clothes and food for the road. A canteen, dented but full, hung from one of the straps. She slipped it on, Tilly watching all the while.

"I can't thank you enough," Polly said.

Tilly held open her arms, and Polly collapsed into them, crying soft, dry tears. "After what you've been through, it's the least you can expect from your own kin. There's an address in there. You write when you get settled or even when you don't, you hear?"

Polly promised as they left the humble cabin, finding Blue saddled and ready for travel. James hugged her and settled her pack before helping Polly onto the horse.

Blue stood there, gently, as Polly settled herself. She sat atop her new horse, but something troubled her. "You said Blue had a history, Uncle James. Dare I ask it?"

James just smirked and leaned against a fence post. "I was afraid you'd never ask, Polly!"

Chapter 36

"Did you ever hear about that Indian uprising down to Fort Dalles last year or so?"

Polly shook her head. "Pa hasn't actually kept up on much goings on with the Oregon Trail ever since he got off it," she confessed.

James nodded and continued, "Well, a year or two ago, one of the local tribes kidnapped one of the Indian agents from the government. They crucified him, Polly, mounted him upside down on a cross. They did this on the hill the opposite side of Fort Dalles and skinned him alive. This stunned the community.

"However, later, we all come to find out that the agent was actually stealing from the Indians. The government would issue twenty or thirty horses to the agent to give to the Indians. The agent sold a majority of them, kept the money for himself, and then handed over two or three to the Indians. The Indians were not dumb and found this out quickly. After he'd been doing this for years, they got fed up with the agent and finally did him in. Doing it in front of the community was their way of warning.

"Well, the army was still about six months away so the community raised a posse, a small army of volunteers—about fifty people. One of the volunteers was a young man by the name of Daniel Butler. You would have liked Daniel, Polly. He was about your age, seventeen years of age and quite a hell-raiser. A regular patron of the saloons and houses of girls where he heard there was a small band of Indians over near Snake River. He and two other young men, who were drinking heavy with Daniel, decided to kill some renegades so they jumped on their horse and headed east.

"A day later, the three of them found tracks of Indian ponies heading south. Daniel and his friends thought there were three or four Indians in the small pack of raiders. Typical of the time, the Indians raided farms and stole their horses and cattle.

"Daniel and his two friends thought this was going to be an easy 'kill' and they would be heroes to the local community. Their ego prevailed. As they headed south following the tracks, they came over a small ridge and found themselves in the middle of the Indians...all thirty of them!"

Polly gasped. By now, she felt as if she knew poor Daniel. "Whatever did they do, Uncle James?"

"Well, Polly, naturally everyone was surprised. The Indians were stunned that three white men are in the middle of their camp, and, of course, you can image the shock of Daniel and his two friends staring at thirty Indians. As soon as the shock wore off, the dust began to fly; Indians scrambled to their ponies, and Daniel and his friends began running through the maze of horses, cows, and Indians.

"They headed south with adrenaline rushing through their veins as their horses were in the same state. The rolling plain gave few hiding places, so all they had was their horse (which was not too rested due to their last day-and-a-half ride). The three boys ran their horses hard, as fast as they could ride; the thirty Indians behind were always inching nearer.

"About half an hour later, they felt the fatigue entering their horses and the Indians were moving ever closer. The boys hollered among each other in loud voices and decided that they must take a risk if any of them were to survive. They finally decided to split up, heading out in three different directions. Their hope was that the band of Indians would follow only one of them and leave the other two to escape to their freedom. Once it was decided, the boys split off in three different directions. Sure enough, the Indians, banding together in the safety of their tribe, turned slightly and pursued only one…It was Daniel Butler."

Polly gasped, holding tight to the reins of her new horse as if she, too, were galloping alongside poor Daniel. "What happened next?"

James continued, "Another half hour full of terror followed, Daniel riding his horse into a lather. Daniel sees the Indians so near that he is trying to determine where to make a stand and fight till death. He is hoping that he will kill a couple before his untimely death but is more worried that they will take him alive and skin him like the government agent. This drove fear into his heart.

"Over the next hill, he discovers that he is near the Snake River. Known for the deep canyon and sheer walls, he sees no way around it. Skidding to a stop on a rock ledge overlooking the Snake, the river had to be four or five stories straight down! Turning to look at the Indians, who are now speeding up and elated, already screaming in victory to their impending prisoner.

"Daniel does a crazy act that puts his name in history: he jumps his horse over the edge and plunges into the river below. They both go over, man and horse, splashing in the water and coming up for air after dashing to the bottom. Amazing as it is, they both survive. The Indians slide to a stop and look in wonder at the horse and man swimming to the side of the shore. They are not as crazy as the white guy, so they turn and head back to their camp.

"Meanwhile, the current takes Daniel downriver, until wet and exhausted, he eventually finds himself in Bend, Oregon. Daniel ended up in a saloon, gambling and drinking as usual. His story went through the town like wildfire, and he became famous overnight. Unfortunately, gambling never did suit Daniel well, and he quickly became indebted to the local cardsharp.

"The next morning found Daniel negotiating with a family that was traveling by wagon heading for Fort Dalles. He sold his horse to the family. In parting, he trusted a certain James O'Neal to take care of his horse 'Blue,' as he had saved his life many times over."

Polly patted Blue gently. "You mean, I am riding a living legend?"

Uncle James chuckled. "That you are, Polly; that you are."

Polly nodded solemnly. "I can't believe you're letting me take Blue after all he's done."

James patted Blue one last time and smiled. "A horse like Blue needs an adventure from time to time, right, boy? He won't get that around this old farm."

Blue affectionately whinnied, and as if he might change his mind, James slapped the horse on his hindquarters to give him a head start. Blue lurched ahead, and Polly smiled, waving good-bye.

Chapter 37

Blue proved a gentle and trustworthy companion as Polly traveled northwest on the well-worn trail to Fort Dalles. It was late spring now, and even though she still often traveled by moonlight, the land looked grassy and vibrant, its flowers bursting with color. The wildlife was feeding brazenly on the fresh grass, and once, even a buffalo was shambling through the tree line, wary of Blue's whinnies but not leery enough to disappear altogether.

She rode steadily, at peace for the first time in months. There was no Ada to make demands of her anymore, no chores to do other than to sit atop Blue and march steadily toward her fate. The night stretched on, warm and lazy with a soft wind caressing her neck.

Despite the wildflowers in bloom and the occasional antelope or deer flitting at the borders of the trail, Polly was still anxious of a confrontation with Ike, or worse, that he might escape her grasp, but she was also certain that she wouldn't stop until she found him, even if it meant the rest of her life.

If Ike managed to float the Columbia River and elude her, she would follow his trail, cold as it was, even if she had to swim to Portland and track him on the other side of its shores.

She still traveled by night, using the moon as her guide and confident now that a horse like Blue could outrun even the rowdiest band of Indians or cowboys! The trail was long but not unpleasant. She paused often, if only to make sure Blue had plenty of water to drink and fresh grass to eat.

After the first night, she led Blue off the beaten path to a small thicket where she found fresh berries in bloom and a small running stream. She ate of the berries until she was set to burst and then shared the rest with Blue, who lapped them up with his long, coarse tongue.

She took off his tack, laying it on the ground so Blue could rest comfortably during the long, warm day. It was spring now in Oregon, a beautiful and fragrant time, but also warm, especially when the sun was high.

Polly tied him gently to a tree and rested her weary bones against a fallen log, exploring her pack for something heartier for dinner than wild berries from a thorny thicket.

She ate a dry biscuit and chunk of cured ham, washing it down with more water and sharing the crumbs from both with Blue. But he seemed more interested in the wildflowers and thick grass growing beneath his massive hooves.

While stowing away the rest of her food for later, Polly found a hunting knife lying in the bottom of her pack. She took it out of its leather sheath, admiring its long, lethal blade in the early morning sun.

Its leather sheath was large, and she stood as dawn approached, trying to find a place to hide it beneath her skirt or, possibly, behind her back. But it was too large and bulky and made a spectacle of itself no matter where she hung it.

Then she got an idea: if she made a strap for it, perhaps, she could hang it under her shoulder like the gunslingers did. She'd seen a similar holster under the sheriff's arm when he'd come for Ike.

She dug through the pack, excited now, but found only a small handkerchief monogrammed with her uncle's initials. She kept it out just in case, and then looked around for anything else to make a holster from.

She inched toward where she'd left Blue's saddle and tack, his bridle reflected in the early morning sun, and noticed the long leather fringes hanging from the saddle Uncle James had given her. She took out the knife and knelt down, cutting off the longer tassels and gathering them together with her kerchief.

She sat back down, whiling away the morning by knotting the leather thongs together and binding them at the joints with strips from her uncle's handkerchief, which she used like "glue" to strengthen where the leather knots were tied.

It took her all morning—and well past noon—before she had something resembling a shoulder holster from which the knife could hang. At last, she slipped her arm through and, admiring her reflection in the stream at the edge of their thicket, she adjusted the holster until at last it fit in the crook of her left arm.

After several adjustments, she could simply reach over with her right hand and slip the knife from its sheath. She practiced with her jacket off, and once she'd mastered the movement, put on her jacket and shifted the holster so it looked less bulky.

It would never be completely invisible to the roving eye, but after the stories her father, and later her uncle, had told her of the saloons and whorehouses in Fort Dalles, she doubted there'd be anyone paying her much attention.

Still, she shifted and pulled, prodded and readjusted, until the holster was as nondescript as she could make it. Only after she'd perfected the art of sliding the knife from the holster with her jacket on did she feel that the job was done.

Satisfied with the makeshift holster, Polly slipped off her jacket and rested it under her head, lying down in the cool, dark grass as the trees shaded her from the midday sun.

Chapter 38

Polly woke to the sound of Blue stomping his hooves. She rose with alarm, but it was merely the horse's way of telling her he was ready to go. She was glad, too. By now, the sun was setting and she always liked to get a bead on the trail before the sun went down altogether.

She watered and fed him once more before cinching tight the saddle and grabbing the reins. Her holster was going to take some getting used to, but now that she was getting closer and closer to her final destination with each of Blue's strides, she dared not take it off.

They walked from the thicket and found the trail, still dotted with weary travelers who paid her little mind as they trudged, hot and dusty from another long day's travels.

As she rode Blue among them, she saw the weariness etched into their lined faces, picturing her mama in their early days on the trail. How hopeful she'd been when they started, how eager to reach the West Coast and start a new life, full of opportunity and land of their own.

How quickly the trail had beaten her down, Polly's father, too. And no sooner had Polly's mother grown weary and thin from weeks on the trail than had Ada shown up, Ike in tow, clinging to them like barnacles, ingratiating herself, until it was as if Polly and her family had never known true peace.

Only Polly saw the ice in Ada's eyes, the cruelty in Ike's leering expressions and false smile. But she was just a child then, so young and innocent and who would listen to her warnings? Not Ma, that was for sure. And certainly not Pa. After Ike had taken Polly's virtue and Ada had taken her mother, what was poor Pa to do but seek comfort in the only female companionship available to him?

As the travelers steamed steadily toward Fort Dalles, Polly saw that same weariness in their bones. Some still managed to look hopeful, but most looked defeated, hungry, and tired. She wished them safe travels from time to time but kept to herself, never knowing when prying eyes might peer too closely at her.

She had had no word from home since she'd vanished, the homestead burned to rubble, Lafayette's eyes—and arms—insistent. She thought often of his warm embrace, his gentle snores as he lay there on the floor, the perfect gentleman, while she dozed fitfully in his bed.

If only he'd been able to understand her intense desire for revenge, the depth of her hatred for Ike and what he'd done to her, for Ada and what she'd done to poor Bonney, her child, left for dead in a shallow grave.

Apart from Pa, Lafayette was the only soul who'd ever shown her an ounce of affection in Bonney's Canyon, the only man who'd loved her for her and not what he could take from her or use her for.

She found herself smiling at his humble cottage at the back of the schoolhouse, his tidy bookshelf and freshly laundered sheets. He was a gentleman, and kind, and she felt bad about leaving him without saying good-bye.

But as she turned back to the trail, her smile returned to grit and steel. She couldn't risk Lafayette trying to prevent her from her destiny, a fate that grew closer and closer with each of Blue's footsteps.

The night was still young when the smell of fire filled the air; moisture collected on her face as Blue instinctively picked up his pace. She must be close, she thought, as the flickering of several campfires drifted into view.

They were at the base of a small hill and rushing water grew louder and louder as she urged Blue to the top. As Polly rounded the top of the hill, it crested into the mighty Columbia River. The sound was haunting after her long journey on the flat, dusty prairie ground and the sight impressive as the mostly full moon shown down below.

Fort Dalles was a small village with a modest army post on the bend in the river. Farmers who migrated from the Midwest looking for their fortune congregated on its banks, all breaking down their wagons to head down the last and most dangerous parts of their long journey.

Polly wondered how far she'd have to go to find Ike, and the imposing sight of the river did little to dampen her resolve to track him down, as far and as long as it might take.

She dismounted Blue, patting his backside fondly as he bent his head and waited for her to kiss his cheek and finger-comb his long, tangled mane. She took off his saddle and blanket, watching his white skin glow blue under the moonlight as he shook his haunches and nodded with satisfaction to be free of his daily burden.

A small sapling became his hitching post as he bent to nibble greedily on the thick grass at his feet. Now that she was in view of the Fort, in spitting distanced of her destination, she risked a fire for the first time on the trail.

It crackled and glowed as she drank from the canteen her uncle's wife had packed for her and that Polly had been careful to fill at every stop. She rose and went to Blue, filling her hand with water and letting him lap it up gently.

She stood, and they looked out together over the raging river. She leaned close, feeling his heat as she reflected on her long journey. Below them, the town was noisy and ribald, rife with men on the prowl, dusty and dry from their long journeys, looking to wet their whistle and more as they prowled the muddy streets and plied its bars.

She settled down, intimidated by the thought of walking into town and showing Ike's picture as it scowled from the newspaper clipping she kept close to her vest.

She'd been alone for so long, ever since leaving Bonney's Canyon. Her days on the trail had been eventful but also peaceful and solitary. She had had nothing but Blue, wildflowers, and the occasional buffalo, for company for over a week, and the thought of sashaying up to these dirty cowboys and their unshaven faces made her cringe with fear.

She patted Blue once more, took one last look at the town below, and sat by the campfire, staring into its belly as she poked it with a stray piece of kindling, working up her nerve as the day's long travels settled on her weary bones.

Chapter 39

Polly awoke late the next morning, tangled in her blankets and squinting against the midmorning sun. Blue stood, munching grass from around the tree and snorting quietly. She stretched, yawned, and made a fire to brew fresh coffee.

Below, the river gurgled and splashed, sounding ominous with the winter's runoff. She spread fresh oats out for Blue, ate the last of her cured ham and hard tack, and washed her face, gearing up for the day. Her holster was snug under her arm as she slid on her worn jacket.

She walked Blue down from the hill, listening to the hum of the town as she gently entered the throng of people streaming into Fort Dalles. The sound of wagon wheels, creaking leather, and horse's hooves filled the air. Polly felt vaguely refreshed from the long night's sleep and her first day in the encampment.

She was so close to achieving her goal, but now that she laid eyes on the encampment itself, fear and intimidation rushed through her veins. She took to Blue, climbing into her saddle to feel taller and get a better view of the fort. It was a ramshackle encampment, dirt roads muddy and uneven, with rough fellows leaning against the general stores and saloons.

Spittoons lined every front porch and seemed full to overflowing as Polly and her trusty steed, Blue, joined the mass of settlers steadily streaming into town. The air smelled like smoke of all kinds, from cheap tobacco and campfires to the sizzle of animal meat.

Wagons lined nearly every inch of free space just off the main trail, lonely, weary travelers sulking and looking uncertainly at the stores and saloons across the street. From atop old Blue, Polly watched their tired faces.

Children wriggled but dared not stray too far from the wagon. Mothers with their lined and dirty faces looked haggard from the constant hovering, and the fathers paced, torn between the responsibility of family and the temptation to take a much-needed drink after long months on the trail.

Indeed, the town got rowdier the longer Polly rode. She was glad for the knife under her arm as she watched fights break out into the streets, mostly drunken cowboys or scoundrels stumbling from the bars and saloons.

Polly knew if Ike was anywhere in this godforsaken town, he'd be holed up in a bar somewhere, stealing pennies off of drunks and buying himself rounds of cheap draft beer.

She shuddered at the thought and eased Blue up to the nearest general store, a shoddy and worn building that seemed to be leaning to one side. She hitched him to the mossy post out front and patted his muzzle gently. "It's OK, Blue," she murmured, mostly to convince herself.

Inside, the store was cramped and crowded. There was a mix of soldiers and scamps and scalawags, trappers and travelers, a right motley crew. With trembling fingers, she pulled the newspaper clipping from her pocket and approached the shop clerk.

He was a ruddy-faced man with thin lips surrounded by a dirty-blond beard. "Help you, missy?"

"Y-y-es, please," she stammered. "I'm...I'm looking for my brother. He ran away from home and—"

"You buyin' something, gal?" the shop clerk bellowed, arousing everyone in the entire store.

Polly looked around, red-faced, at the seedy men staring at her from all angles. She turned back to the clerk.

"Uh, yes, of course. I'll be having some oats for my horse, bacon for me, and hardtack, please."

He grumbled and set about filling her order. She fiddled nervously with her pocketbook, wrangling some of the last money she still had leftover from her father's sock drawer. She had enough to pay for the three small bundles, which the clerk shoved roughly across the counter.

He reached for the money, and she stove up her courage, pulling her hands back. "About this picture, sir?"

The clerk eyed her warily, licking his thin lips. "Lemme see," he said, spitting into a brass spittoon at his feet. He scrunched up his eyes and regarded the yellow newsprint. "He looks like all the other punks who stumble in here after a few drinks, pinching licorice whips and thumb tacks. I maybe seen him in camp; I maybe not."

He shoved the picture back and bellowed, "Next."

Polly was shoved aside roughly by a skinny soldier clamoring for chewing tobacco. She dropped one of her bags, and when she stooped to pick it up, a young boy grabbed it first.

"Here," he said, hair dirty and teeth dirtier. He looked to be a few years younger than Polly, twelve or thirteen at most.

"Thanks," she said, inching outside. He followed her and, as they neared the last step, inched closer. "I seen your brother, miss."

She stopped, clutching his crusty sleeve desperately. "You did. When? Where?"

The boy chuckled and eyed her packages hungrily. "I'll tell you whether you share or not, miss, but I sure could use a bite to eat."

She shook her head and then nodded. "Here," she said, dragging him toward the side of the building. A slow whinny told Polly that Blue was watching them. For some reason, it made her feel better.

They sat on a small bench, the legs covered in ugly yellow weeds. "Here," she said again, dragging a strip of cured bacon from her sack and breaking off a piece of hard tack.

He gobbled it greedily, and Polly noticed his fingers were dirty and grubby. He smelled like he hadn't bathed in days. Before he was finished eating, he mumbled, "I seen that boy in Murphy's Bar up yonder." Bits of food sprayed her shoulder. She flinched and pressed him for more information.

"When?" she asked.

"Couple nights ago," he nodded, as if agreeing with himself. "Half in the bag, he was. Bumming rummies for free drinks, cadging cigarettes, generally making a nuisance of himself. He'd been banned from three other saloons."

"Did he say anything?"

The kid shrugged. "He was trying to catch a ride down the river, to Portland," he said. "Last I heard, he'd conned some poor settler into taking him along. Must have worked, since he ain't been around bothering nobody ever since."

Polly thanked the boy with another slab of bacon before sliding her purchases into her saddle bag and feeding Blue a handful of oats. He licked her hands greedily, and she fed him some more. "We're getting closer," she said to Blue while hitching up her skirt to avoid the muddy tracks in the road and heading over to Murphy's Saloon.

It was late morning now, and the saloon was noisy and crowded. Polly was greeted by catcalls and whistles as she stumbled in, eyes slowly adjusting to the filmy dark. The large saloon was lit only by gas lamps smoking on the walls, with nary a window open to cast in daylight.

Polly gritted her teeth and wound her way through the tables, face hot and blushing as she approached the bar. She'd grown taller over the summer, and foot on one of the brass rails along the bottom of the bar, she almost met eye to eye with the bartender cleaning out thick beer mugs with a dirty rag.

"You know you ain't supposed to be in here, sweetheart," the man said. He was scraggly and balding and jowly but not unkind. "But I suppose if you're looking for your pa, it's OK if you drag him out of here quickly."

Polly heard the pity in the man's voice and decided to try a different tack this time around. "I'm actually looking for my brother," she said, holding out the picture from the newspaper. "Someone said they saw him in here the other night, scrounging around for passage to Portland. He'd had a row with my pa, and we ain't seen him since."

The man took a closer look but frowned. "I'm sorry, dearie, he just looks like so many other boys that come in here talking tough and running their mouths."

She looked at the picture. Ike's corn-yellow hair was fuzzy, and his scowl downplayed in his mug shot. Polly realized it didn't do him justice. "He's a big boy, spiky blond hair, piggish eyes, would have been louder than just about anybody and twice as boastful."

The man's watery eyes narrowed as he struggled to recollect. "Two days ago, you say?"

"He'd have been haggling with some unsuspecting settler, looking to get out of town fast—"

Suddenly, the man's eyes lit up. "Yup, yessirree, I know 'zactly the boy you're wanting. Big fella, chip on his shoulder, can't hold his liquor?"

Polly smirked. "That'd be Ike."

The bartender nodded, putting down his glass. "Last I remember, it was closing time and he was stumbling out with this one fellar, who had spent all week turning his wagon into a raft to float the Columbia River. I seen them the next morning, too, heading out on the contraption as I was walking into work."

Polly's head hung in disappointment. Not only was Ike gone, but he had two days on her. Still, she supposed, it could have been worse.

The barkeep cleared his throat. "I wish you luck in finding him, miss. I really do."

They both looked toward the swinging batroom doors at the same time. Suddenly, Polly noted the rushing sounds of the Columbia River just down the block. "I hope you're not trying to follow him this time of year, missy. Better to wait until summer, when the spring runoff is over and the river calms down."

She looked back at him sadly. "I wish I could, mister."

Chapter 40

Polly stumbled from the saloon into the streets, eyes nearly blinded by the noonday sun after parlaying with the barkeep in the dark tavern. She walked back to the trading post and unhitched Blue. She fed him a few more handfuls of oats and then mounted him as they inched slowly through the crowded streets of Fort Dalles.

Polly was grateful for the company of Blue and for the knife she kept safely hidden beneath her jacket. By this time of day, the streets were alive with beggars and swindlers, the black market thriving with catcalls from soldiers stumbling by, intoxicated at midday from drinking their lunches.

She inched Blue through the crowd, easing toward the riverbank. It was dotted with families, their wagons dismounted, lashing their wagon boards together to make makeshift rafts. Men hammered, women tied, and children used mud to cram the gaps between boards in a vain attempt at making the crafts watertight.

Polly watched them enviously. If only she could hitch a ride with one such family, she could get to Portland and hopefully catch up to Ike. Still, each time she approached one of them, they looked at her as if she were Ike, eager to take from them something she did not deserve.

While she'd been so brave in striding into that saloon, big as you please, she seemed to have used up all her energies and now turned from the shore, feeling defeated and shy.

Polly figured she'd return to her camp, watch the shoreline, and maybe scout for a family from there. Already, she felt drained from the stress of the morning, in a way that days on the road hadn't tired her.

As she strode atop Blue back toward the maddening crowd lining the streets, she saw a little girl standing off to one side. Her hair looked stringy and her face muddy, as if perhaps she'd fallen. Polly kept waiting for some frantic young mother to come claim her, but after two full minutes, it seemed as if the crowd was impervious to the young girl's cries.

Polly dismounted Blue and led him over to the girl. The girl saw her and stopped crying in that way children will, huffing instead as if she might start crying all over again any moment.

Polly offered a wide smile and said, "I'm Polly. What's your name?"

"Beatrice," said the little girl, wiping her eyes and leaving dirt trails above her chubby cheeks. "But everyone calls me 'Bea,' though."

"Can I call you Bea?"

The little girl nodded. "Where's your mommy, Bea?"

Suddenly, the little girl began crying again, big fat tears rolling down her cheeks. Polly tried to quiet her, but the girl would have none of it. "OK, well…" Polly stumbled, trying to decide what to do. "I have a horse here, Blue. Would you like to meet him?"

The girl nodded as Polly took her hand and led Bea to Blue. "He's not Blue at all," the little girl said, making Polly laugh.

"Wait until you see him in the moonlight," Polly promised as Bea reached out a hand to stroke Blue's smooth white coat.

"I'd like that," Bea marveled.

"Would you like to ride him?" Polly asked.

Bea looked up at Blue's flaring nostrils and nodded.

Polly hoisted her up onto the saddle and then joined her, urging Blue slowly through town and hoping someone might spot the little girl and come claim her.

As they inched forward, Polly scanned the crowd but found only whiskey-soaked beards and sweat-stained bowlers. The sea of men looked up, drunkenly or angrily or bored. Suddenly, Polly heard shouting.

"Beatrice!" yelled a young woman, black hair tangled in her face as she ripped off her bonnet to wave in the sea of ill-tempered young men. "Here, Beatrice. It's Mommy!"

Polly steered Blue toward the frantic woman, who ran up to the horse and clung desperately to Bea's legs. "Oh, thank goodness Mommy's found you."

Polly inched Blue toward a quiet side street and helped Beatrice off into her mother's waiting arms. "Oh thank you, thank you," said the woman as Polly slid off her saddle and tied Blue to the branch of a nearby sapling. "I was trying to cross the street to get to the general store, and we got separated. I tried to find her but this town is so filthy and crowded and *no* one would help!"

The woman was crying to herself now, and Polly tried to intervene. "I'm Polly," she said. "I'm alone here myself and know how Beatrice felt."

"Oh, goodness," said the mother, reapplying her bonnet and extending an appreciative but still trembling hand. "My name's Sally Gilhousen. Did you… did you say you were alone? Please, join us back at the wagon and share a proper supper. It's the least we can do for you finding little Bea for us." Polly's stomach rumbled audibly, and even Beatrice laughed.

Polly walked alongside Blue as Sally led them all back to the Gilhousen camp. It was, like most, a shoddy affair. The wagon looked like a cattle carcass that had been picked apart by buzzards.

The wagon cover had been removed, as had the wheels and several of the baseboards. It looked as if the waterproof tarp was being used as a makeshift tent. A short man, wiry but strong, rose and dusted his hands off on his dirty pants when Polly approached.

"My husband, Bill," said Sally as the man shook Polly's hand. He had kind eyes and shook his head sorrowfully as Sally breathlessly told him the tale of how she and Polly had met.

Bill hugged Beatrice tight and murmured, "The sooner we get out of this town, the better."

"You're floating the river?" Polly asked, perking up.

"As soon as we can." Sally sighed, sitting down around the fire Bill had going. Polly joined them around the fire, drinking fresh coffee and resting her bones. She'd been traveling so long, on the run, avoiding people, it felt good to sit out in the open, jawing with others, eating hot beans and cured bacon as she shared her larder with her new friends.

As the afternoon wore on and Beatrice lazily played with a dirty rag doll, Polly found herself telling Sally and Bill her story—not all of it, but enough of the truth so that they knew she was out to find her brother, that he had a two-day head start, and she needed to cross the river.

Sally and Bill looked at each other, sharing an almost relieved glance. Polly could almost hear them exhale. Hesitantly, Sally suggested, "Well, I've got little Beatrice to watch all day, and I'm not very handy to begin with, so... we really could use a hand converting the wagon into a raft." She looked to her husband for confirmation and, when it was received, added, "If you wouldn't be averse to helping us build it, we wouldn't be against asking you to join us as we cross the river."

Polly almost gasped to hear the offer. "I'd love to," she said, rolling up her sleeves. The thought of Ike wandering around Portland, possibly eluding her grasp, made her anxious all over.

Bill chuckled and rose from the fire. "Well, I was going to start lashing some of these boards together before the light gives out," he explained. "If you want to lend a hand?"

Chapter 41

Polly woke to the smell of fresh coffee and the rustling of fabric long before dawn the next morning. A small fire crackled, and she sat up from her blanket, stretching. Dampness filled the air, and as she woke more fully, Polly could hear the rush of water.

She stood, stretching her back, finding Bill Gilhousen staring at the nearby river as it rushed along beneath the rising sun. He heard Polly stir and turned, handing her a fresh cup of coffee.

"Thanks," she said, sipping it even though it was hot. It was good and fresh and strong, just like she liked it.

"Black's the best we can do after spending most of our savings on supplies for the raft," he apologized.

She waved it away. "Just like I like it," she said.

He nodded and sipped from his own cup, pointing to his wife and daughter still sleeping in the half-tarp-half-tent farther up the riverbank.

"I normally wake them when I get up," he said gently, "but since you offered to help…"

She set the coffee cup down on one of the large, flat rocks ringing the fire. "What do you need me to do?" she asked, tugging her bonnet from her pocket and slinging it on her head.

Bill rasped out a chuckle. "I need you to have a good breakfast with me," he said, pointing to a fried egg and thick cut of bacon cooling in a greasy skillet near the fire. "You'll need your energy, I suppose."

Polly's stomach rumbled, and she sat, devouring the breakfast in five big bites. It was nice to have something other than stale biscuits and jerky for a change.

Between the coffee and the hot breakfast, Polly felt stronger than ever as Bill led her down to the riverbank. It was clear they weren't alone at this ungodly hour, as several men toiled under the fading moonlight to ready their rafts for floating the treacherous Columbia River.

"We're all eager to beat the spring runoff," he explained, handing her a makeshift tool belt that looked suspiciously like one of his wife's hand-me-down apron pockets. Inside was a hammer and nails.

Bill approached a stack of fresh lumber, thick pine boards, and two-by-fours. It was surrounded by twine, and from the twine, hung little bells. "It took a lot of bartering to buy these boards," he explained. "I watch them like a hawk." He pointed with his own hammer down the riverbank, where men just like him—honest, hardworking, tired, and drawn—hammered and sawed into the quiet dawn. "We all take turns, patrolling the riverbank, keeping an eye on each other's life savings."

Polly nodded and helped Bill slide two boards out from their holding pen. "You turn the clean side over, like this." He showed her, lining them face down and next to each other so that the rough, knotted sides were facing up. "Then you take these smaller strips and we nail the boards together, two at a time, until we've got enough to fit all of us. Then we'll lash everything together and use tar to waterproof the cracks. At least, that's the theory."

Bill chuckled easily, stretched his back, and bent to work. He waited until Polly bent across from him and then began hammering. When he was done, she copied him on her side, looking up at him for approval when she was done. In reply, she found a broad smile waiting for her.

They bent to their work, hammering and nailing, securing boards into strips of two and then stacking them back in their "pen." The work felt good and reassuring, as it meant Polly would soon be in Portland—and that much closer to Ike.

They worked through the morning, hammering, sawing, and stacking, until she heard someone behind them clear her throat. Polly looked up, sweat stinging her eyes, to find Sally, two blue tin plates in hand, heaped with steaming potatoes and scrabble. Beatrice handed a cup of coffee to her pa and ran back to the campsite to fetch another one for Polly.

They all sat, dry on the riverbank, eating lunch together and watching the river go by. "We're gonna ride that?" asked Beatrice, sitting cross-legged next to Polly. The little girl was so close their knees touched. It made Polly smile.

Nearby, Blue munched on old hay next to the Gilhousens' old nag, Chester. Both were tied to a gnarly tree just south of the campsite.

"All the way to the other side of the Cascade Mountains," said Sally, straining to keep the nervousness out of her voice. Polly knew how she felt; the sound of the river was getting stronger every day.

When lunch was over, she and Bill couldn't get back to work fast enough.

Chapter 42

"You mind if I use some of these scraps, Mr. Gilhousen?"

Bill wagged a calloused finger. "Bill, Polly. How many times do I have to tell you, you can call me Bill!"

Mr. Gilhousen—Bill—looked down at the crooked or too thin or too thick strips of lumber he'd deemed unworthy of the family raft. "I don't see why not," Bill said. "But…aren't you ready to knock off for the night?"

Polly looked at Sally and Beatrice, nestled by the fire, Beatrice playing with an old rag doll while Sally sang softly in her ear. "I'll be sure not to keep anyone up at night."

Billy tucked her under the chin. It was a fatherly gesture, and the warmth of his touch, the rough fingertips, and the smell of fresh sawdust on his knuckles reminded Polly of her father. "That's not what I meant, girl. I mean, aren't you tuckered out yet?"

Polly stole a glance at Blue, standing awkwardly by the gnarled old tree, tugging at his rope. "I've got just a little more work to do."

Bill arched one eyebrow, opened his mouth to ask another question, and then thought better of it. He clucked his tongue and walked over to the fire.

Polly borrowed Bill's hatchet, which he'd left hanging from a tree branch next to his precious stash of lumber, and began splitting the long pieces of wood into thinner "rails." Then she began laying them out, in a rectangular shape, closer to the river on level land.

Hammering as fiercely as she could, working alone in the last of the day's light, Polly got as far as halfway around the rough rectangle. At last, her back sore, her legs wobbly, she gave up.

Blue waited patiently, standing idle, as he had all day. "Tomorrow, Blue," she promised him. "I'll finish tomorrow."

The next morning, Polly was the first to rise and put on the coffee before Bill began stirring in the half-tent he'd erected from the family's own wagon cover.

She handed him a cup of coffee and tucked a stray lock of hair under her bonnet. "My Pa always said I was an eager beaver," she said brightly, already halfway through her own mug.

Bill nodded and took a large gulp. "So tell me, Polly, about your family."

Polly nodded tensely; she'd anticipated this moment.

"Not much to tell, really. Ma got sick and died on the trail. After that, Dad gave up on going any further west and stuck up stakes not far from where she'd fallen ill. He took another wife, who had a son about my age, a little older. Pa worked hard, all on his own, got too sick and, well, passed away. My stepmother kicked me out, and I went to live with my uncle, Pa's brother. But he had a wife of his own and a new baby, and one more mouth to feed didn't cotton to well. I heard my stepbrother had up and left the farm and set up stakes in Portland, which is where I'm headed. He's my only kin left, after all."

Bill had finished his coffee and started on breakfast. "I'm sorry to hear that, Polly. Sally and I know many a child that was orphaned on the trail. We're just glad you found us first. Lots of unsavory characters in a place like Fort Dalles."

They ate quietly and quickly after that and then set about to work. The raft was nearly done now, but just after noon, the sky grew dark and a slight drizzle complicated their work. Bill and Polly covered the wood pile as best they could, but when Bill joined his family under the tarp, beckoning her to take shelter, Polly only shook her head and returned to her pet project.

She was already busy hammering away when Sally braved the downpour to hand her a rain slicker. "At least *try* not to catch pneumonia," she said, retreating back to the tarp.

The rain came and went, as did the clouds and the sun. She took her rain slicker off as much as she put it on, but by midday, the rail fence was complete. Bill, taking advantage of the dry spell, came out to join her and inspect her work.

"Very nice," he said, finding the fence sturdy and chest-high. "Your Pa teach you how to do this?"

Polly nodded toward the horses. "It's a pen, so they can stay closer to camp and rest on level ground."

Bill frowned. "They look just fine to me, tied up the way they are."

Polly shook her head. "If it's all the same to you, Bill, I prefer not to tie up old Blue." It was true. Ever since they'd been riding together, Blue didn't really need a guide. Though she tethered him up whenever they were around others, out on their own or along the trail, Blue simply followed her wherever she went.

Bill looked toward the horses, huddling together near the old gnarled tree just up the hill. Even he had to admit they looked uncomfortable. "Be my guest," he said.

After scrambling up the hill, Polly untied both horses and led Chester down the hill. Quietly, obediently, Blue followed, impressing Bill as well as Sally and Beatrice, who came out to watch the meager procession.

At last, the two horses were in their pen and, swinging the gate shut, Polly looked down at her craftsmanship proudly. In the distance, she heard hammering, and when she turned toward the source, she found that Bill had pulled the half-finished raft and was already hammering away.

Polly patted Blue, happy in his new pen, and took up her hammer. Joining Bill, she bent to her work and ignored the rain as it drizzled on her back.

Chapter 43

The days passed, then a week, then one more. With each passing day, Bill and Polly rose earlier and stayed later. At night, they hung lanterns from nearby tree branches or tree stumps, desperate to work one more hour, then two, for the water was rising with each passing day.

Polly had first noticed it early one morning. She rose from her sleeping bag, rubbing her eyes against the predawn darkness. Something had woken her, a noise, laced with dread, splashing and coursing down river. She looked around, wondering if scoundrels or maybe even Injuns, had invaded the camp, but it wasn't a human sound; it was something far more monstrous.

She'd risen, only to find Bill and several other men already in their shirtsleeves, hammers in hand, appraising the river as it swirled and rushed on by.

They'd acknowledged her as one of their own, grumbling in the dark. "Won't be long now before she gets out of hand," one of the men had glowered, spitting tobacco at his feet. It took a second for Polly to realize that he meant the Columbia River, not her!

"It's already out of hand if you've got old folks or little kids on board," said another, turning to his work.

Bill had nodded and smiled at Polly. Turning to their raft, he pointed with his hammer. "Guess we better step it up, huh, Polly?"

And so they had. Now there were two rafts, one for the family and one for the horses, tied and lashed, hammered and nailed, tarred and dried and ready for the egress across to the other side and, for Polly, a second chance at tracking down Ike.

The bank was buzzing with activity as she and the Gilhousens stood, the rafts packed, the horses at the ready, facing the churning waters. Polly's heart was in her chest. Beatrice looked so small, clutching Sally's hand as her mother stood, face grim, bonnet tight, staring at the rushing water.

"Bill?" Sally asked, voice small. "Are you…sure about this?"

Bill's expression, grim and resigned, was also uncertain. "It's the only way," he confessed as Polly helped him drag the first raft to the water. She was stronger now, the soreness in her muscles gone after those first few long days hammering and sawing, lashing and binding. She felt like she had grown as well, standing nearly to Bill's shoulder as they stood, out of breath now, both rafts at the edge of the shore.

They looked at each other, and Bill cracked a rare smile. "I never thought I'd say this," Bill joked, slapping her on the shoulder with his large, calloused hands, "but you're a good man to have by one's side in a pinch, Polly."

She chuckled as they bent back to their work. Bill was stocking the larger raft with the brunt of the supplies: whatever was left of the wagon they'd dismantled and cannibalized for its canvas, slats, and buckboard. A small area in the back, cobbled together with odd pieces of wood and the last of the horse pen, roped off the Gilhousen's horse, Chester.

Blue seemed anxious to leave and was the first to board the smaller of the two rafts, standing and staring down the long river while Polly and the family climbed aboard. Polly made sure that her loyal and faithful companion was securely fastened to his own hodgepodge of a horse pen before loading on Sally and her frightened daughter, Beatrice.

"It's OK, Bea," Polly said as, at last, they were all on board and pushing off into the Columbia. "You'll see. It's just like a toy boat bobbing in the bathtub, promise."

Although it was far from placid, the river seemed at peace this early morning. Polly steered the claustrophobia-inducing raft with a large birch branch,

196

much like a gondolier in Vienna. She worked hard to keep pace with Bill. The larger, heavier raft picked up momentum as the day wore on.

Bill had hoped to get through the terrible Cascade rapids before the night was upon them so that they could float, uneventfully, the rest of the way to Portland and then on to Oregon City. Polly felt vaguely relieved. Although the water was thick and turgid, the raft seemed to have a balance to it, making it easier to steer as she pressed her long pole against the river bottom.

Trees lined either side of the river, casting quiet pools of shade as they passed. Behind her, Beatrice played with a flour-sack doll while her mother, Sally, whispered occasionally to Blue, keeping him calm.

The first half of the day was mostly uneventful. Native Indians were seen at the bank of the river gorging themselves on fresh salmon, the flesh vibrant and as orange as fall pumpkins.

The river seemed alive with salmon, causing their own whitewater as they pushed upstream, thick like herds of cattle or wild horses. Beatrice had yelped upon first seeing them, but as she grew used to their occasional flashes, she giggled each time.

Polly was thankful the Indians seemed oblivious to the rafts and their cargo. Hundreds of Indians seemed to be in a ritual and continued to gorge themselves on raw salmon. Polly shivered to see this feast—and hear it. The event was lively, and she watched as Sally sheltered little Beatrice as they passed.

Everyone was happy they passed by without any incident. But Polly was perhaps the most relieved. The scene on the riverbanks, the Indians lost in ecstasy as they gorged on the fresh, orange salmon flesh, reminded Polly of the stories her mother had told her of evil possession of a man's soul.

Chapter 44

The sound began shortly after they passed the party of hungry Indians: the gurgling of water that had woken her that early spring morning less than a week ago. And then, there it was, the source of the rushing sound: whitewater, frothing between high canyon walls and dashing over slick, moss-covered rocks.

The first rapids seemed merciful as they easily skirted past them without any issues. Blue whinnied, steadying himself in his makeshift pen. Beatrice laughed, once or twice, water splashing her face as Polly effortlessly guided the raft through the giant rocks with the dripping end of her birch paddle. Then, ominously, the roar of the water deepened. The river was becoming narrower as the sheer rocks that lined the treacherous canyon seemed to close in. Even before Bill shouted a warning over his shoulder to "look out," Polly knew they were approaching the infamous Cascade Rapids.

Ahead of Polly and the rest of his family, Bill was in the lead with his larger raft. Polly watched carefully as Bill was trying to guide the raft to the right along the sheer rock wall avoiding what was looming around the next corner: a whirlpool the size of four wagons. Polly had heard around Fort Dalles that this was the spot where the most loss of life occurred.

Polly watched in horror as the raft dipped unnaturally, sending Bill's horse flailing and much of the supplies shifting to follow the downward projection.

Suddenly, it righted itself, but Polly felt in her bones that disaster was right around the corner. What was worse, she knew that she was destined to repeat Bill's dangerous course; there was no way for her to "steer" her way out of his calamity!

As the roar became a deafening blast, the water seemed to rise up and over the rafts, covering everything with a cold, wet coat. Confusion led to panic as Bill's raft caught an overhanging limb hung up between two rock boulders near the rock-faced wall. His raft tipped violently down, and the ever-flowing force of the river began to spin his raft to the left, toward the roar of the endless bottom of the whirlpool.

Sally screamed, grabbed her daughter, and hugged the corner of the raft. Polly leaped to the rudder and pushed with all her strength. There was little she could do by now but hold on for life. Next to her, Blue began to dance, sensing the impending danger.

As the raft tumbled like soap suds going down the sink drain, Polly reached for Blue to keep him steady and not lurch over the edge of the raft. One hand on Blue and the other hand on the tiller, she saw, seemingly in slow motion, Bill's raft breaking up in the extreme force of the water and being sucked down the black hole of the whirlpool.

All at once, everything seemed to go to pieces: the cracking of the raft's logs as they smashed against the looming rocks, Sally screaming, Beatrice crying, Chester plunging over the side, supplies and all their personal possessions being sucked down the river.

Trembling hands wet and shaking on the tiller, Polly pulled with all her might to move the raft as close to the right side as possible but not to get caught in Bill's raft, which by now was mere pieces of wood. Bill was nowhere in sight and neither was his horse Chester. What seemed like minutes only took a few seconds, and then the raft was gone.

"Bill!" Sally screamed desperately, on all fours, the raft tumbling forward on its inevitable course. Beatrice screamed, and Polly caught her as she tumbled off her perch, dress soaking wet and eyes wide with horror. "Beatrice!" Sally grabbed her, soothing her hair, eyes just as wild and looking at Polly's pleadingly. "Please," she gasped, struggling against the rocking motion of the raft as the rocks neared, "do something!"

But Polly's weight was no match for the force of the water. The raft hit the bank of rocks with such force it splintered into two pieces. Missing the whirlpool by what seemed like only inches, their raft was pushed past it and broke up as it rounded the following corner. Whitewater seemed to swallow them up as everyone and everything from the raft struggled to survive.

Polly felt the scratch of a rock as it brushed past her cheek, felt the tug of the water beneath her heavy leather boots, felt branches and twigs or even pieces of their raft tug at her faded blue skirt. Something caught it, a log from the raft, perhaps, or a rope still tied tight to a hundred pounds of supplies being sucked into the whirlpool between the looming wet rocks.

The water muffled the roar as Polly tried to untangle herself while being pulled under by the violent forces beneath her. She remembered the knife she kept so carefully near her left underarm and quickly cut herself free. The current forced her to the churning surface, and Polly herself was thrown violently into a white wall of water and rocks.

Gasping for air among the turbulent waters, Polly frantically fought her way to a nearby outcropping of rock and hung on for dear life. Looking back, she could see Sally and Beatrice, clinging to Sally's back. Sally was being pulled away from the left bank of rocks. Polly could see terror in her face as her hands clutched and slipped futilely from the moss-covered rocks. Polly could see impending death in Sally's face. Sally glanced toward Polly in a last plea for help before she slipped below the surface.

Without thinking, Polly pushed off from the rocks. Underwater, her heart racing, she frantically searched the murky water for any sign of Sally and accidently caught a handful of Sally's dress. Hanging on, she pulled herself toward Sally and was abruptly pushed to the surface by the changing rapids. Catching her breath as the turbulent waters spattered around her, she pulled Sally and her daughter into her arms.

Together, they were dashed from rock to rock, reaching out with bloodied, icy fingers as one bend in the river led to another and then another. Polly fought hard to direct herself to the rock wall, but her efforts were as useless as the raft's rudder in these violent waters.

Suddenly, Polly was reminded of the advice her father had once given her long ago: if she fell into the river, she was not to fight the current but use it to her advantage instead.

Desperately clinging to Sally and Beatrice, Polly kicked out with her aching feet, rushing with the current as it sped them along. Pushing off mossy rocks with her drenched leather boots, she somehow guided her path onto a short outcropping of rocks, and with her left hand gripping tightly to Sally and her daughter, she wedged her right arm into two rock outcroppings.

The pain was instant, and even above the rushing water, she heard the tear of something in her arm coming loose. Still, she fought through the pain to hold her position. But the water was too strong.

After only a minute, she knew she was in trouble as her sprained arm was slipping from the rock. No longer able to swim, she knew that she would soon drown if she could not reach the shore. As Polly tried to determine if Sally and her daughter could survive on their own, she heard a familiar snort up river.

It was Blue, struggling against the current, only his head and glistening wet mane visible above the rapids. Blue was being pushed downriver, along with all of the debris from the two shattered rafts. He struggled against the current, sensing Polly's terror and pushing hard toward her.

Taking a leap of faith, Polly let go of the rock, and Blue suddenly surged to her. With her last strength and able hand, she reached out and grabbed onto his mane as the current surged and fought to pull her away. It was as if it had been planned. The horse was suddenly beneath them as Polly pulled herself up, clenching tightly to Blue's mane, and the girls found themselves on Blue's back, holding on for their lives. Polly lay low and flat on his back, holding on to Sally and her daughter with her left hand.

At the next bend in the river, Blue surged into an eddy and came upon a sandy alcove, which he lurched onto with wobbly, dripping legs. Like potatoes from a sack, the women fell onto the sand. Gasping for breath, both Sally and her daughter lay on the beach, winded and trying to gain their composure.

Polly sat up, coughing water, blinking. Sally's screams began to peel forth as she remembered that her dear husband, Bill, had been swept away and was gone forever. Next to her, Beatrice huddled, the two lost in misery, consoling each other as both took turns wailing well into the night.

Polly thought of starting a fire but knew she wasn't up to it. She wondered if Indians, scoundrels, or worse patrolled the riverbanks, looking for the lost and vulnerable, but there wasn't much she could do about it in her condition.

She lay on the beach, exhausted, head pounding, lamenting that all their supplies were gone. All that was left were their bodies, bruised and broken, and the clothes on their back—wet, ragged, and torn.

Polly lay beside the front legs of Blue, nursing her sprained right arm. Blue lightly nudged her to ensure she was safe. Polly looked up into Blue's eyes and knew their bond was unlike anything she had ever experienced before.

Chapter 45

As night approached, Polly roused herself. They had slept, fitfully, from sheer exhaustion, all three alternately sobbing and snoring. Polly yelped when she rolled over onto her sprained arm.

She sat up, finding the day gone and the horizon tinged with the fiery orange-blue of sunset. Sally lay on her back, motionless, with Beatrice curled up at her feet.

With great effort, Polly rose, only to plunk down again immediately on the trunk of an old, downed tree. She yanked the hem from her skirt and wrapped it around her neck, forming a crude sling for her sprained arm. If only it had been her left instead of her right. She had so much to do and could ill afford an injury.

Blue looked up from a patch of fresh wildflowers and whinnied, reminding her that if it hadn't been for him, she'd have much more to worry about than a sprained arm.

There was a chill in the air, and Polly stood once more, using her good hand for momentum.

"Sally," she hissed, gently, rousing the young mother as she rose, eyes red and puffy from crying. "I hate to bother you, but I'm going to need your help if we want to make it through the night."

Sally nodded; both women agreed to let Beatrice sleep. "I need wood for a fire," Polly said as Sally stood, motionless, expressionless, silently. "I'll scour the riverbank before we lose the light completely and see if I can salvage anything."

Sally nodded and left without a word. Polly wondered if she'd ever speak again. She walked away listlessly, leather boots still squishing from their dunking, sand covering her powder-blue skirt, bonnet gone forever and hair stringy and sandy across her slumped shoulders.

Polly limped toward the shore. Her ankle was sore, but the splint was strong and she was getting used to using only one hand. She broke off a long, heavy branch from a neighboring tree and used it as a walking stick until she reached the shore.

The water still rushed, but it was slower here, more eddy than whirlpool. Sure enough, some detritus from their doomed voyage had collected in the reeds and along the banks. She worked until she could no longer see, promising herself she'd come back at the day's first light.

She sorted through piles, tying sacks together and dragging them back as best she could with one good hand and hardly able to see. Somehow, Sally had started a fire, and now, Beatrice clung to her as they sat on a log bench the mother must have dragged over for them to share.

Beatrice sprang to life the minute Polly returned to the campsite. "Polly!" she cried, tears fresh on her face. "We thought we'd lost you, too!"

"You'll never lose me, Beatrice," Polly assured her as Sally stared forlornly into the fire. "Me or Blue."

"Good," Beatrice said, eager to help. Together, they dragged the sacks next to the fire for a closer look.

Polly opened them, one by one, as Beatrice watched closely and Sally ignored them both. There was a single shoe; a useless and clumped sack of waterlogged flour; a measuring cup, already rusting; a pink petticoat and a blue bonnet; a knife; and a bowl.

"Look!" Beatrice said as Polly dragged a bit of wet jerky from the bottom of a flour sack. "Can we eat it?" the little girl asked.

Polly opened up the bag and saw that the jerky was moist but didn't seem any worse for the wear. "I don't see why not," she told Beatrice, handing her two strips. Without being told, the little girl raced to her mother to offer her one. Sally barely looked up.

Beatrice returned and handed one of the strips back. "She didn't want it."

"She will tomorrow," Polly said in a high, reassuring voice, though she wasn't quite sure if a grieving Sally would ever eat, or talk, again. "We'll just save it for her, OK?"

Beatrice beamed, and together, they spent a few pleasant minutes alternately chewing and complaining about the toughness of the recovered jerky. The fact was, it was quite a find. Normally, Polly would hunt or forage for food, but with her sprained arm, that would prove to be quite a challenge.

Although she had little appetite, Polly forced down the jagged strip of dried beef for the sustenance it would provide. After all, her journey was only beginning.

"Look," Polly said, digging to the bottom of one sack and retrieving a damp but otherwise unharmed stuffed doll. It was homemade, cobbled together from strips of fabric and an old flour sack, the thread that bound the arms and legs to the torso heavy and coarse. One button eye was moving, and the yarn hair was still dripping, but other than that, it looked much as it had before the accident.

"Mavis!" Beatrice squealed, accepting it as Polly handed it over. The girl hustled it over to show her mother, but Sally only glanced at it quickly, before returning her gaze to the unforgiving river that had taken her husband.

Beatrice slumped against the back of the tree stump her mother was sitting on and spoke quietly to her doll, so quietly Polly couldn't hear their "conversation."

When she looked up a few minutes later, after sorting through the last of the bags, Beatrice was curled up at her mother's back, clutching her damp doll and snoring gently.

Polly, having now slept and eaten, quickly got to work. She stretched damp linen and clothes over tree branches, tried her best to dry out waterlogged hard tack by placing it on a log next to the fire, and sorted the junk from the salvageable—and all with one hand.

She worked through the night, lighting a torch and going back to the riverbank repeatedly until every last scrap of cotton and tin fork was recovered. When at last Sally and Beatrice rose, Polly had sorted three bags—one for each of them to carry—and had bundled Blue's saddle with two more.

Chapter 46

Sally followed listlessly as Polly led the way, Beatrice on one side of her, Blue ambling along on the other. The rapids had dumped them out at a tidal pool that was only a few steps away from a fresh trail cut through the brush that lined the riverbank.

Just on the other side, up a short hill and through dry woods, awaited a clean trail, dusty with frequent use and wide enough to hold two wagons rumbling side by side. It was empty at this hour, but as they made steady progress, Polly could see other travelers, damp and road weary like themselves, off in the distance ahead of them.

Beatrice chatted amiably with her doll while Blue kept pace with Polly's limping progress. They stopped at a trading post after only a few miles, and with several of the contents she had managed to salvage from an open coin purse that had landed ashore, Polly stocked them for the long walk into town: a little coffee, some sugar, cured ham, and dry biscuits and, for Beatrice, some penny candy to hold ransom lest she misbehave.

They camped on the first night, just off the trail, a large fire and Polly's trusty knife on hand should any unsavory visitors spot the fire and decide to investigate. Sally had yet to speak since the accident, and even Beatrice had retreated to the far reaches of the fire, playing with her doll, feeding it crumbs from her dinner and speaking quietly until she finally fell asleep.

"Sally," Polly said, tidying up the few stray dishes she'd managed to salvage from the riverbank after her own meal. "I don't mind the silent treatment, but your girl's gonna need a mother shortly."

Sally gave her an indignant flash and seemed to grow even more silent. Polly slept soundly and rose early to find Sally sitting in the same spot, staring at a smoldering fire that had long since gone out.

There was a small stream to the south of camp, and Polly helped Beatrice clean her face and hands and change her socks for the long day's walk. When they got back to camp, Sally was standing next to Blue, waiting patiently for them.

They had walked for nearly half a mile before Polly realized that Sally had left her sack back at the camp. It held little but damp socks and bonnets and the stray tin cup, but Polly was most angry at herself for letting it happen.

She took one of the sacks from Blue's back and handed it to Sally instead. She hoisted Beatrice on top of Blue, and they walked silently for the rest of the morning.

By late afternoon, the trail was heavy with other travelers—families, mostly, tuckered out and dirty, their own supplies dwindling, their faces joyless and slack.

Even the children were muted as they teetered along in stiff and dusty shoes. The weather was warm, and faces were lined with sweat and dirt from the dry, dusty trail.

The town of Portland loomed ahead, and though quite a bit larger than Fort Dalles, from half a mile away, it had the same desperate sound of a frontier town: loud women and drunk men, laughing—or crying—children shouting, dogs barking, fires burning.

As they approached town, Polly's stomach clenched. It was early afternoon now, plenty of light left in the day, and her passion to find Ike had only intensified, if anything, over her weeks-long journey out of Bonney's Canyon. And yet, now that Portland was so near, Polly dreaded dredging up old skeletons from her closet.

The time with Bill and his family had restored Polly's faith in what a family—a real family—could look like, could feel like. In many ways, Polly was mourning her own family as she watched Bill go under in those swirling rapids and never come back up to the surface. In a way, she was mourning still.

"Bye, Polly," Beatrice said, forcing Polly to dry her eyes and focus on her fellow travelers. While she had been standing there, watching the other travelers stream into Portland, Sally had taken Beatrice down from Blue, and with a sack over each shoulder, they both looked back at Polly.

"Come here, Pumpkin," Polly said, voice quiet as she knelt to accept the little girl's arms as they clung tightly to her neck. "I want you to be brave and take care of your mom, OK?"

Beatrice wiped her nose and nodded, standing in front of Polly for a brief moment before rushing to take her mother's hand. Polly stood and watched the woman and child walk away.

But then, after only a few steps, Sally turned. "Thank you," said the grieving widow, finally looking into Polly's eyes. "I…I wouldn't have survived Bill's death if it hadn't been for you, Polly."

Polly smiled and shook her head. Patting Blue affectionately, she said, "Just remember, Sally, if it wasn't for Blue here, none of us would be alive."

Sally nodded. "Just the same," she said, clutching Beatrice's hand. "We both owe you a debt of gratitude."

Polly nodded and watched them go. Once she could no longer see them, Polly sighed. A gurgling stream beckoned just off trail, and Polly followed its sound until at last it appeared in a beautiful green clearing.

She and Blue both drank deeply, and after taking off her boots, stockings, and bonnet and pulling her tattered skirt up to her knees, Polly waded in. The water was deliciously cold after the long, hot trail, and she bathed as best she could within earshot of a dozen or more passing travelers.

Blue feasted on wildflowers and fresh grass while Polly washed down the last of her jerky with fresh, cold, stream water. They lazed, the sun high above but sheltered by the outcropping of trees. Polly dozed briefly, but, as if on instinct, Blue woke her with a plaintive snort well before darkness fell.

She stood and laced her shoes, patting her faithful horse's muzzle. Blue had been so good to her since they'd met. He was such a noble beast, quiet and loyal to the end. She literally owed him her life, and she wasn't going to let him down now.

"It's time," she said, leading Blue from the clearing, both of them watered and fed. In minutes, they would be in Portland, where she could once again resume her quest for Ike.

Rested, fed, and rehydrated, her loyal companion at her side, Polly was finally ready to put the past to rest—even if it meant facing her past in the bargain.

Chapter 47

Portland, Oregon.

Polly was finally here. But the question remained...was Ike?

She'd been through so much to get here, had almost died, and had buried her entire family—mother, father, even her daughter—hundreds of miles of trail and a raging river away.

She had hidden from Indians; found a best friend in Blue; walked, ridden, and then floated through two territories; worn holes in her shoes; and nearly had her arm yanked off. But would it pay off? Was Ike here, in Portland, the end of the Oregon Trail? Or had he split for parts unknown, hooked up with some other ruffians, heading farther west to terrorize some other young gals?

As Polly strode into town, she knew she couldn't rest until she found out. Polly looked out of place here on the crowded, busy streets of Portland. Drinking dens, bordellos, and gambling houses lined every intersection. The men outnumbered the women thirty to one, but she didn't fear the hard-eyed drinkers, gamblers, cowboys, grifters, and lowlife thugs, who whistled as she hurried by.

She'd come too far to be bullied or postponed by any two-bit hustler now. She unfolded the clipping, miraculously still intact after her travels, probably because she'd kept it wedged just inside the leather sheath beneath her arm.

Ike's face stared back at her, unwholesome and repulsive, making her shiver even in the heat of day. She entered the first saloon in her path, pushed her way through, and ignored even louder, rowdier catcalls as she walked purposefully toward the bar.

The barkeep saw her coming and waved a dirty bar rag in her face. "You know you're not supposed to be in here, darling. Now, run along before I call the law."

Polly fixed a grim smile to her face and tried her sweetest voice. "Please, mister," she oozed, practicing the story she'd been working on since she got into town. "My brother, Ike, ran off one night as the rest of my family slept on the trail. Have you seen him, mister? If you don't want to talk to me, I can go get my pa and you can talk to him."

She looked at the man's sweaty face with hopeful eyes, until at last his furrowed brow grew smooth and he took the clipping from her trembling hands.

The bar was hot, almost stifling, and sweat ran down the barkeep's dirty face. The light was dim, and as the man began shaking his head, Polly interjected hopefully, "The clipping's old, but I think he might still be in town."

The bartender scratched his rotund belly beneath a dirty apron and shook his head. "'Fraid I don't recognize him. Now, unless you're going to buy something, I suggest—"

Polly was reaching for the clipping back when a tall, thin man lounging in a nearby barstool leaned over. "Let me see that," he said.

He had an open vest covering a dirty shirt and a dirty bowler covering his greasy head. He smelled like cheap beer and cheaper whiskey, but Polly was desperate so she passed the clipping over to the curious stranger.

Polly turned a cold shoulder to the disinterested bartender and directed her attention toward the thin man. "Do you know him?"

The stranger squinted his eyes and took a closer look at Ike's picture. "No," he said, crushing Polly's hopes. Then he added quickly, "I ain't never seen him in my life. But if he's in town, I know where you can find him."

He slid the clipping back across the dirty bar, and turning, Polly absently folded it and began slipping it back into her pocket. Then the curious man laughed out loud, sipping liberally from his half-empty beer mug and slamming it down on the bar.

Polly turned to him, unable to hide the desperation in her voice. "Sir, please tell me. I have to find him and put my family right."

The man turned to her, eyes surprisingly alert as he trained them on hers. He leaned closer to where she stood defiantly, fists clenched at her sides. "Well, look here, it's like this. How old are you anyway?"

Polly said nothing, just stood and stared him down. The man chuckled dryly and continued, "Never mind. A man travels west to make his fortune. He ain't married, don't have no family to support, ain't no women here anyway. Where do you think is his first port of call?"

Polly tilted her head curiously, but instead of answering, the man only spread his arms out wide. Angry yellow stains lurked under his scrawny arms. "That's right," he continued energetically, downing the last of his beer. "The saloon. He comes to forget. To drink. To solve his problems with his pistol. And when he's had enough of making merry what d'you think he does then? Well, let me tell you he goes to the whorehouse to—"

Flustered, Polly tipped her bonnet in the man's direction and babbled, "Th-th-thank you for your honesty, sir."

Polly could still hear the man's drunken laughter as she hurried from the bar and out into the hot, dusty streets of Portland. She stood just in front of the saloon, staring down at her dusty, dirty boots, tears threatening to spill down her hollow cheeks.

She was low on money, her arm still hurt, and she was hungry, thirsty, had nowhere to stay, and—

Suddenly, a clod of chewed tobacco landed at her feet. She took an involuntary step back and quickly looked up to find where it had come from.

From just behind her, a crusty voice croaked, "You looking for Ike O'Neal?"

Polly gasped and spun to find its speaker, an older white-haired man staring squarely at Polly. He was rough mannered and ill tempered, his face weathered by sun and age, narrowed eyes hidden by the shadow from his cowboy hat.

He was tall, and Polly had to look up at him to nod. "Yes, sir."

He nudged his hat higher on his head with one calloused knuckle and looked down at her suspiciously with a wrinkled brow. "Who sent you? Ike owe you money or somethin'?"

Polly opened her mouth to spin her rehearsed tale, but something in her gut told her this old salt wouldn't fall for it. Instead, she played her cards closer to her chest. "No, sir. No one sent me. I'm just a relative. By marriage only."

She squinted up at him, standing her ground. He squinted back down at her, spitting another wad of juicy tobacco at her feet as he considered her words. Unconsciously, she inched away from the dark stain on the bleak, dirt street.

The man scared Polly but not enough to make her run. If he knew Ike, it would be worth the fear to find out all he knew. That is, if he would tell her.

After a long silence as they stared each other down, the man finally nodded, tugging his cowboy hat down lower on his forehead. "Find Missy," he said, nodding toward a dusty row house near the end of the street. "At Madam's whorehouse. If she likes you, she'll help you."

Polly covered her eyes with her hand to get a better look at the nondescript, two-story building. "Thank you," she said, turning back to the mysterious old man. "But...who are you, sir?"

At last, the man smiled, joylessly. "Someone who wants to see Ike O'Neal dead and buried." He lowered his voice as he inched closer, weathered cowboy boots kicking up dust in his path. "From the look in your eyes, I can tell you want that too."

The man doffed his hat, bowed slightly, slipped it back on, and turned to beat a hasty retreat. Polly watched him go, shoulders stooped from years on the range, legs bowed from decades on a horse.

When at last he had rounded a corner and disappeared from view, she turned toward the end of the street and marched, slowly, toward Madam's.

Chapter 48

Siobhan rolled her head from left to the right, trying to ease the crick in her neck. Inside the City Hall records department, the light was dim and the air was musty, but she was determined to scour as far and as wide as she could to get to the truth.

The microfiche machine was almost as old and stubborn as Siobhan. She rattled and slid through the years, putting Polly's history in context. It took some getting used to, the sliding in and out of the microfiche machine; the ancient language of the old newspapers; the thick, heavy-leaded newsprint, but finally, Siobhan found the month she was looking for: the time of Ike's breakout from the Chester County jail.

Her heart almost leaped from her chest when Siobhan discovered the same story Polly had cut from the local newspaper—Ike's face, piggish and defiant in the ancient photo.

She inched her tired neck closer to the article, reading the headline: "Jail Break Shocks Local Community," in the old style typesetting—"Sheriff's deputies were baffled by the midnight jailbreak and scoured Holcomb County until the break of day as the missing prisoner eluded them well past dawn..." She continued rereading it until she almost had it memorized.

She could picture Polly using her stepmother's shears to carefully snip the article from the paper, folding it carefully and slipping it away under her pillow, staring at it in her darkest hours, living on the only passion she had left: revenge.

An older woman cleared her throat and, momentarily startled, Siobhan jerked upright, turning toward the reference room door. The librarian slid her bifocals down her nose and said, sweetly but firmly, "Library's about to close, dear."

Siobhan was almost relieved and after clicking print, stood impatiently by the ancient printer as it wheezed out a copy of Ike's breakout story. She grabbed it as it finished and thanked the librarian on her way out the door.

When she arrived home, Siobhan rushed up to her room and grabbed Polly's journals off of her bed. She walked into her father's room to find him staring out the window. Siobhan wondered if he'd watched her come in and what he thought about all day.

The room was quiet and dark, and when Siobhan cleared her throat, her father blinked but otherwise didn't move. She walked toward him, sensible heels clacking on the wooden floors as she strode toward her father's wheelchair.

"I brought you these, Zachariah. I thought we might talk."

Zachariah stared at the journals for a moment with disgust, and then he pushed Siobhan's hand away. The journals fell to the floor, cracked leather binding creaking and yellowed pages fluttering as Siobhan reached to retrieve them, almost protectively.

Zachariah scowled at her, shaking his ancient head. "I should have burned them when I had the chance. The poisonous ramblings of a madwoman."

Siobhan stood, clutching the journals to her chest. Zachariah chuckled dryly. "I see you've been keeping yourself occupied snooping around."

"I wasn't snooping. I did some research at the county hall. The fire. The baby. It all checks out. I just don't understand why Polly's been eradicated from our lives. Why do you hate her so much?"

Zachariah glared back at her. "Because she ruined the future for all of us and not one of us can atone for her sins."

"What are you talking about?"

"She's inside you. I saw her the first day you arrived at the ranch. She's a curse. And the curse lives on."

Siobhan ignored the old man's insults and ordered, "Tell me what she did."

Zachariah looked back out the window, as if staring back in time. "She was a murderer."

"I don't believe you," she said.

"Do you think I'm confused again?" Zachariah asked, turning from the window and leering at her with a curious smile. "Do you think the dementia is making me invent things?"

He reached down with his leathery paws and grabbed his wheels, turning his chair toward her and staring her in the face. "I'd be glad to forget about Polly. Why can't the dementia make me forget the things I hate the most?"

Siobhan tucked a curl behind her ear and bit her lip. She clutched the journals tighter to her chest. "Polly's story ends with the fire at the ranch. Polly was reunited with Lafayette."

Zachariah offered a wry smile. "That's not the end of it. It's just the beginning."

"Tell me what happened," she insisted. "I really need to know."

Amazingly, Zachariah obliged. "Polly set out after her stepbrother. She couldn't let it rest. She was consumed with getting her revenge. Settling the score."

"But Polly was brutalized by Ike for years," Siobhan insisted. "He killed her mother."

"She was bitter," Zachariah agreed. "She never got over it. It drove her insane. And don't bother looking for the details. I burned the last journal a long time ago."

Siobhan stared aghast at him.

"You can't relate to her one little bit, can you? Is it because she's a woman?"

Zachariah chuckled joylessly. "You see her as a hero."

"She is a hero," Siobhan insisted, looking down at her father, shaking her head. "Look at you. You blame women for everything. Always have done. From the day my mother died, you made my life a misery. Do you know how I've felt all these years, thinking that her death was my fault? She died of cancer, Dad. Why did you blame me?"

Zachariah's face drained as Siobhan's words landed. His voice was dry and humorless as he explained, "As I said, it's Polly's fault. Some wrongs cannot be set right."

She waited, feeling Zachariah's ire roll off of him in waves. "Leave me alone, Polly," he said. "Get out of here. Leave me alone."

Chapter 49

It might have looked humble from the outside, but inside Madam Jasmine's Goodtime Emporium was as opulent as Polly had ever seen—not with her own eyes, of course, but in ladies' magazines her mom used to read.

Polly sat in a lavish parlor. Oil paintings and French furniture lined the walls. A crystal chandelier hung from the ceiling, filling the room with soft orange light. The smell of tobacco and the sound of pouring drinks echoed in the background.

Polly's throat felt dry. She watched as a woman in a flowing pink dress, her waist cinched within an inch of its life, and a matching hat swept into the room as if she were onstage. Feeling the urge to stand, Polly started to get up, but the woman motioned with a gloved hand and Polly sat back down.

"Polly, is it?" asked the woman in a stilted Southern voice.

"Y-y-yes, ma'am," she stammered, nervous from the long wait.

"I'm Madam," said the woman proudly, taking off her gloves dramatically and laying them across her lap. "Madam Jasmine. So, Polly, what brings you to my…Emporium?"

"I'm new in town," Polly began as the woman sank delicately into a brocade love seat across from her. "I heard there was work here. I can clean and cook and wash real well."

Madam Jasmine pursed her lips, bright red beneath her cheeks. She looked to be in her late fifties, face lined with age and experience, eyes dark and sharp as a hawk's.

"You heard correct," she said. "But I'd prefer someone a little older. This isn't the most suitable place for...children."

Polly's voice grew high with emotion. "You're quite wrong, ma'am, if you'll forgive me for speaking out of turn," she began. "I'm nearly sixteen years old already. I don't even need to sleep here in the house. I'd much prefer the barn where I can sleep with my horse, Blue. All I'm looking for is a job so I can study at night."

Madam hung her head, the hat taking the place of her face as it began to quiver and then shake. Laughter rose from beneath the hat until it rose, and Madam stared back at her, shaking her head curiously.

"My dear," Madam chuckled. "Do you even know what this establishment is?"

Polly blushed and confessed, "No, ma'am."

Madam's voice grew firm and authoritative. "Then allow me to make something absolutely clear. My boardinghouse here comprises three fire-places, a saloon, a champagne cellar, and twelve suites filled with imported furniture from Europe. I provide each of my employees with a wardrobe that includes a fur coat, four tailored suits, eight hats, two dress coats, twelve pairs of shoes, twelve pairs of gloves, seven evening gowns, and seven negligees."

Madam's eyes were wide, her voice high as she paused to catch her breath. "I offer my ladies free health care, legal assistance, housing, and meals. Now what in the name of God makes you think I would want you to sleep in the barn with your horse?"

"I'm sorry," Polly said, hanging her head. "I just thought—"

Madam sat back, looking at Polly carefully. "Yes, I can see you did. Not many people do nowadays, so at least I can give you credit for that." The old woman widened her eyes and asked, "What are you studying?"

"Midwifery," Polly said, blushing a little. She rarely had the chance to talk about herself. "I want to help people."

Madam nodded and lit a cigarette. She crossed her legs and blew out a plume of smoke, studying Polly carefully. Polly felt like a bug under a microscope.

After a moment, she put the cigarette out in a thick glass ashtray on the end table beside her. "Come back in the morning," Madam said, a half-smile on her face. "If you're as good as your word, the job is yours. But I'm warning you, it doesn't pay much. You know you have the looks for this kind of work," she said, sizing Polly up. "If we cleaned you up, that is. Trained you."

Polly stuck her chin out and looked back at Madam. "I'd rather use my brain than my body."

Madam stared right back. "My dear, where exactly in the history books does it say that a woman has ever been valued for her brain?"

Polly opened her mouth to answer, but Madam cut her off: "Do you know how much you can make in a factory? Five dollars a week? My girls make that in an hour."

Madam lit another cigarette and studied Polly from between puffs of thick, acrid smoke. "You obviously have neither the looks nor the head for business," she decreed.

Polly wasn't offended by Madam's words; she'd been insulted by worse. "That may be so, but I have morals."

Madam snuffed out another cigarette and stood, dramatically, slipping her gloves back on and straightening her hat. When she was through, she looked down at Polly and decreed, "I'm afraid morals won't get you far in this town."

Chapter 50

Polly heard the tinkling of the ivories down in the main parlor as the pianist, Big Slim, breezed through a familiar tune, a melody she couldn't quite place. He played from five until midnight, seven days a week, and was the highlight of the last few nights as Polly hustled fresh sheets and linens to the ladies in their boudoirs.

"Ladies," Madam Jasmine called them, not "women."

"Boudoirs," Madam Jasmine called them, not "bedrooms."

"Learn the language," she'd told Polly on her first night shift three days earlier, "and you'll learn to love the Emporium."

Polly had been quick to learn the lingo but hadn't quite fallen in love with the Emporium as much. Still, it was a paying gig and steady. There was no hurting for business here, that much Polly could see.

All day and night, the men came and went. The parlor oozed with sweat and desire as Big Slim plunked away at his piano and Madam poured the libations, cheap Scotch in sparkling crystal glasses.

The more they drank, the louder—and rowdier—they got. But that was a good thing, the ladies said. The drunker they were, the quicker they...finished their business and left the Emporium, broke, but happy.

Polly finished folding her latest batch of clean linen and shut the closet door at the end of the upstairs hallway. She was trundling past the closed doors, ignoring the sounds of passion from behind, when one door flew open and a scantily dressed blonde stumbled out, clutching her silk nightgown to her bare chest.

"Get back in here, Missy," a voice chastised from inside the dimly lit bedroom.

Polly perked up. *Missy.* It was the same name the crazy old coot outside of the saloon had given her.

The leggy blonde turned toward the door, shimmying in her see-through negligee. "I'll be right back, Judge Hawkins. Quit your bellyaching."

Polly stood in the hallway, arms loaded down with linen, transfixed. The girl was beautiful and otherworldly with milky pale skin, flushed cheeks, long legs, and a straight, white-toothed smile.

She shut the door behind her and suddenly noticed Polly standing transfixed. The girl put her hand out, ladylike. Polly, loaded down by clean sheets, arched one eyebrow. Missy helped her put them on a parlor chair between bedrooms and took her hand.

"You must be the new girl, Polly. I've heard a lot about you. I'm Missy. Pleased to make your acquaintance."

Polly nodded nervously. "And yours." Polly felt the need to curtsy in her presence, for reasons she couldn't explain.

Missy nodded and dragged her farther down the gaslit hallway. "What brings a nice girl like you to a place like this, Polly?"

Polly shrugged, noting the older woman's breezy tone but suspicious eyes. "Seemed like as good a job as any," Polly said, giving her pat answer.

Missy nodded, but her eyes said she wasn't quite satisfied. They arrived at the end of the hall, where an open window let in a gentle night's breeze through rustling curtains.

Missy leaned on the windowsill, sticking her face out the window and sniffing deeply. "Uh, ma'am," Polly ventured. "What are we doing here?"

Missy brought her head back in, leaning back on the windowsill daintily. "Nothing much, Polly. But it helps if you keep the client waiting just a bit. Makes 'em want you all the more when you get back to the room, you know?"

226

Polly chuckled as Missy sighed and then marched straight back to her room, where Judge Hawkins greeted her with a giant whoop and holler. She picked back up her linens and returned to her duty. Back near the open window at the end of the hall, she listened in at the nearest door before knocking gently.

"Fresh linens," she announced, awaiting a reply. When there was none, she opened the door and shimmied in. The rooms were small but ornate, with red velvet chairs and sagging beds covered in frilly blankets and curtains to match.

On each nightstand was a fresh bottle of homemade whiskey with two crystal glasses and on every dresser, a porcelain pitcher of water in a matching basin for freshening up. Candles flickered and glowed from every corner, casting dancing shadows over the ornate wallpaper.

Polly opened up the bottom dresser drawer to slide in a fresh pile of sheets and pillowcases. As she was putting them on top of the last batch, her hand ran into something cold, hard, like metal.

She lifted back a top sheet and gasped. Inside was a pistol, tucked toward the back of the wobbly wooden drawer. Polly sat back on her heels, gazing at the polished steel. She listened closely for approaching footsteps and, hearing none, reached in and carefully slid the gun back out.

It felt heavy and cool in her hand. It had a wooden stock and a long, black barrel. It was cold and, she knew, deadly. Was it loaded? She was about to check when the sound of footsteps in the hall made her slide the gun back in between the sheets and look up, forcing a "Who, me?" expression on her face.

Preceding the footsteps was a waft of expensive French perfume, and Polly straightened to find Madam standing in the doorway momentarily. Her eyes were sharp but kind as she poked her head in, her peach-colored hat hardly fitting in the narrow doorway.

"Hi, Polly," she said breezily. "I was just checking in on my new girl. Everything all right?"

"Hunky dory!" Polly snapped breezily, carefully patting down the frilly white apron she wore over her stiff black French maid uniform.

Madam wrinkled her nose at the "country" expression but nodded none-theless. "Carry on, dear," she said with a smile. "I'm hearing good things!" With that, she and her cloud of expensive perfume drifted back down the hall.

Polly stood, quietly approaching the doorway and poking her head out-side. The doors were shut, the only sound the hollering and whooping from the men downstairs, and Big Slim's frenetic piano playing.

She returned to the drawer, sliding it back open and quickly slipping the gun into her apron pocket.

Chapter 51

A few nights later, Polly sat at her simple wooden desk, fiddling with the wick of her burning oil lamp. When it was bright enough, she slid the glass top back down and returned to her anatomy book. It was thick and still smelled new, maybe because she'd bought it with her first week's pay. She'd had little leftover after the hefty price tag, but it didn't much matter.

It might have been a "house of ill repute," as her stepmother would have called it, but Madam Jasmine's Goodtime Emporium took care of pretty much all her essentials: a roof over her head; three good, hot meals a day; and all the free piano music she could stand!

She paused in her studies to use her favorite knife to sharpen her pencil and then put it back in her holster beneath her shoulder and continued scribbling notes in the book's ample margins in her tight, careful script.

She was practicing her spelling of "aorta" when a soft knock came at her door. Startled, Polly raced to cover up her thick school book when the door opened, revealing Missy standing there in a tatty burgundy robe.

"Polly…"

Missy took in the giant book, the row of carefully lined pencils, and the eraser dust. Polly hadn't told anyone but Madam Jasmine of her studies and didn't brag about it to the other girls. She hadn't wanted any of them to know.

Now her secret was out. Missy inched in, her face hardening with every step. "Can I…" she began. "Can I come in for a minute?"

Polly had barely nodded when Missy slammed the door behind her, covering it with her back. Nostrils flaring and eyes wide, she hissed, "Who sent you?"

Polly noted the tone of concern in Missy's voice and blurted, "No one sent me. I'm here to pay for my schooling; that's all—"

Missy inched forward, cheeks flushed with emotion. "Yes, they did," she interrupted. "Someone sent you to spy on me, didn't they? It doesn't take much working out. A young girl like you shows up at a brothel, asking for a job, studying anatomy. Please! I'm not going to fall for that. It was my father, wasn't it?"

Polly shook her head vehemently. "Missy, honest, I don't know what you're talking about."

Missy hardened her eyes even more and bore down on Polly. "Yes. You. Do!" she spat, emphasizing each word more than the last.

Polly stood from her desk, glad for the sheath beneath her shoulder. She'd faced harder women than Missy in her own damn family and wasn't going to back down from a common harlot!

But Missy showed her mettle as both women refused to back down. "Yes! You! Do!"

Polly tried to reason with the irate hooker. "No, I don't. It certainly wasn't your father, whoever he is. I thought if I became your friend, you might…help me."

"Tell me the truth, Polly. Or I'll tell Madam and you'll be out of here before you know it."

"Tell her what?" Polly asked.

Missy toyed with the corner of the anatomy book, smiling slyly. "I'll think of something, dear one."

Polly shook her head. "It is the truth. I'm not here to spy on you. I'm in Portland…looking for someone."

Missy changed her tune. "Who?"

Polly hemmed. "Just…someone…who needs to be found. I know he's in Portland, or somewhere nearby. I have to find him. I thought you could help me."

Missy made a face, contemplating Polly's latest revelation. "Why me?" she asked. "Who gave you my name?"

Polly shrugged. "A man in one of the bars in town."

"Who?" Missy pressed.

Polly shook her head. "He wouldn't tell me his name."

Missy wouldn't give up, asking, "What did he look like?"

Polly racked her brain for an accurate description. "Old. White hair. Crazy-eyed. Ringing a bell yet?"

Apparently, it was—and not in a good way. Missy frowned and sank onto the sagging single bed shoved against the wall of Polly's tiny room. "That's Joe Dowd," Missy explained when not chewing the fingernail she promptly shoved in her mouth. As her eyes focused on a spot just above Polly's head, Missy's voice trailed away; she was lost in some long-forgotten memory. "He was the father of one of the girls here. My best friend, Katie." Then she refocused on Polly and asked, "So who are you looking for?"

The atmosphere in the room had shifted. Missy sat, deflated, on her bed. Polly slumped down in her chair and stared at her evenly. "Ike O'Neal," she confessed.

Like a shot, Missy sat up bolt straight. "I know the bastard," she seethed. "Tell me, what are you going to do when you find him?"

Polly's voice was as cold as the steel of the gun barrel hidden away in her unmentionables drawer: "Kill him."

Missy's eyes matched her icy tone: "I'll help you."

Chapter 52

Siobhan crossed her legs and then uncrossed them. She was nervous and couldn't help fidgeting. She hated lawyers, and while Joseph Cotton, Esquire, was young and kind, he was still a lawyer and her reason for being here for a second time was no more pleasant than her visit.

It was late afternoon, and the weak sun filtered in through the half-open blinds. Across from her, Joseph Cotton, sat just as uncomfortably in his own leather desk chair.

Siobhan's voice was harsh and insistent, even to her own ears.

"I've really tried to make my peace with him, Mr. Cotton, but he won't have any of it. He's confused most of the time now. I think the best thing I can do is put the house and land up for sale as soon as possible."

Cotton ran long fingers through his short hair. "I'm sorry to hear that. Everyone in town will be sorry. The land has been in your family for what was it…five generations—"

"I know all that," Siobhan blurted, cutting him off. "I've been through this. Do you think I'd be here if I hadn't thought it through first?"

Cotton looked back at her, one eyebrow arched but saying not a word. She castigated herself, counted to ten, and pulled it together.

"I'm sorry," she added. "I…I don't mean to snap. It's an emotional time."

The young man nodded, straightening the knot in his cheap paisley tie. "I understand. I lost my father too recently. This was his practice for over fifty years."

Cotton looked around at the plaques on the walls, as if seeing them for the first time.

"I didn't realize," she said, softer this time.

He shrugged weak shoulders in a powder-blue dress shirt. "It's all right. How could you? It just makes you a little more aware that time is short, if you know what I mean."

"I do," she agreed. She smiled then, wry and bittersweet. "You know, it's so strange. Everyone around here has always loved my father. Absolutely everyone I meet. And yet, in all my years, I have never seen that side of him."

Cotton gave her his own version of a wry smile. She noticed his eyes were as green as the accountant's lamp on the corner of his desk. "Sometimes," he said diplomatically, "certain people, they're not really cut out for parenthood."

She gave a chuckle that was dry and humorless and bordering on bitter.

"I used to think that, but now it just seems like some lame excuse. Anyway, I guess, there's no point in keeping on revisiting old ground."

They slipped into an awkward silence until, a few seconds later, Siobhan asked, "So…how long will it take you to draw up the papers?"

Cotton nodded, picking up a pen and tapping it on his desk blotter. "We'll get straight onto it," he said, finally summoning some lawyerly gusto.

She nodded, clutched her purse strap to her shoulder, and stood. She felt awkward in her new dress skirt and matching blazer. Both were new; she hadn't brought any fancy clothes with her.

"Thank you," she said, tempted to reach out a hand for him to shake but thinking better of it. "I…I hope you don't think less of me."

He stood abruptly and offered his own hand, as if reading her mind. She shook it energetically. "Of course not," he scoffed.

She slipped her hand from his and turned toward the door.

He cleared his throat, causing her to turn back around. "Siobhan. While I remember. We also have some papers in our possession. They were deposited a long time ago by your father. What should I do with them, now that you're taking possession of his estate?"

She cocked her head curiously. "What are they?"

He nodded perfunctorily. "They look like personal items. Letters. A notebook. Your father didn't want anything to do with them if I understand correctly. He asked my father to keep them…"

Suddenly, her curiosity was piqued. "Can I see them?"

His relieved smile forced wrinkles around his green eyes. "Of course," he answered, pressing a buzzer on his desk phone. "I'll get them for you."

Siobhan drove home less than an hour later, a pile of letters and the journal on the seat next to her. She was anxious to get back to the ranch, up to her room, where she might dig into the treasure trove of new documents Mr. Cotton had presented her with.

The sky had darkened on her way out of the lawyer's office, threatening rain that was soon delivered in droves on her way out of the humble parking lot. Now the wind gusted and drove the rain down in sheets as, to the west, thunder rumbled, echoing over the hills.

The road back to the ranch was deserted, not a car in sight, her headlights doing little to illuminate the drenched road in front of her. She eased down on the accelerator, eager to drive through the rain rather than linger inside of it. Why did her father insist on living so far out of town?

The wipers did their best, but as the weather steadily worsened and the rain came relentlessly, it was everything Siobhan could do to see three feet in front of her. Then, lightning, cutting a jagged scar across the sky, illuminated her path. As Siobhan strained her eyes on the road in front of her, a young girl suddenly stepped out from the graveled shoulder and straight into Siobhan's path.

She wore traditional clothes: a black dress, bonnet, and long apron. The girl looked up, oblivious to the rain, eyes wide, and for a brief moment, through the raging downpour, met Siobhan's frightened glance.

In that moment, Siobhan knew it was Polly, staring straight back at her. Siobhan panicked and hit the brakes. She skidded sideways, the seat belt clenching tightly against her chest as she bucked forward, face stopping only inches from the steering wheel as the car careened and skidded to a stop in the middle of the vacant road.

She gasped, quickly finding the seat-belt release and flying from the car. She rounded the front, instantly drenched as the rain pelted her from the sky, wiping wet hair from her eyes in a vain search for the girl, for Polly. Siobhan circled the car, even looked underneath and ventured to the roadside; there was no one, nothing. Siobhan was alone.

She stood, bathed in the car's headlights, rain drumming on her head, calling out in vain, "Polly! Polly?" The only answer was a rumbling of thunder through the dark skies from a distance.

Siobhan got back into the car, cinched her belt, and pounded the steering wheel in frustration. She was soaked and her new outfit completely ruined. Putting the car back into drive, she raced home, nearly taking out the mailbox as she careened into the long, winding drive that led her up the road to her father's ranch.

Later, showered, a hot cup of tea by her bed, hair drying in a tightly wrapped towel, clinging to the collar of her robe with one hand, she reached for the cracked leather volume that marked the final portion of Polly's journal.

She'd nearly gasped when she found it in the stack of letters and papers Mr. Cotton had given her earlier and forced herself to bathe before reading it, if only not to catch her death of cold before she could finish it!

With a trembling hand, knowing she wouldn't sleep until it was done, she opened the cracked cover and began to read...

Chapter 53

The town was quiet as Missy led Polly out of the Emporium and down the street. Gas lanterns lit their way sporadically, and the street was dry and dirty from another night's revelry.

As they skirted the elevated sidewalks in front of the town's quiet shops, a well-dressed gentleman stepped from the shadows and cleared his throat. Polly stared at his handsome face, gleaming under the nearest lamp. His eyes were alight but only for Missy.

Polly nudged her older, wiser companion, but she barely gave the distinguished-looking gentleman a glance. Instead, she only hastened her pace, grunting, "Come on, Polly," as she trudged in her heels and danced forward.

As Polly quickened her pace to catch up, the gentleman stepped from the sidewalk and Missy broke out into a full run. Polly chased after her struggling to keep up, turning only once to watch the man's shoulders crumble as he turned and retreated back into the local hotel.

"I think…" Polly gasped when at last, Missy rounded the corner and slowed to a walk, "I think he wanted to talk to you."

Missy spat like a man into the soft dirt at their feet and slowed a little more. "Damn cretin's there every day."

"Who was it?" Polly pressed.

Missy shrugged. "Don't matter."

"One of your clients?"

Missy spat again, this time a laugh. "Hardly. It was my father."

Polly paused to hear this news, but Missy only grabbed her sleeve and hustled her along toward the end of another, darker street. Polly hadn't wandered through town much since arriving in Portland and still hadn't fully gained her bearings. She was familiar with the saloon, the Emporium, the bookstore, maybe the general store, but that was about it.

As Missy dragged her through town, she realized she hadn't missed much. There were a few more saloons and gin joints toward the edge of town, seedier and scruffier than those on Main Street, and not much else.

Just past the last saloon, the street just seemed to end, deteriorating from smooth, flat dirt to rougher patches, marred with thick vegetation and the odd dip, bump, or curve. It was like nobody bothered much with anything past the city limits.

But it was far from uninhabited. As the clouds parted to reveal a full moon and Missy led her closer down a particular dirt track, Polly saw a crooked row of one-room, makeshift homesteads. They were shabby little things, many not much bigger than outhouses and hardly more appealing. They had slanted porches with thick, dirty windows behind greasy oil lamps partially covered by sagging, faded curtains.

Missy stopped her, turning abruptly so that their noses almost touched. "Stay down," she ordered, voice hardly above a whisper. "Don't make a sound."

Polly nodded feverishly before croaking, "What are we looking at?"

Missy inched closer, pointing toward one dilapidated building. "That cabin right there with the oil lamp in the window."

Polly nodded absently. "Why?"

Missy looked back at her. "It's where Ike O'Neal hides out."

Polly flinched, her fingers absently clutching at the collar of her blouse. She wasn't scared, just…surprised. She'd wanted little more than to study her anatomy books after another long day of scrubbing out washbasins and refreshing old laundry when Missy had showed up at her door. Now, here she was, on the verge of finally realizing the objective she'd set for herself ever since leaving home so long ago.

"I can't stay here like this," Polly gasped. "He might see me."

Missy shook her head. "He's not home."

"How do you know?" she asked.

"He ain't been home in weeks," Missy explained. "Law is on his tail, so he left town. But he'll be back, cos' he always makes the same mistake."

Polly's eyes narrowed. "What's that?"

Missy nodded knowingly. "Women."

Chapter 54

The night was soft and quiet as Missy and Polly walked, side by side, back into Portland proper. The streets were empty, and gas lamps flickered here and there. A full moon followed them as they strode openly down the middle of the street.

"What happened?" Polly asked.

"Ike was a regular client of the Emporium," Missy recalled, "but Madam Jasmine banned him in the end. Too many complaints from the girls. He was small fry to her anyway." Missy paused, lingeringly by a shop window to gaze at a satin bonnet. "I remember one time he asked for me, and boy was he rough. His eyes went completely black, you know…in the act. I ain't never seen nothing like that on no one. The only time I ever felt afraid in this business, I kid you not. Was lucky to get out alive."

Polly shivered but kept her face impassive. "And Katie?"

Missy clucked her tongue. "They found her dead. I told her from the start Ike was trouble. But she wouldn't listen. She was a good person, but she was messed up."

Polly pictured the weathered cowboy in the middle of the street her first day in Portland, his haunted eyes and haggard voice. "Old Joe never got over it," Missy said, as if reading her mind. "Knew the minute they found her body, dead and cold, it was Ike had done it. We all did. But there was no way to prove it."

"There's no end to his evil." Polly shook her head, pondering out loud to herself.

Missy turned to her, eyes curious. "So what makes you think you can take him on?"

Polly opened her mouth to answer and then realized…she couldn't. She had never thought about the how, only the "why." Missy nodded, as if she understood. They moved on from the storefront and walked toward the well-to-do side of town.

Polly felt restless and anything but tired. Missy seemed to share the sentiment. They paused outside a big impressive house surrounded by iron gates. From the street stretched a grassy lawn, leading up to a three-story Victorian home that was so fancy, it almost looked out of place.

Missy gazed up at a large living room window on the ground floor. Polly turned to her and pressed, "Why isn't the sheriff looking for Ike? He's on the run, isn't he?"

Missy shrugged her shoulders. "We're all on the run here. All running from something."

"But what about justice?" Polly muttered.

"Justice?" Missy scoffed. "Out here, they make it up as they go along. I mean, how much do you think the law cares about Ike O'Neal anyway? He targets prostitutes. Men who assault whores are punished far less severely than if they had assaulted 'respectable' women…"

Missy's voice trailed off as she looked from Polly back to the lighted window in the fancy house. "But he's sure made a whole lot of enemies along the way. And those things have a way of catching up with you…"

Missy's voice trailed off, and her face lit up as a young nurse crossed in front of the picture window. Polly followed Missy's gaze to see the young woman cradling a baby in her arms. She was rocking it to sleep, lips moving as she whispered what was surely a pretty lullaby to the pampered child.

Polly nudged Missy, wondering if the tough "working girl" was just putting her on. "What are we looking at?" she whispered.

But Missy wasn't putting her on, and from the wistful expression on her young face, Polly could guess at the answer. "Is it…yours?"

Missy nodded, watching the young nurse's every move through the large living room window. "They forced me to give him up for adoption."

Polly placed an instinctive hand on the older girl's shoulder. "I'm sorry."

Missy, never taking her eyes off the child or his nurse, plucked up her shoulders and stuck out her chin. "It's for the best," she said, defensively, as if trying to convince even herself. "He'll have a better life here than any I could give him, an' that's the truth."

Polly nodded and watched as, midstep, the nurse gazed absently out the window. Her eyes met Missy's, and for a moment, neither woman moved. Then Missy nodded, and the nurse moved out of view. Moments later, the light went out in the window.

In the darkness, Missy turned to Polly, face as hard as her voice as she asked, "Why do you want to find Ike?"

Polly stared back. "He destroyed my family."

Missy offered a wry grin. "Don't give me that, Polly," she countered. "I asked why *you* want to find Ike?"

Polly held firm. "I just told you."

"What did he do to you?" Missy asked, trying again to understand Polly's fierce determination.

But Polly wasn't biting. "The whole story ain't fit for anyone except me and God."

Missy nodded anyway. "Then I think I understand."

She left then, expecting Polly to follow; she did. They walked silently through the gaslit streets back to the Emporium, in through the empty front room, and up the stairs into Missy's room.

From beneath her mattress, Missy pulled a gleaming Colt Peacemaker. She held it in her palm and handed it to Polly.

"When Katie died, Madam realized things were getting too dangerous. Now we all have guns in the bedrooms so we can protect ourselves if we need to."

Polly held the gun, admiring its glossy sheen, expert craftsmanship, and long metal barrel.

"There's some that say you can't rape a whore," Missy said. "But they're wrong. Dead wrong." She nodded toward the gun in Polly's hands. "Learn how to use it."

Polly nodded silently, wondering if Missy was speaking from experience...

Chapter 55

Lafayette was desperate, almost wild-eyed, as he paced the polished wooden floor of George Patterson's home on the outskirts of town.

"I've heard all kinds of gossip," Lafayette pressed, admiring the well-fed gentleman on the plush green sofa. "I want to know the truth."

George Patterson was pensive, hesitant. "Why do you care so much? I mean, no offense, but you were her teacher, not her—"

"I'm sorry, sir," Lafayette interjected. "When Lizzie died, it affected the pupils badly. And now we're looking into what might have caused Polly's disappearance, too."

Mr. Patterson looked offended at the mention of his daughter's name. Lafayette nodded but pressed on nonetheless, "I'm sorry to ask this, sir, but I was wondering if—before she died—Lizzie ever mentioned Polly."

The gentleman put down his drink on a polished end table and put both hands on his knees, leveling a harsh gaze at Lafayette. "Now look here, Lafayette, I think it's rather poor manners for you to show up at this house unannounced to probe me about my daughter's death."

Lafayette choked back a sob and apologized. "I'm sorry to remind you of such desperate times, but I fear for Polly. I don't know what's happened to her, and nobody seems to care. I wouldn't—" Lafayette looked around the gentleman's parlor, the polished oak cabinets and fine crystal glasses on the bar. "I wouldn't be here at this hour, troubling you like this, if it wasn't urgent. Please, tell me, sir, do you know anything at all?"

George stood from the couch, regarded his glass, and filled it from a fine crystal decanter resting on top of the smooth, wooden bar. He kept his back turned to Lafayette as he splashed in two quick streams of soda from his spritzer and added two uneven ice cubes from a frosty bucket.

When at last he turned to Lafayette, he was stirring the drink absently with his finger, staring at a spot just above the teacher's head. "Other than my belief that the stepbrother should hang for his crimes, I do not. Drink?"

Lafayette was sorely tempted but wanted to keep his head. He shook it, indicating Mr. Patterson should go on. At last, their eyes met and Lizzie's father said, "Ah, yes, I forgot. A man of God renounces all vices...at least, in public."

Lafayette frowned. He hadn't come here for a sermon; he wanted information. Mr. Patterson hastily downed his fresh drink in a single, desperate gulp.

He held the crystal glass between both hands, leaning back on the bar rail in his well-fitted parlor, studying Lafayette as he swirled the melting ice cubes around at the bottom of the glass.

"The boy is evil," George Patterson finally spat, returning from his private reverie. "Who can say what Polly must have endured at his hands? The girl is either dead or far away from here. Either way, she's in a better place and should be left to rest."

"That seems a little harsh, sir."

Patterson scoffed and set his glass atop the polished bar. "That may be so, but the fact remains: I can't help you."

The portly man shuffled by Lafayette, taking out his gold pocket watch and looking at it pointedly as he made his way into the foyer and opened the large, glass door. "Good day, Mr. Davis."

Lafayette stood his ground, lingering near a large table in the foyer featuring fresh fruit.

"In town, they say Polly was pregnant."

"Nonsense," George blustered, turning to face Lafayette with a blushing scowl. "The girl was all of fifteen years old. It's just the gossip mongers fuelling the fire. Let me show you out."

Lafayette nodded in resignation. It was clear George Patterson would reveal no new information about Polly—or anything else for that matter. No wonder the town's mill owner was so successful; he was a shrewd and unwilling negotiator!

Davis doffed his hat, waving it at Patterson as he descended into the street just outside the big man's even bigger home. It was almost dusk, and the squeaking wheels of a metal baby carriage caught his attention. Lafayette turned to see a pretty younger woman, bundled against the evening chill, pushing a newborn baby in a black iron pram.

George Patterson must have spotted her as well. Rushing down the stairs to stand next to Lafayette, he seemed to want to shield Davis from the young woman. Or vice versa. Either way, he stood red-faced and flushed, between them.

"George!" said Rose Patterson, clutching her gloved hand to her chest. "You gave me a fright."

George's face was blustery and red as he stammered, "Come inside, woman. Come inside. Don't stand on ceremony. You'll catch your death of cold."

But Rose did stand on ceremony, nodding in a half-curtsy to Lafayette. "Mr. Davis. How lovely to see you."

Lafayette nodded back to her, clutching his hat between both hands. "And you, madam." Staring down at the pram, Lafayette noted the tiny, pink fingers of a red-faced infant, bundled up against the cold in a soft white blanket and matching cap.

He stooped a little lower, noting a tiny lock of red hair poking from the tiny pink cap. Patterson cleared his throat, and looking from husband to wife, Lafayette couldn't help but notice they both had dark hair.

"A new arrival?" Lafayette asked curiously, inching closer to the pram. "Boy or girl? She must help you a lot under the circumstances."

"Girl," Rose gushed. "She was a miracle. She reminds me of my Lizzie."

Lafayette smiled at the beautiful baby, so calm and with piercing…blue… eyes. Suddenly, a thought crossed his mind. He looked up at Rose, so young and slender. He couldn't remember seeing her with so much as a single extra ounce on her in the last nine months. "Forgive me, I…I did not realize you were with child."

Rose grew pale as she brushed at her cheek with one small, gloved hand. It trembled, slightly, against her cheek. She avoided Lafayette's eyes and stared down into the pram, struggling with a reply.

Her husband interrupted, rushing to her side and sliding an arm protectively over her shoulder. "We kept her inside," he blustered defensively. "Rose's health was fragile, wasn't it, my dear?"

Rose nodded and reached for the pram handle as George steered her toward the house. "Good day, sir."

Lafayette watched Rose disappear into the open doorway. To George, who held the door open for his wife, Lafayette called out, "You'll let me know if you hear anything?"

George made sure his wife was safely inside and the pram along with her, before closing the door and turning toward Lafayette, red-faced. "Stay away from that Polly girl. I'm warning you, Davis. Nothing good follows anyone who touches her."

Lafayette wore a knowing smirk. "With respect, I disagree. Good day, sir."

Several days later, Lafayette looked up from the stack of students' papers he'd been preparing to grade in his tiny shed tacked onto the back of his one-room schoolhouse.

The knock at the door was steady and persistent, continuing until he'd stood and crossed the floor. "Mr. Patterson?"

George Patterson, looking gruff and flustered in his crisp, three-piece suit, dabbed a linen handkerchief across his flushed forehead. "I've got news," he said, barging past Lafayette and pacing anxiously around his tiny room.

"News?" asked Lafayette, shutting the door but standing near it. "News of what, Mr. Patterson?"

Patterson waved a hand distractedly. "We're both grown men here, Lafayette. Call me George, for Christ's sake!"

Lafayette chuckled humorlessly. "Fine, George. News about what?"

"They found the remains of the baby."

Lafayette nodded. There was no need to ask whose baby. George wouldn't be here if it wasn't to talk about Polly. He cleared his throat anyway, aware that George was awaiting some type of response.

Not getting any, George added, "It was buried on the property. Near the old barn. In a place called...Bonney's Canyon?"

Lafayette reached a hand out to steady himself against the wall. His stomach felt like it was in knots. His palms were clammy, and he felt like he might be sick.

He could only picture Polly, poor Polly, alone and crying, burying her own child, sadder than any young child ever had a right to be. He blinked his eyes and looked at George. "I have to find Polly."

George rolled his eyes, waving his damp handkerchief dramatically. "Look here, man. I'm the wealthiest landowner in the region, if not the state, and I've heard enough of Polly O'Neal for one lifetime. If you want your job and your life to continue as it is, stay away from her. Nothing good ever touches that girl."

Lafayette felt the urge to lash out at George Patterson, to berate or even strike him, but he stood, stock still, unsure of what to say or do. Lafayette knew that George Patterson was the least of his worries, and regardless of what the man said, he would have to do something, anything, to let Polly know that she wasn't alone in this world.

Chapter 56

Portland was a city in a forest, surrounded by roaring water and towering trees. It wasn't hard for Polly to find a deserted and isolated patch of scrub pines to her liking.

With rusty tin cans from an old trash pile rattling around in the burlap sack she'd been hauling over her shoulder ever since sneaking away from the Emporium, Polly spied the secluded spot and let them down with a rattle.

She slid the big knife from her secret holster and used it to hack down several small trees in the middle of the clearing. Setting a tin can on top of each freshly cut sapling trunk, Polly took out the gun Missy had given her and took aim.

The Colt .45 was heavy in Polly's small hand, but she was determined to master the weapon so that she would leave nothing to chance when she finally confronted Ike.

She steadied her gun hand with the other and squinted one eye until the first can was dead in her sights. With a steady aim, she pulled the trigger. The gun exploded in her hand, making an awful "*Blam!*" filling the air in front of her face with acrid, wafting smoke and knocking her back several paces.

"Damn!" she said, spotting the tin can still standing exactly where she'd aimed at it.

Her right shoulder hurt, and she knew it would be sore tomorrow, but she braced herself, spread her legs a little more for balance, raised the gun again, steadied herself, and fired.

The recoil was less shocking this time, her aim more steady, but still the can stood right where she'd sighted it. Polly sighed, gritted her teeth, and fired once more.

This time, the explosive shot preceded a faint "ding," and when the white smoke cleared before her eyes, Polly cheered to see the first can, dented and lying on the ground.

She smiled eagerly to herself and aimed once more. This time, her arms felt strong, her focus was clear, and she allowed herself the luxury of picturing Ike's face as she fired at the next can—and the next and the next. Each time, it went down with a satisfying belch of smoke and tinny "ding" in the distance.

Polly practiced until her ammunition was gone and then used her knife to dig a shallow grave. She buried the tin cans and the burlap sack, covering the freshly dug hole with the branches of the saplings she'd cut.

On her way back into town, Polly stopped by the general store. A ruddy-faced gentleman in shirt sleeves and an open vest beamed at her from behind the counter.

"What'll it be today, little lady?"

Polly blushed. She'd forgotten that, to others, she was still the picture of a young girl, wholesome and fresh scrubbed and pretty. Never mind the eight-inch blade tucked under her arm or the pistol hiding in the bottom pocket of her apron!

"My pappy ran out of ammunition for his Colt .45," she said, batting her eyes.

The shopkeep looked at her curiously. "I'm not sure I like selling bullets to women, especially young women such as yourself."

Polly forced herself not to roll her eyes and instead pulled out the wad of cash she'd managed to make during her first three weeks of employment at the Emporium. "Really?" she said, holding the wad of crumpled bills as if she didn't know how much she'd earned, down to the penny. "Well, I guess I'll go tell him, but he gave me all this money and—"

"How much ammunition does your pappy need, little girl?" asked the shopkeeper while Polly smothered a smile behind her free hand.

"At least a couple dozen rounds," she said, before adding a few licorice vines and root beer barrels to the order.

Walking away from the store with enough ammunition to kill Ike several times over, Polly felt good for the first time in a long time. It was evening now, and soon she would start her nightly rounds at Madam Jasmine's Goodtime Emporium.

Polly didn't mind much. The work kept her busy, and gossiping with the "girls," as Madam called them, was fun for Polly. She'd never been much for friends back home. Too much work to do on the farm, it seemed, and once her father remarried, well, she'd given up school for good.

But now she was surrounded by women, women who treated her, if not exactly as an equal, then at least as a friend. And that was good enough for Polly.

She heard the energetic twinkling of ragtime music on the piano as Big Slim tickled the ivories. He tipped his emerald-green bowler at her as Polly sidled by, giggling at the attention while a gaggle of nervous men already filled the plush salon.

Upstairs, Polly headed straight for her room, eager to slide the Colt .45 and the ammunition she'd procured for it safely back in the bottom of her dresser drawer.

But her door was already open. Not much, but just a crack. And as much as she considered the Emporium home these days, she had too many secrets to trust the other girls with an open door; she always shut it tightly when she left.

Polly held her breath outside the door, but the cheers from downstairs as Big Slim's manic piano playing reached a crescendo made it impossible for her to hear whether anyone was inside or not. She inched closer, took a deep breath, and pushed the door open.

"Missy!" Polly gasped, finding her newest friend standing near the window, moonlight spilling over her shoulder.

Missy whirled around, a "Wanted" poster stretched between two hands. Polly gasped; her face was on it this time, not Ike's!

"I want the whole story right now, or I'm taking you in."

"Wh-where did you get that?" Polly asked.

"Where didn't I?" asked Missy, shoving Polly's clothes in a pillowcase. "They're all over town. Says here you're wanted for torching the family homestead back home. Is that true?"

Polly's stomach clenched, her lungs fighting for air. She felt like she'd been punched by a giant! "Technically..." she stammered, following Missy down the busy stairs and out the back door.

In the dark, stealing away from the Emporium for what could be the last time, Polly didn't even have a chance to look back. Missy yanked her forward by her free hand while Polly clutched her meager belongings in the other.

"Lie to me and we can go left, toward the sheriff's station. Tell me the truth, and we'll go anywhere you want."

Polly, stomach clenched, knees wobbly, went right instinctively, toward the clearing where she'd lined up the tin cans earlier in the day. It was as remote as could be, yet within walking distance of town. They walked in silence for a while, Polly looking over her shoulder every so often to make sure no one was following them.

"It's not like it sounds," she began, whispering though within minutes they were already free of town. She told Missy the story, every last detail, even ones she'd been too afraid to tell herself. By the time the tale was told, Polly and Missy had arrived at the clearing.

It looked different at night, smaller, even more secluded. It was a place to make a last stand or hideout until she could take a stand.

A fallen log made a convenient bench as Missy and Polly fell onto it, crying into each other's arms. "Now do you believe me?" Polly asked.

Missy pushed her away gently and offered her a handkerchief, drying her own eyes with the sleeve of her dress. "At least your child is still alive," Polly reasoned. "He may not be with you, but he's being cared for. Mine is...mine is..."

Polly could barely continue. The lump was too thick in her throat as she tried to stop her voice from cracking. "I'm not even sure where she is buried."

Missy slung a familiar arm around Polly's shoulder as they sat, on the log, in the dark. "I'm so sorry, Polly." Missy reached down and clung almost desperately to Polly's hand. "What do we do now? If they find you, they'll haul you back home. And who knows what might happen then? They might even blame you for the fire!"

Polly's voice hardened. "I can take care of myself, Missy."

Missy clucked in a motherly way. "How will you defend yourself? You'll go to jail if you go through with this."

Polly shook her head, reaching down into her apron. The Colt .45 felt solid and reassuring in her hands as she brought it out of her pocket, the barrel shining in the moonlight. She placed her thumb on the hammer and cocked it backward.

"I'll wait. They'll never find me here. They can't even find Ike in plain sight. I'll wait until the dust settles. They'll forget about me, and then soon enough, Ike will come back and he'll slip up again. And when he does…"

Polly aimed the gun at the three fresh stumps she'd cut by hand only a few hours earlier, when the sun seemed as bright as her future. She closed her left eye and carefully took aim in the moonlight. Seeing only the rust from an earlier tin can staining the fresh tree trunk, she curled her index finger around the trigger and squeezed. The hammer snapped forward and the sound of the gunshot and the bullet connecting with the tin piercing and ringing out through the silence of the night.

Chapter 57

TWO YEARS LATER

"Blam!"

"Ding."

"Blam!"

"Ding."

One by one, the dented, rusty tin cans fell from the tree trunks, two years older now, two years taller. Polly aimed down the barrel of her trusty Colt and snipped off another two cans, one after the other, before striding on jaunty legs toward the row of tree trunks to line more cans up for another round of target practice.

No longer the coltish lass who wore pigtails and bonnets, Polly had let her hair grow long and let one of the other girls braid it. She wore makeup now, too, a little of it anyway. Her clothes were fancy, her walk purposeful as she lined the cans up once more and, returning to her firing point, the grass beneath her feet worn yellow and dry by years of routine, she quickly let loose the trusty Colt.

"Blam!"

"Ding."

"Blam!"

"Ding."

One by one, the tin cans fell, until Polly's eye was tired of squinting and her thumb was chafed from firing. She left the cans where they fell, no longer bothering to bury them or cover her tracks. This was her spot, and in the two years since she'd confessed to Missy, no one had found it or followed her or so much as borrowed it for his or her own use.

She walked confidently back to town, using a familiar trail, her smile sly and lonely and sad in the waning sun. Her shift would start at the Emporium soon, and she didn't want to be late.

It was a pleasant spring evening, the parlor windows open and Big Slim's tinkling piano filling the end of the street with vibrant music. Madam Jasmine was waiting for her as she walked through the back door, eager to get upstairs and freshen up before she started her shift.

"Madam?" Polly balked. The grand dame never lingered long by the servant's door, but tonight, she looked downright flushed.

"You have a visitor, Polly."

Polly paused, the door barely half open. Her story was well-known now, all the girls working hard to keep Polly's true identity a secret. Even Madam Jasmine had pledged her undying allegiance when she'd heard the poor girl's miserable tale.

"Me?" Polly asked, somewhat surprised. No one ever came to visit her, and she knew no reason why anyone would.

Madam Jasmine fanned her face, flustered. "I told him you're on duty. But he insists he must talk to you."

Polly nodded dutifully and patted her hair down. *Who could it be?* she wondered as Madam led her along the servants' quarters and down toward the parlor, bustling as always. *Ike?*

Polly followed along, her vision partly obscured by one of Madam's oversized hats. When at last Madam bowed to present her, Polly gasped. "Lafayette!" she gushed, rushing into his arms. He was waiting for her, smelling clean and fresh and familiar and nothing like Portland. He picked her up, spun her around, much to the chagrin of Madam and the other men awaiting their ladies of the evening.

At last, Lafayette put her down and shoved her away, smiling as he drank in her face. "I couldn't stay away from you any longer."

"I thought you'd forgotten me," she confessed as she rushed back into his arms, laughing with relief to see his familiar face, smell his familiar smell.

"How could I?" he gushed, dragging her into a secluded corner of the parlor. His eyes, and tone, grew serious. "Forgive me, Polly."

"Forgive you for what?"

"I should never have let you go."

Polly looked up toward her room, face growing flushed. "I know a place where you'll never have to let me go."

She raced from him then, daring him to catch up. "Polly!" Madam Jasmine called from downstairs, but she ran up them anyway, two at a time, ignoring her boss and confidante.

"Polly?" Lafayette questioned, catching up to her at the top of the stairs.

She kissed him then, on the lips, as full and soft and sweet as she'd always imagined them. "Don't worry," she sassed, grabbing his hand and leading him toward her room. "No one will bother us here."

He had barely followed her in before she slammed the door shut and dragged him to her bed. Her heart was racing, her palms clammy. She'd never wanted to hold anyone, kiss anyone, caress anyone, so badly before.

He responded, gingerly at first, kissing her on the mouth, then her neck, hands around her back and pulling her close. She gasped at the sensation of his skin on hers and then even louder as he began nibbling her ear.

"You don't know how long I've dreamed of this moment," he whispered in her ears, even as his trembling hands began undoing her blouse.

Now it was his turn to gasp as his eyes, wide and wet, took in the sight of her milky-white flesh, nearly bursting from her bustier. "Polly, you're a woman," he said, feasting his eyes on her from a distance.

She put on a mock pout, like she'd seen the other girls do. "Isn't that a good thing?"

He stopped untying her bodice, pushed himself away to the edge of the bed. "I…Polly, I'm a man of God. This…this is wrong."

261

"Wrong?" she contested, standing up abruptly and covering herself back up. "What the hell did you come here for then? To preach to me?"

Her voice was harsh. He looked shocked and then…disgusted. His expression soured as the lamp from the nightstand filled his handsome face with eerie shadows. "A whorehouse? It's even worse than I thought. I must pray for your soul."

"Whores?" she spat, pacing the floor. "You've got a nerve. These so-called 'whores' have been more like family to me than you ever were."

His sneer faltered, and his lower lip began trembling. Polly could see that he was hurt, that her words had stung him. She hadn't intended to speak so harshly or condemn him so quickly.

Still, hers weren't the only words to sting. Her face was flushed as she hid behind the fuzzy wool shawl she kept at the foot of her bed. "Why did you come?" she pressed. "Why now? Nothing has changed."

Lafayette's eyes drank her in, his voice tender and soft. "I couldn't wait any longer. I had to see you. There's so much I needed to tell you. My conscience—"

"I don't care about your conscience," Polly scoffed.

He was hurt again, wounded, as he stammered "I…I…feel like I don't know you anymore."

This time, Polly didn't feel quite so sorry. She clucked her tongue. "Did you think I'd stay a girl forever, Lafayette?" she asked. "I grew up. I'm a woman. Not a little girl. Don't you like me this way?"

She let the shawl covering her chest slip just a bit. He noticed, the color rising to his cheeks again. "Of course I do."

She shook her head, almost sadly. "No. You only loved me as your little schoolgirl crush. But I am not a virgin any longer, Professor." She watched him flinch with the truth. "It's too late for that. Years too late. If you don't like me now, as I am, you wouldn't like me if you knew the truth."

He stared at her and then away, both of them falling into an awkward silence. When he looked back at her, he said, "I do know the truth."

Her voice was steel. "Well, then, no wonder you are praying for my soul."

She turned away from him then, her face reflected in the bedroom window. But there were no tears running down her face, only ice in her veins. "Ike must pay," she decreed.

"An act of violence will change you forever."

"It's already changed me," she scoffed. "I'm not like you. You're so good. So righteous. So perfect." She heard the squeak of a floorboard as he approached her and then stopped midway across the room. She turned back to him, eyes flashing anger. "Oh, why don't you just go? I never want to see you again."

There, midway across the room, Lafayette opened his mouth to protest. Just then, the sound of tiny pebbles hitting the glass windowpane at her back made Polly flinch. She turned, yanking open the window only to find Missy standing beneath her window.

"Ike's here," she said, urgently waving Polly down. "He's back in town. Come now, before it's too late."

Polly turned, sharing her glee at the news with Lafayette. His face looked positively horrified. She noticed. "I don't need to be judged by anyone," she said in a steely voice, no longer a student to her teacher." Brushing past him, she hissed, "Get away from me, and if you know what's good for you, don't ever come back."

He stood, long after she'd parted, staring at her things. Sad and alone, he left the room and walked quietly down the stairs. No one noticed him as he left or wondered why his tie was on so straight, his cheeks so wet.

Chapter 58

The night was dark and quiet in the little cluster of cabins on the outskirts of town. Every sound was magnified by her fear and apprehension, even as the blood pounded in her ears at the thought of finally reaching the end of her journey.

Polly crouched beside Missy outside Ike's cabin. The oil lamp flickered in the greasy window as a cheap, gauzy curtain flapped in the open window.

"Where is he?" asked Polly.

Missy clucked her tongue. "Where is he ever? Out drinking in town."

Polly nodded her head resolutely. "I'm going inside. I want to see what I can find."

Missy's eyes grew wide in the dark. "Are you crazy? I'm not letting you do that."

Polly inched forward. "Just try and stop me." Before she could, she slipped onto the warped doorstep. Looking down at Missy, crouched beneath the open window, Polly said, "Keep a look out. If he comes back, find a way to warn me."

Missy cursed and shook her head. "This is a bad idea, Polly."

But it was too late; Polly was already on the stoop, trying the doorknob. She knew the door would open even before it did, and even if it hadn't, she would have found a way to slip into the open window.

The room was squalid to start with and made even more so by Ike's presence; it was everywhere. She could feel it, oozing off the walls, sticking to the floor, stinking up the joint.

There was hardly a stick of furniture beyond a sagging cot, a chair next to it, and a table by the window missing a chair. There was the oil lamp, overturned whiskey bottles, a deck of cards, piles of greasy clothes, and not much else.

The oil lamp didn't help much, casting long shadows in the squalid room, black smoke curling from the flame and staining the cheap wallpaper above the windowsill.

She shivered, realized this was the closest she'd been to Ike in years. She thought maybe some of his power might have waned over the years, but instead, Polly found herself nauseous, her throat dry, her hands trembling.

None of it would stop her from her course, but she couldn't help but feel disappointed by the weakness of her reaction. She cursed herself, clenched her fists at her sides, and got down to business.

Her eyes had adjusted to the flickering lantern light, but what she saw wasn't very inspiring; the few sticks of furniture and piles of greasy, sweaty clothes didn't promise many hiding places. But then, out of the corner of her eye, she noted an old tin box sitting isolated on a shelf beside the window.

It had some obscure tobacco company name stamped on top, like it had been a giveaway from the company or some kind of fancy holiday packaging once upon a time. Now it looked dented and meager. She opened it anyway, the scent of newsprint and mold instantly filling her nostrils.

She leafed through a thin stack of news clippings before finding several letters addressed to Ike. She reached for one, carefully unfolding it when, outside, Missy cleared her throat; Polly froze.

"Well, if it ain't Ike O'Neal," Missy said, loud enough for Polly's benefit. "Long time, no see."

Polly froze, the tin box in one hand, the letter in another. She'd fought so long to get here, had worked so hard to find her man, and now he was just on the other side of a flimsy plywood door.

"Missy." Polly's stomach dropped at the sound of Ike's voice. It had been so long since she'd heard it, and yet the sound of it brought her right back to those dark and scary places, Ike sneaking into her room, beating her…raping her.

Polly ditched the tin box, slipping the letter back inside and sliding the top on before shoving it back on the shelf. Crossing the room in two strides, she leaned against the greasy wall and peered outside the window.

Ike still looked like Ike, broad-shouldered and big-boned. His hair was limp and greasy, nose reddened and skin pockmarked by his love affair with the gin bottle. But he still looked hale and hearty enough to put up a good fight, and the sight of him still put the fear in Polly's heart.

Not enough to distract her, but enough to get the butterflies in her stomach good and riled.

Ike's voice was slow and easy, like he'd just stumbled from an evening at the local saloon. "What you doin' round these here parts?" he asked Missy.

Missy's voice was sugary and sweet. "Business," she said sassily.

Ike chuckled, low and easy. "Really? You can come inside if you're looking for business."

"Oh, Ike," came a strange voice, feminine, breathy, and loud, not unlike some of the new girls back at the Emporium. Polly stiffened; Ike had a woman with him!

There came the scratch of footsteps in the soft sand below the window as Polly squeezed against the wall, wondering what to do. Ike would be at the door in no time and how could she bolt through the window without him spotting her? She clung with her back to the wall, cursing her rash and stupid notions.

Missy had been right all along; this was a bad idea!

For her part, Missy's voice grew oozy and low. "Come and talk to me a while, Ike," she insisted.

But Ike was firm. "I'm sorry, Missy. As you can see, I already got company tonight." Then came a dry chuckle and, icily, Ike added, "Respectable company. For a change."

Ike's companion giggled breathily. But Missy hadn't worked at the Emporium all those years to still have a thin skin. "Can't be so respectable if she's with you," Missy spat.

Ike's tone grew icy and familiar; it was the same one he'd used to threaten Polly all those years ago. "Hush that mouth now, Missy. Or I'll be forced to hush it for you."

Polly gripped her fists tighter at her side, hearing the tone in Ike's voice shift as he cooed to his female companion, "Here, darlin', Let me show you inside." Heavy footsteps sounded on the short stoop as Polly looked around.

She had nowhere to go, and as the door creaked open, she panicked, leaping beneath the bed even as Ike stumbled forward, drunk, falling onto the floor as his cheap date chuckled, helping him up to lean against the wall.

"Careful, sugar," she cooed, grabbing the wallet from his back pocket and rifling through it to grab his last few bills. "You don't want to pass out before our date."

Ike chuckled and Polly, through clenched eyelids, peered out to see Missy looking through the door. Only briefly did their eyes meet before Ike's companion slammed it shut and led him to the bed.

Polly bit into her knuckle as the mattress sagged above her, covering her ears as the sounds of kissing, fondling, unbuttoning, and more filled the tiny room. The woman squealed with delight at first, until Ike began treating her roughly.

The cheap iron frame squeaked as the mattress sagged; the woman choked, gasping for air as she gulped, "Don't do that, Ike; it hurts like that."

Ike grunted, enjoying himself. "I'm not joking," said the woman, fear gripping her voice. "Get your hands off me. I can't breathe."

"Shut your mouth," Ike grunted as Polly tried to reach for her knife. In the small space under the bed, she couldn't get to her hidden holster. She cursed and lay, frozen in fear, roiling with disgust.

As the mattress bucked and wheezed, the woman yelped, "I said, be quiet," Ike hissed. Then, she heard a startling and all too familiar sound: Ike's beefy hand swiping through the air and striking the woman, slapping her hard and heavy into silence.

The slap seemed to excite him, and the squeaking of the bed frame intensified. He yelped as he finished, like a cowboy, huffing and puffing as his body slid off the woman and sagged on his side of the bed.

He chuckled cruelly, the sound of a cigarette lighting. "No wonder your husband ain't around."

Chapter 59

Polly's back hurt, and her throat was dry. Ike and the woman had been snoring for over an hour, but she wanted to give them plenty of time to reach the deepest, darkest depths of sleep before making her escape.

At last, when she could take it no more, Polly inched from beneath the bed. The room was silent save for Ike's and the woman's snores, so every sound Polly made as she slid and scraped her way across the hardwood floor sounded ten times as loud as it probably was.

Still, she could afford to take no chances. At last, she squeezed herself from beneath the bed, standing for the first time in hours. Sprawled across the mattress, Ike lay on his back, arm over his head, snoring loudly, face greasy and wet with perspiration.

Next to him, a woman a good ten years older did the same, sheets clutched against her naked chest, makeup smeared, hair a mess, face a mask of sleep, and nostrils flaring with each loud snore.

Polly grimaced and inched away, careful not to let the soles of her shoes scrape the hardwood floor or bump into a piece of furniture. The lamp was almost empty now, the wick still burning weakly as she hastened to the door.

Her hand was long past trembling as she turned the knob and slid the door open only to hear it creak as loud as a rooster crowing "Good morning." She yelped and turned, only to find Ike and his companion in the same position, passed out, snoring, half-covered by the sheets in the sagging bed.

She breathed a sigh of relief, wondering to herself, *How could they not have heard?* And yet, there they lay, still passed out, spent from their late-night aerobics. About to leave, Polly turned, the lamplight flickering on the tin box she'd abandoned earlier.

She reached for it, curious, gently prying off the lid. With every inch, she watched Ike sleep until, at last, it gave. Preoccupied, she looked down, retrieving the stack of letters she'd been forced to abandon when Ike had stumbled in hours earlier.

The corners scraped along the box, but the door was open; she'd soon be gone and—

A hand, heavy and thick, clamped down on hers. She gasped, turning, to find Ike grinning in his long johns, chest covered in perspiration. His eyes were cold and fierce, just as they'd always been.

Her heart had literally stopped. "What in tarnation do you think you're doing?" he bellowed, voice thick and rank with the sour stench of old gin.

The noise awakened his lady friend, and sitting up, clutching the sheets to her chest, she saw the two of them in the flickering lamplight and screamed.

Ike flinched at the sound, head still thick as she struggled to wriggle out of his vice-like grip. When he opened his eyes again, he peered down at Polly, blinking steadily, eyes cloudy with confusion and...then...a glimpse of something else.

"Polly?" he gasped, blinking in confusion.

Realizing the tin was in his hand, Polly slammed the lid down, hard, on his sausage-like fingers. Ike screamed in pain, and the minute his grip loosened, Polly yanked her arm free.

Ike lashed out, face red with pain, with shock, with embarrassment, nearly missing her face as she managed to duck out of the way of his flying fist. Just then, the door opened, and Missy flew in, eyes wide. She took one look at Ike, wincing in pain, stumbling after Polly, and did the first thing she thought of: Missy kicked Ike dead between the legs.

He stopped, midstride, coughing, red-faced, falling to his knees and puking out whatever misery he had been drinking all night. It smelled like an outhouse and burned like a furnace, steaming on the floor as Ike slumped and then fell face first into the steaming, putrid heap.

The girls fled, pounding down the steps, into the dirt, running until their lungs burned. When they were safely around the corner from Ike's cabin, Missy jerked to a stop and yanked Polly around to face her.

"Jesus, girl," she gasped, wide-eyed and panting. "Until I heard Ike scream and saw you standing there, I thought you was a goner for sure!"

Polly grabbed her hand, yanking her along. "We're not out of the woods yet!"

The girls ran off into the night, the sound of Ike's screams fading behind them. Polly led Missy through the underbrush, turning only once to find Ike, circling the foot of his doorstep, as if uncertain which way they'd gone.

He kicked the dirt, cursing, waving his injured fingers in the air as if to cool them off. Only when he spat onto the ground and tumbled back up the steps, slamming his door shut after him, did Polly at last breathe a sigh of relief and lead Missy from the brush.

Polly's heart couldn't stop beating fast, but, if anything, it was Missy who seemed the most upset. "I darn well told you it was a bad idea, but would you listen?"

Polly turned to her friend as the town of Portland came into view. "He recognized me."

Missy sighed and then groaned, tossing her hands up helplessly. "Now what do we do?"

Polly shook her head. "I have no idea. This obviously wasn't the plan."

"What plan?" Missy scoffed, and before Polly could answer, she said, "He'll come looking for us. He'll find us, and he'll kill us."

Polly spoke through gritted teeth. "Not if I kill him first."

Missy grabbed Polly by the shoulder and spun her around to face her. "Who is the insane one here, Polly? You or him? Just tell me that."

Polly didn't answer; she couldn't answer. She merely turned toward town and continued walking. Missy followed her, grumbling, "I'm clearly the insane one for helping you, right?"

Chapter 60

Polly woke the next morning, somehow amazed she'd lived through the night. Her room at the Emporium was Spartan but clean. Bright morning light filtered through the curtains.

She blinked her eyes, aware that she'd been roused from slumber by the shouting sounds spilling from the street below her window. She thought she'd been dreaming, but as she slid her feet into her slippers and approached the door, the shouting only grew louder.

Polly flung open the window and looked down to find an unruly mob milling about in the street. They had blood on their eyes and threats on their breath as they packed the square in front of the courthouse. Polly dressed quickly and joined them, rushing through the crowd to find the nearest paper vendor.

"What's going on?" she asked, as more and more irate citizens continued to crowd the square.

The newsman pointed to the front page of that morning's *Oregonian*. "The mayor's wife was found dead," said the paperboy, handing her a copy. "A suspect has been charged."

She tossed down two bits for the paper and then inched away, leaning against a lamppost to read the story; she never quite got that far. Under a banner headline she couldn't quite focus on, Polly saw a picture of the dead woman: it was the woman in Ike's bed just the night before!

Polly heard her name being called even as the courthouse doors opened and the crowd hustled in. "Missy!" Polly cried, seeing her friend and shoving the paper at her. Missy tried to read on the fly as they followed the crowd into the courthouse.

She gave up as a fellow Lookie-Lou knocked the paper out of her hand. Polly and Missy joined the throng inside the courtroom, managing to find spots against the back wall in the standing-room-only space.

They had only just settled, Polly wishing she'd thought to bring her bonnet, when a door opened and two bailiffs hauled Ike, sweat-stained and worse for the wear, toward the convict's box.

Polly left her spot along the wall as the room rose to its feet to get a better look at the man whom the police had arrested for killing the mayor's wife.

"Polly!" Missy cried out as her friend made headway while approaching the front row. "Don't! Stay back. Don't let him see you!"

Polly turned, smiling purposefully toward her concerned friend. "It's OK," she assured Missy. "I know what I'm doing."

A plan forming in her head, Polly made her way across the courtroom like a panther stalking her prey. Through the crowds of onlookers, she zigged and zagged, pushed and pulled, and, at one point, even ducked between the legs of the crowd before reaching the front of the gallery.

The judge was an older man, face red below his white mop of hair. He banged his gavel on the bench trying to calm the crowd, which finally quieted after repeated bangs of the gavel.

"Order!" the judge bellowed at them. "Order or I'll remove you from this court!"

Polly smirked, thinking to herself, *Good luck!* Ike was in the convict's box, a cell within the courthouse. A young man dressed in a cheap, ill-fitting suit stood outside, explaining motions or sentencing or God knows what to Ike, who wasn't listening.

His piggish eyes, dark still but scared now, scanned the crowd nervously. At last, they fell on Polly, who stiffened but managed to keep her expression neutral. Ike on the other hand could not maintain his composure. As Polly caught him out of the corner of her eye, he seemed scared as hell!

Chapter 61

It was visiting day, and Ike sat across from her, furtive in his jailhouse blues. Polly settled into her seat, watching as the guard—rifle slung over his shoulder—leaned against the far wall.

Ike waited until his own guard had joined the other before leaning forward to confess, "Sure did scare me to see you there at the courthouse the other day, Polly."

Now, however, he seemed calm, even at home, as he slid the toothpick from his mouth and began to clean out his dirty fingernails. She grimaced as he chuckled to himself. "Thought you were there to testify against me."

Polly shook her head, hardly trying to hide her blatant disgust. "Ike, I didn't come here to testify. I came to find you 'cause I have news from your momma."

Ike looked up from his disgusting fingernails, suddenly a big-eyed puppy in a dog-store window. "Momma? What's wrong with her?"

Polly slid her eyes toward the guards and, seeing them occupied, inched forward to whisper, "She asked me not to tell you until we get you out of here."

Ike's eyes grew big as he leaned in as well. "Get me out of here? I'm due to hang in a couple of days, or didn't you hear?"

Polly said nothing, merely cocked one eyebrow to refute him. Ike seemed interested, inching forward even more. "Why should I trust you?" he asked, crossing his arms over his barrel chest.

Polly narrowed her eyes. "Because you have something I want."

"I do?" Ike sputtered.

"The truth," Polly explained.

Ike grinned, nodding understandingly. "Indeed, I do. Had it in safekeeping all these years."

Polly granted him that much. "And if I know you, Ike, you ain't gonna just hand it over to me, are you—not without striking a bargain beforehand. So I've decided I'll trade you: your life, for the truth."

Ike suddenly seemed concerned. "The truth about what?"

Polly shook her head. "First answer me this: why, Ike?"

Ike flared his nostrils in confusion. "Why what?"

Polly inched closer with teeth clenched. One of the guards eyed her carefully, but she whispered forcefully, "Why did you do it? To all those women? To me? Why, Ike? It makes no sense."

Ike's black, piggish eyes sat blank and squat in his round, sweaty pie face. He cleared his throat, stalling for time, as though he'd never considered the question until that very moment. He smirked, toying with her.

"Honestly, Polly? Because I could," he said.

Polly dug her fingernails hard into her palms. If she hadn't had a plan to keep herself focused, she would have leaped through the bars and strangled him where he sat, saved the hangman a trip to the gallows.

Ike knew it. What was more, he seemed to enjoy it. He sat back in his chair now, cocky. "What else do you want to know?"

Polly hissed through gritted teeth, "What happened to my baby?"

Ike nodded. "I can tell you that."

Polly wanted to be sure. "How do you know?"

Ike licked his lips smugly. "Ma writes me all the time."

Polly shook her head. "She can't write."

Ike looked unfazed. "Your pa can. I still have the letters."

Polly thought of the tin back at his rented room, all those letters. If only he'd stayed passed out long enough for her to read them herself, she might have been rid of Ike, once and for all—or at least her need for him and his information.

Ike leaned forward once more, breath as sour as the gleam in his eyes. He hissed through his teeth, careful for the guards not to overhear, "Get me out of here and you have a deal."

Polly felt pleasure as Ike took the bait. "I thought you might say that."

She rose, the straight-backed chair she'd been sitting in sliding out from beneath her. Before the guard could notice and arrive to escort her, Polly leaned down and whispered, "Tomorrow night then, Ike. At the jailhouse. Be ready."

Ike smirked, sitting back in his chair as the guards slowly moseyed over. "Tomorrow it is. Until then, pretty Polly."

She glared at him, leaning close enough so Ike could hear her. "Call me that again," she answered, discreetly patting the bulge in her apron pocket, "and I'll shoot you dead right here."

Chapter 62

Polly sat on her bed, concentrating and toying with a loose thread in the hem of her skirt as Missy paced anxiously around the compact room.

"He's calling your bluff, Polly. He doesn't know anything."

Polly knew Missy could be right but trusted her own instincts. "Maybe," she said, surprisingly calmly. "But if he does…"

Missy paused, midpace, to sigh and throw up her hands. "You'll end up in jail yourself if you're not careful."

Polly couldn't argue with that. "That's why I need your help."

Missy widened her eyes and began nervously pacing once more. "Now what?" she asked.

"I have a plan," Polly replied calmly.

Missy chuckled humorlessly, shaking her head and staring out the bedroom window into the empty square outside the courthouse. "I hope for your sake it's better than the last one."

Polly regarded the watch in her apron pocket and sighed, standing. "Let's find out, shall we?"

"Now?" Missy gasped, following her out into the hall.

"No time like the present." Polly winked, leading her down the back stairway and out through the kitchen door.

The streets were empty outside the jailhouse, the crowds all gone home, the furor dead now that the sheriff had locked up the prime suspect in the murder of the mayor's wife.

Polly and Missy sidled up to the front entrance, trying to look inconspicuous should anyone be watching from an open window above.

"Tonight is their poker game. They'll all be playing in the back room. Try and distract them while I get inside."

Missy leaned into Polly and confided, "Howie, the deputy who minds the front desk, he's a doll. Just a boy, really. And a little in love with me, too," she admitted. "He would put his fingers in the oven if I told him to."

Polly nodded. "Just do your best to keep him busy, Missy. Then get yourself back to Madam's as quick as you can. Don't let anyone see you."

Missy grabbed Polly's shoulder before she could run off. "Hey, that wasn't part of the plan. I'm not leaving you alone with Ike O'Neal. God knows what will happen."

Polly shook her head. "Missy, if you want to help me, leave me to it. I don't want you caught up in this. He's done enough harm for one lifetime."

Missy reluctantly agreed, but her expression said she didn't like this plan any better than the last. As she slunk around the side of the building, watching Missy approach the jailhouse door with a toss of her curls, Polly couldn't exactly disagree with her.

Polly watched as Missy tossed open the door and once she was inside, crept up to the only window facing the street. Crouching so as not to be seen, she watched her friend's bravura performance with an appreciative eye.

Missy strode through the door in a hurry, startling Howie, who was truly more a boy than a man, baby-faced and swimming in his stiff blue uniform. He looked up from the evening paper with wide eyes, stumbling to his feet as Missy approached him.

In the few steps it had taken her to approach Howie's desk, Missy had somehow worked up enough tears to choke her throat and even smear her mascara.

"Howie!" she railed, loud enough for Polly to hear her through the front door she'd never quite closed. "I've just been robbed."

Howie's face dropped as he suddenly realized this wasn't a social call. "Robbed?" he cried in a squeaky voice. "On these here streets?"

Missy nodded and turned, motioning outside with her fancy white gloves. None the wiser, Howie followed her out.

"It happened…" Missy began, descending the jailhouse steps until they were standing in the street, facing in the opposite direction, "down a yonder."

Howie stood closer, consoling the poor gal with a sensitive arm around her shoulder as he shushed her and said, "Just calm down now, Missy; we'll get him. How far down a yonder?"

As Missy worked up more waterworks and turned Howie just a little farther away from the door, Polly crept up behind them and in through the jailhouse door.

The jailhouse was hot and crowded and bursting with testosterone. From the back room, she could smell sweat and whiskey as someone, perhaps even the sheriff himself, recited a ribald limerick. Polly was well past blushing; she'd heard far worse at the Emporium.

She crouched along the outer wall, ducking behind Howie's desk as a guard walked by, blue jacket unbuttoned, hat crooked on his sweaty forehead.

"Found it!" he cried, wagging a half-empty bottle of rum on his way toward the back room. Polly waited for the crowd to cheer his return before spotting the jail keys hanging from a hook. She snatched them nervously, flinching as they jangled loudly in the quiet reception area. She waited, impatiently, to see if anyone had noticed but was met only with lusty laughter from the other room; the storyteller must have just finished his limerick.

Polly clutched the keys tight to her blouse, softening the jangle with each step as she entered the hallway and inched toward the back room. Inching out into the light so she could get a better look, she peered through the open door at the end of the hallway to see the sheriff and several deputies gathered around a desk, lamps lighting their faces, studying their cards, deeply entrenched in their weekly poker game.

The guard who'd located the rum bottle rejoined the game, taking his seat and lustily imbibing straight from the bottle before dolling out shots to his fellow players.

Inching away, Polly turned back toward the cells at the other end of the hall. She raced toward them, keys jingling freely now, knowing she had only a few moments to complete her mission.

Her heart raced as she flew by the row of six cells in the jailhouse, expecting Ike to be in at least one of them. Possibly the last? But they were all empty. She stamped her foot, biting her lower lip. *Where the hell could he be?* she thought to herself.

Then, it occurred to her: a lynch mob! The sheriff must have moved Ike for safekeeping. No sooner had the thought occurred to her than she heard voices outside in the back alley—loud, drunk, angry, violent.

She ran back toward the reception area, slowing as she neared the back room, glad she'd left the keys stuck in the last cell in the row so as not to give herself away. Inside the back room, a young deputy stood, staring out a greasy window into the street.

When he turned, the deputy's face was ghostly pale and damp with sweat. "Sir, the lynch mob is approaching. Almost on our doorstep now."

The sheriff, growling in disgust, tossed his greasy cards onto the desktop. "I'm out," he growled, turning the stump of a wet cigar around in his mouth. "Did you take the boy to the hotel like I told ya?" he asked the deputy at the window.

The deputy nodded. "Yes, sir. They'll never find him."

The sheriff nodded. "OK then, let's deal with this crowd." He grunted, pushing himself up out of his seat. "It's clearly not my Goddamn night tonight. Neither for cards nor for justice."

Polly was just ahead of him and raced through the open door using the unruly crowd for cover as the sheriff and his deputies strode angrily onto the front porch.

As he bellowed orders at the crowd, Polly did her best to blend in, shuffling among them as she made her way steadily toward the edge of the building. It was an unruly mob, as ugly as it was drunk, as sweaty as it was smelly.

The sheriff tossed his cigar stump onto the ground and bellowed above the riotous noise, "He's not here, so y'all can go home to your beds and wait for justice to be served in the morning."

The crowd surged forward, nearly taking Polly along with it. Fortunately, she had just reached its end when the crowd erupted into shouting and yelling in response to the sheriff's news.

"Do you hear me?" the sheriff shouted, pulling the pistol from his holster and cocking it for all to see. "You can disperse right now. Get away with you."

But the crowd wanted blood and wouldn't be swayed so easily. They pushed forward still, even as one of the deputies fired off a warning round from his rifle, high above their heads.

Missy caught up to her just as Polly rounded the side of the building, bolting into the street and heading for the edge of town. "Polly!" she shouted after her friend. "What's happening?"

Polly shook her head, not wanting Missy to follow. She called out as she mounted Blue, who was waiting patiently outside the local stables, "He's not here. They moved him."

Missy stumbled in pursuit, crying out as she sank to her knees, "You'll never find him, Polly. Just give it up. Let the law deal with him."

Polly scoffed, shouting almost to herself as she kept Blue marching steadily forward, "He's at the hotel. I reckon he'll just shoot his way out. I have to stop him."

Polly was relieved when at last she saw the sign for the Portland Hotel, brightly lit against the midnight sky. But her relief was short-lived. Almost as soon as she arrived, hitching Blue up to a nearby saloon and slipping from his saddle, she spotted a lone guard sitting on the hotel's front stoop, smoking a cigarette.

He looked casual—that is, until gunfire erupted from behind him, inside the hotel. Polly ducked behind a gas lamppost as the guard turned, dropping his cigarette from one hand while cocking his pistol with the other. He never made it inside. There, in the doorway, a single bullet ripped through his chest.

Red spatter coated the stoop as the guard stumbled, falling into a heap. Ike appeared momentarily, eyes wild, a pistol in his hand, spotting Polly right away.

"Can't have them come after me," Ike bragged. "Just making sure of it."

Polly shivered and took to Blue as Ike followed, leaping onto the back of the guard's horse as the two raced away from the hotel into the night. It wasn't far from the edge of town to the wilderness, and that was straight where the two headed.

Almost instinctively, they both guided their horses into the hills. Ike was an able horseman, but his mount was nothing compared to old Blue. Polly followed closely, watching Ike's furtive glances and beady eyes.

They rode until the hills were high and the town of Portland, torches blazing as a search party formed, was far in the distance. As the hills leveled out, Ike slowed his horse to a trot and then a walk. Polly followed suit, Blue pulling right alongside Ike as she huffed, "You set me up. You knew they would move you."

Ike shrugged next to her. "Who cares? Let's call it my little insurance policy. Anyway, it's done now. I'm a free man. They ain't gonna catch me again."

Polly thought of the dead guard and shivered. "No, Ike, you made quite sure of that."

Ike turned toward her with hard eyes. She steeled herself for what was coming next. "You know, Polly, I been thinking. You saw me escape. That makes you a witness."

"No," she corrected him. "I actually helped you escape. That makes me an accomplice."

"Maybe better to take the bullet then." Ike raised his pistol and pointed it straight at Polly. She couldn't say she was surprised. If anything, she'd been expecting it from a low-down dirty dog like Ike.

Polly shrugged indifferently. "You can kill me if you want, Ike, but then you ain't never gonna hear the news from your momma. And it must be pretty important news for me to come all this way."

Ike tried to smirk, but there was too much hesitation in his eyes to make it very effective. She knew he was desperate to hear what she had to say. And he better be; it was the only card she had left to play.

"What news you talkin' about, Polly?" he asked and, before she could answer, added, "I know you're lying."

"When did she last send you a letter, Ike?"

288

Ike scrunched up his face as he thought. "Dunno," he hedged. "In case you haven't guessed, I moved around a lot."

Polly dug in. "It's been awhile, hasn't it? What, at least a couple of years? Amazing how time flies." It was her turn to toy with him now, aware he was hanging on her every word. Her voice was icy as she confessed, "She's dead. Your mother's dead, Ike. She doesn't even have a grave. Wasn't worth one. I burned the witch. You'll never see her again."

In the darkness, Polly could almost watch the color drain from Ike's face. His eyes had even managed to grow pale as well. "You're...you're lying!" he sputtered.

"Try me," Polly threatened, watching closely the way Ike had lowered his pistol without even realizing it.

He turned to her instead, eyes pleading. "Don't make no sense. Ma dead? Why, Polly? Why would you do that?"

"She was a murderer."

Suddenly, Ike's eyes flashed with anger, even as he shook his head and stared down at his stolen saddle, trying to work it all out. "Ma was no murderer. No, she's not dead. Nobody could outwit her. You're lying."

Polly used the distraction to raise her own pistol from her apron. When Ike looked up at last, it was straight into her barrel. "Drop your weapon now, Ike. Or I will shoot you dead on the spot, and don't even think of trying to outdraw me. You're not quick enough anymore."

Ike looked up to see the barrel of Polly's gun trained on him. She nodded at him, unflinching. "Tell me the truth, Ike. What happened to my baby?"

Ike pleaded with her, hands raised. "I swear to God, Polly. Ma was no murderer."

"Liar!" she hissed.

Suddenly, it seemed to dawn on Ike. "Is that...is that what this is all about?" Seeing an opportunity, he pounced. "Your baby's still alive."

Polly's face flooded with relief as she began to lower the pistol, momentarily letting down her guard, but Ike being Ike, he couldn't just leave it at that. He practically drooled, egging her on. "You enjoyed it, didn't you? You enjoyed what I did to you. You used to beg for more. All you women, you're all just whores."

Polly raised the pistol again and felt it tremble in her hands. "Shut up, Ike!" she said, but he just stared back, pig-eyed, thick-lipped, and jittery.

He chuckled then, taunting, "Go on, Polly, fire that pistol. You look pretty handy with it. Bet you been practicing, night and day, waiting for this moment. Well, go on then! Fire away!"

Now the gun trembled in Polly's hand, Ike gloating all the while. At last he spat at her feet and raised his own pistol. "I knew you didn't have the salt," he said, raising and pointing it at her chest. "Shooting a human's a lot tougher than firing at a target, ain't it, pretty Polly—"

Blam! The sound of the gunshot tore like thunder through the air, and Ike blew off his saddle, landing feet away in the dirt, half of his left shoulder ripped away, blood forming a crimson pool and oozing into the ground. Dazed, Polly looked at her own pistol. The air was sharp with the scent of gunpowder and blood, but her weapon was cold. She'd never pulled the trigger.

Ike's horse immediately bolted as Polly slipped from Blue, who skittered away at a nervous gallop. Polly fell to Ike even as the brush rustled, and footsteps followed. "Stay where you are, ma'am!" commanded the sheriff, and Polly let the pistol slip from her hands into the high grass.

Polly turned to Ike as the men approached, and she found him sputtering. "Y-you couldn't shoot," he choked, blood oozing from his thick lips. "I knew you couldn't. That's cuz you're better'n me, I suppose…"

"Quiet, Ike," she said, pressing the edge of her apron against his wound to try to stop the bleeding.

"Get away from him, miss!" ordered the sheriff as he drew nearer.

Ike's eyes rolled back in his head, and then he returned to focus his gaze on her. "Your baby ain't dead, Polly," he gasped, wincing at the pain. "Mama and I…we sold that little gal."

The sheriff arrived, and then his deputies helped her to her feet. She could still smell the gun smoke from his twelve-gauge shotgun even as he tried to haul her away.

"No!" she spat, clinging to hold on to Ike's blood-splattered shirt. "Tell me who, Ike? To who?"

Ike looked up at the sheriff and then turned his head and spat blood on his shoe. "Some rich family in town, Polly. Their baby had just died, so…switcheroo, see? That's who Mama buried, Polly, not you'rn…"

Ike seized, body growing rigid as the sheriff fell to his knees. "Don't you die on me, killer!" the sheriff ordered as his deputies pulled Polly away. "Don't you die on me before Portland gets to see you hang!"

But it was too late; Ike was gone. What she'd worked so hard for, what she'd wanted so much to do, in the end, had been beyond her. Lafayette had said an act of violence would change her forever. That was what she'd remembered as her finger had frozen on the trigger; those were the words she'd heard, not Ike's last hateful message.

Lafayette had never said what not committing an act of violence would do. But now she knew. Had she shot down Ike, put a bullet right between his eyes like she'd wanted, he'd never have confessed. He would have gone to his pauper's grave with the knowledge that he and Ada had sold little Bonney so long ago. Had he been gloating when he confessed? Somehow, staring down at the satisfied smile covering his bloody, lifeless lips, Polly didn't think so.

Chapter 63

Polly guided Blue to the edge of town. She would have ridden her trusty steed as far and as fast as she could go, but Missy was at her side and, from the way things were looking, it might be the last time the two ever spoke.

They walked quietly past the Portland Hotel, where a black wreath hung on the front door in honor of the fallen deputy. Polly's eyes misted to think of how that young man had lost his life just to ensure that Ike had a little peace of mind.

And look how far that got him. "So what now?" Missy asked as they began approaching the sheriff and his men.

"Madam gave me a little severance for my troubles," Polly admitted, patting her saddlebag. "And I've been saving ever since I started at the Emporium, so…I should be OK for a while."

Missy watched her feet as they walked, slowing down to give them time to talk before the sheriff took over. "But…where will you go?"

Polly looked up at her friend and smiled, sadly, kindly. "Missy, for the first time in I don't know how long, I have no idea." Blue stopped, as if he knew Polly had more to say. Her eyes welled up as she admitted, "I've spent so long chasing Ike, I never stopped to think about what might come after…"

She looked past Blue to the men waiting at the edge of town, rifles slung casually over their shoulder, eager to make sure Polly kept her promise to leave by nightfall.

"Now that it's here," she said, "I have no idea what I'll do with my life."

"But your studies, Polly, that anatomy book you've been studying when you think nobody's looking. What about that?"

Polly shrugged. "Not sure if I can stand the sight of any more blood, Missy."

Missy snorted humorlessly, not sure if her friend was joking or serious. Polly hitched up her skirt and nodded toward the sheriff. "I best be going before they change their mind and lock me up for obstruction of justice."

Missy nodded. "I'll miss you, Polly O'Neal."

The two fell into a sloppy hug, both crying and sniffling, until Polly broke it off first, shoving Missy away to get a better look at her. "I know one thing I won't be doing," she said to her friend, staring her right in the eye. "I won't be wasting any more of my time on grudges or revenge."

Missy blinked twice before wiping her eyes, not sure what her friend meant. Before she turned and walked Blue to the edge of town, Polly said, "Go see your father, Missy. Talk to the man. I don't know what he did to you, Missy. But give him a chance. I can tell he's a good man. Don't leave it too late to make your peace with him while you still have the chance. I know I'd give anything to say one last thing to my pa."

Missy nodded as Polly led Blue away. The two walked for a few minutes, and when Polly turned, Missy was nowhere to be found. Polly smiled sadly; it was probably better that way.

The sheriff was waiting, sitting high atop his horse, the butt of his rifle resting against his swollen belly. "Evening, ma'am," he said sarcastically. "Thanks for not making us come and get you."

Polly nodded, quickly hopping into Blue's old, familiar saddle. "I hope you're a man of your word, Sheriff."

He nodded, as if offended. "I said if you left town and never came back, we'd forget everything that happened between you and Ike."

Polly clucked a tongue dryly. "I wish I could do that, sir."

The man looked uncomfortable, not quite understanding. "Well, it wasn't you who shot him, after all," he insisted. "I'd rather the saga of Ike O'Neal end with you leaving town before sunup than sticking around raising eyebrows at Madam Jasmine's Goodtime Emporium, if'n you know what I mean?"

"Yes, sir," she said. "And…thank you."

The sheriff nodded, satisfied, tipping his greasy leather hat as she and Blue trotted by. She guided him slowly up the same hill she and Ike had traveled not so long before, until they reached the plateau that would lead them out of town. When she looked back, the sheriff and his men were already gone, heading back to the jailhouse, torches flickering in the dim light before dawn.

Chapter 64

The saloon was rustic and bare as Blue came upon it early the next morning, and Polly saw Lafayette leaning against the hitching post, a bouquet of cheap flowers in his hand.

She didn't know whether to laugh or cry, so she did both.

"I heard they were running you out of town on a rail," Lafayette said as she hitched Blue to the post. "I figured this might be your first stop."

"Little early for a drink, don't you think?" Polly joked, though her heart was not quite in it.

He nodded toward the hotel next door, where the smell of fresh coffee beckoned. "Thought you might be ready for a little breakfast before your trip."

"That I am," she said, following him inside. He looked prim and proper, as if he'd spent the night there. Her suspicions were confirmed when a pretty waitress appeared, blushing to see him again.

"What'll it be, Professor?" the young girl asked, hardly paying Polly any mind.

"Two continentals, if you please," he ordered for her.

Before the girl could leave, Polly cleared her throat. "Excuse me, ma'am," said Polly. "But I'd like steak and eggs, if you please, with a side of hash and breakfast potatoes and a stack of toast with fresh jam."

The waitress looked her up and down. "You expecting company?" she joked but mostly to Lafayette. Polly ignored her and turned to Lafayette.

"I guess you've come to gloat," she said, shaking her head.

Lafayette looked offended, choosing not to speak until the waitress had placed down their coffee and a basket of hard rolls with fresh butter. Polly tucked into them something awful, having not eaten since...well, she couldn't remember when she last ate.

"I've come to see what your future might hold," Lafayette said, sipping his coffee and trying not to marvel at the size of Polly's appetite.

"What future?" she asked, washing the rolls down with coffee.

Lafayette crossed his legs and slid his hat onto the top knee. "Exactly."

She looked at him uncertainly. "You mean...you're not mad at me?"

He smiled. "Whatever for. From what I can tell, you chose forgiveness over violence. Is what I heard wrong?"

"Not exactly," she hemmed, diving into the plate of steak and eggs as soon as the waitress set it down. "By that I mean," she elaborated in between bites, "I set out to do violence for the sake of revenge. When I was about to kill Ike, I realized it was an imperfect moment. I really was facing my dark side when I realized I had to let it go...to refuse...refuse to allow it to define the rest of my life. It was the secret for me to find my freedom. I cannot forgive Ike for what he has done, but I refuse to live the rest of my life without happiness."

He shrugged. "As I said, forgiveness over violence, same difference."

"Is it?" she asked, cryptically. She rolled her eyes, the food doing its work. "Please, Lafayette, this is no time for riddles."

He nodded, hands up apologetically. "You're too right, Polly. You forgave yourself, you saw your mistakes, your dark side, but you did not identify with your superiority or your inferiority."

She nodded. "All I can ask now, Lafayette, is your forgiveness."

"Oh, not mine," he scolded playfully over his coffee cup. "Yours, that's the only secret to a bright future."

Chapter 65

Polly slid the shades up and turned the "Closed" sign to "Open" in the front window of her humble midwifery clinic. It wasn't much more than two rooms separated by a thin curtain—one for waiting and one for delivering—but it was hers, bought and paid for with her own money, and it was everything to her.

Well, almost everything.

She was arranging fresh flowers in the parlor window when the door opened, a little cowbell ringing above. Polly looked up with a smile, blinking twice to make sure what she was seeing was real.

There, in the doorway, stood a well-dressed woman with a familiar smile. Clinging to her left hand was a young girl, dressed as if she were going to church.

"Missy?"

Missy squealed and hugged her, tightly, the moisture of tears covering both their cheeks. "How have you been?" Polly asked. "How did you find me?"

Missy waved her free hand. "It wasn't hard, girl. You're only Oregon's best, most popular, and most famous midwife. So I thought I'd pay you a visit and see how you've been."

"It took you six years to get from Portland to Bonney's Canyon?"

"Mommy?" the little girl interrupted the women's laughter.

Missy gushed, "Well, I've been busy." She glanced down at the small girl, quietly holding her hand and blinking up at Polly with blue eyes and blond hair like her mother's. "Polly, meet my daughter, Estelle."

"Hi, Estelle!" Polly exclaimed.

Estelle blushed and hid behind her mother's coattails. Polly pulled a lollipop from her apron pocket and lured her out for a better look.

"She's gorgeous," she said as the little girl smiled, took the candy, and voraciously unwrapped it. "Like a miniature version of her mother!"

Missy nodded, eyes full of pride for the gorgeous three-year-old girl with her eyes and pert nose.

"Let me look at you," Missy said, nothing but admiration and fond remembrance in her eyes. "You haven't aged a bit."

Polly chuckled, sitting across from Missy in the cozy reception area. "I wouldn't go that far," she said coyly.

The two women excitedly began reminiscing and catching up at the same time. It seemed to Polly that hardly any time had passed at all, so familiar was their chatter as little Estelle leaned against her mother's lap, silently napping now, one thumb stuck squarely in her mouth.

Polly's heart filled with pride to see Missy happy, married, a mother at last. They had come full circle, both women. Now both were happy, healthy, and together again.

And to think, once upon a time, facing down Ike's gun in the dead of night atop that Portland hill, Polly had thought she'd never see Missy again.

The little girl played in the small yard as the two women moved to the porch to catch the morning sun. Polly watched her, eyes growing misty with a flood of bittersweet emotions.

"What's wrong, darlin'?" Missy asked, patting Polly's hand.

Polly looked at her, no longer hiding her tears. "I've been keeping something from you," she confessed. "All these years."

"What is it, love?"

Polly looked at her old friend, gripping her hand tightly. "You know I grew up here, right, Missy?" Missy admired the fine front lawn and the stirrings of the town beyond. She nodded.

"When I came back for good and set up shop here, I received an unlikely visitor one day: the sheriff. He told me that my father hadn't killed himself after all." Missy's face registered the shock Polly herself had felt upon hearing the news.

"Then who?" she asked. "How?"

"He'd been murdered by a man here in town, George Patterson. When Ike and Ada sold my baby to the Pattersons, apparently, my father tried to stop them. He'd tried reason, at first, but Mr. Patterson was the richest man in town and not one to take 'no' for an answer. He shot my father and took the baby anyway. By the time the authorities put two and two together, the Pattersons had hopped a boat headed for China."

"China?" Missy gasped. "But it's so far away!"

Polly nodded ruefully. "I suppose that was the point."

"And they took your baby with them?"

"Afraid so. Now I'll never know where she is or what happened to her."

Missy's eyes grew suspicious. "That's not all you'll never know, Polly."

"How do you mean?"

"I see that look in your eyes, girl," Missy explained. "It's the same look you had in your eyes whenever I mentioned Ike—"

"Mommy!" cried the little girl, interrupting the two old friends. "I scraped my knee!"

Polly chuckled to relieve the tension. "Lucky I've got a medicine bag right in the front room!"

She patched up little Estelle and, by the time she was licking on a fresh lollipop and staring at her new bandage, Missy said it was time to go.

"I wish you could stay longer." Polly sighed as the two women hugged.

Missy agreed, and so did Estelle. "You have the best lollipops!" she answered when Polly asked her why.

Watching them leave for the trip back to Portland, Polly felt a heavy sadness fall over her heart.

On the way home from work that day, Missy's new address folded and carefully slid into her apron pocket, Polly paused to admire the sunset over Bonney's Canyon.

A man, handsome and alone, stood next to a gnarled old tree, tracing a heart carved there long ago.

"Come here often, sir?" she asked coyly as Lafayette, face bathed in the waning sun, broke into a smile to see her. Their embrace was long, tender, and meaningful.

Then he took her hand to help her trace the shape carved into the tree's ancient trunk. "See?" he asked gently, standing behind her, warm and solid as always. "The heart you carved in the tree trunk, it's still here."

"And so am I," she said, turning to kiss him once more.

"Thank God!" he gasped, clutching her hand for the short walk home. "I waited for you long enough..."

Polly sighed contentedly, but regret lingered like a cloud over her perfect day. Ever since confiding to Missy earlier that day, she hadn't been able to get the thought of little Bonney or her father's murderer out of her head. Even now, as she and Lafayette walked through the pastoral sunset, her mind was racing with the familiar thought of revenge...

Epilogue

Siobhan closed the last page of Polly's journal and doubled over, racked with tears. She couldn't imagine what Polly had gone through, and at such a young age. And she marveled at the poor girl's strength in not killing Ike, after she had suffered such pains and set her sights on revenge for so long.

But Siobhan's tears were not just for little Polly, but herself as well. She stood, drying her eyes, and crossed the room to look into the vanity mirror. It was early afternoon, and in the pure orange light that sifted through the bedroom window, her eyes looked dark and drawn. She pulled her hair back and reached for a sweater, sliding her arms into it as she slipped down the stairs.

Her father's room was in the back wing, his nurse resting peacefully on a leather wing chair in the foyer just outside. She looked up to see Siobhan's shadow filling the doorway and smiled softly.

"He's resting," she said, marking a page in her thick romance novel before sliding it onto her lap.

"Could I...could I see him?"

The nurse narrowed her eyes and smirked. "Promise no fireworks this time?"

Siobhan snorted, verging on tears again. She merely nodded and walked by the nurse. As she did, she put out a comforting hand, gripping the nurse's shoulder in silent appreciation for all she put up with for the old man.

She walked in, hating the smell of old that filled the room—old air, old man, old pill bottles, old bed linens. The shades were up, and the room was spacious and bright with the afternoon sun, her father was sitting in his chair, gazing out at his ranch.

He must have heard her approaching from behind.

"All this land..." he croaked, reaching down to spin his wheelchair around to face her. "And I can't even make it to the mailbox. How's that for irony?"

She shrugged. "There's no shame in getting old, Dad."

He looked up at her, scowling. "Spoken like a young person."

She ignored the vitriol in his voice. "I didn't come here to talk about your legs, old man. I came here to forgive you."

"Forgive me?" he snapped. "For what? Providing you with a roof over your head? Food in your belly? Clothes on your back?"

She was tempted to sink onto his bed but knew with the heaviness in her limbs she might never get up.

Instead, she leaned her hip against the bed and sighed. "I appreciate all that, Dad. But we're not animals. Sometimes a daughter needs more than the clothes on her back to survive. There were times...times when I needed your love, not just your allowance."

He sniffled, rolling his shoulders. "Damn kids today, always want everyone to be so emotional. You think my old man ever gave me the time of day? Think he ever did anything better than put a roof over my head and clothes on my back?"

She shrugged. "Isn't it our job as parents to do better for our children?"

His eyes got big. "How the hell would you know?"

The words stung—and stung deep. She stiffened but kept her resolve. If Polly could forgive Ike everything that had passed between them, Siobhan felt she could forgive her father for being a heartless thug. Didn't mean they'd be having breakfast together every morning from now on, but perhaps in his last remaining months, or weeks, or days, she could at least give him peace of mind.

"I love you, Dad," she said through gritted teeth. "And not just because I have to. For what you did and didn't do, I forgive you. And I hope, whatever you think I did or didn't do, you could forgive me as well."

"Damn daughters," he railed at her back, voice tight with emotion. "Always so emotional. I don't need your forgiveness any more than you need mine. We're grown, ain't we? Let the past be the past…"

His voice was stern, like his withered face. Before opening the door, she turned once to stare back at him.

"That's what I'm trying to do," she said, leaving him there to his thoughts.

Siobhan heard the rustling of the nurse's paperback on the arm of the couch but didn't look back to engage. Instead, she clutched her sweater tighter to her chest and walked out through the front door.

The air was cool, but not chill. Her comfortable flats carried her away from the ranch, and on and on until she looked up, realizing she was back in Bonney's Canyon. Her heart ached to stare at the gnarled old tree, and she ran her fingertips along the trunk of the big Oregon Oak, tracing the faded heart carved there so long ago.

Weariness overtook Siobhan as she slid down against the tree trunk. It felt warm and familiar against her back, the land soft and gentle beneath her legs. She stared at the canyon, dyed pink by the dusk and laced with shadows as the sunlight waned.

A feeling of calm fell over her, warm but unfamiliar. She'd been living out of a suitcase for weeks, wondering where she might land, where her next journey would take her, but she knew she had already found her destination.

Her father would be gone soon, the ranch passed on to her. She had been thinking of selling it, taking the money, and moving as far away as possible. But she knew there was nowhere to run. This was home, for better or worse.

The ranch was her father's legacy to her, and she thought she could be a good steward. She would stay and be with her father to the end. She would assure him that she would stay and run the ranch in his stead. Maybe that was what he wanted so badly. Maybe that would convince him to forgive her, or possibly even…like…her. Either way, she would do what she had to do and make a life for herself.

Images of Mitch and her dancing in the moonlight appeared in her mind's eye. Lost feelings rushed through her body…happy, romantic, and intimate. Tears welted up quickly as she realized that she had passed through the dark barriers of grief and guilt to find love and forgiveness on the other side. This quickly transformed into a warm anticipation to see Mitch again with open arms.

The thought pleased her, and she placed her hands in the rough, sandy earth, pulling herself up. Something soft and unfamiliar pressed her left palm, not a leaf or a vine but something man-made, a string or some yarn. She leaned over to look closer and saw a faded piece of twine, knotted at the end, lingering among the dead leaves at the base of the tree trunk.

She tugged it gently to see if it was attached to anything. It was. Tugging harder, she felt the dirt give way, revealing more of the string as it pulled the object to the surface. She moved closer now, on all fours, like a child digging for buried treasure.

She yanked the string harder, careful not to let it break, watching more dirt give way as she dug with her fingertips and free hand until enough earth had been displaced that what was buried began to emerge.

The string was wound around an ancient red handkerchief. Siobhan cleared the earth around it, lifting it gently out of the shallow hole and placing it carefully on the ground beside her. The handkerchief was badly faded, and wiping the earth aside, she opened it with care.

Inside the silken fabric were three thin volumes, leather-bound. Her heart raced as she opened the first one to see Polly's handwriting! She clutched them to her chest, relieved to be able to read more of her old friend's adventures.

She closed the journal, noticing it had a strange symbol on the front. Looking more closely, she saw that the other two leather-bound volumes did as well.

She stood, abruptly, clinging to the journals for dear life as she raced back to the ranch. The sun was setting, the sky orange at the horizon, her shadow long and stretched before her.

About the Author

My first memory of Great-Grandma Polly was when my father took me to see her. He would always bring her something from the farm, and this day, he brought her some butter.

When the door to the old house on Ninth Street opened, it revealed a small, frail-looking lady sitting on a daybed in the living room. She was unwinding her hair, which she washed every month. This event had me in awe; her hair rolled off the bed, down the floor, and almost reached the door before the final strand of gray stretched out as if it were a morning yawn.

Her age faded quickly as she smiled upon us and spoke optimistically and with gentleness unlike I have ever heard.

Great-Grandfather Lafayette was 101 years old at the time and was soon to pass peacefully away. It was my father at his bedside when he passed away, and he listened to his fading heart until it no longer pulsed with life. He told me their story many times with tears in his eyes. Lafayette was his hero.

Great-Grandma Polly was to live on until she turned one hundred. Up to the time she passed away, she was always giving to the poor, either with food (butter from my father, which was quickly passed along to other needy people), teaching Sunday school, or sitting with those who could not care for themselves.

The many stories about Great-Grandma Polly were spun so many times that myth became fact and facts disappeared in myth. My mother was quite fond of Polly, and she always wished she would have written down the many stories that Polly shared with her.

Her daughter Maggie (Maggie "Bonney" McClure) was constantly with her mother during the time of elder years and was with her up to the time of her death. Maggie was never the same after Polly's death. My mother took care of Maggie until her death at ninety-eight.

In the brief time I remember Great-Grandma, she gave me a sense of compassion and dedication rarely ever seen today.

This picture was taken around 1950. It is the only photo I have of Polly. My  sister and I held Great-Grandma in high respect. I remember that I was concerned that I might be too heavy for her to pick me up, and she quickly said, "You are easy to pick up...easier than putting a saddle on Ol' Blue, besides, if you quit squirming so much, I will tell you a story how Ol' Blue saved Pa's life in the snowstorm of ninety-eight." I could hardly wait to hear the story.

All other characters in this book are fictional but display many family elements. Siobhan is one such character. The name is derived from the Anglo-Norman "Jehanne," which was introduced to Ireland in the Middle Ages and is pronounced as "Shi-vaun." She is a combination of all of us.

Polly and Lafayette had three children, the only boy was named Lafayette Irl Davis (my grandfather). My father was named Irl, as was I. The story about our name came from Great-Grandma Polly, who decided that there should be "Irish" in our remembrance of the family. "I-R-L" is the abbreviation for Ireland, and she wanted everyone to remember her father, Patrick O'Neal.

I.M. Davis is the fifth generation on the family farm in north-central Oregon. After graduating from college, he traveled extensively throughout the world. Between 1984 and 2005, he created and managed his manufacturing company in China and distributed products in over seventeen different countries. In 2005, he sold his companies and he and his wife, Laila, relocated to the family farm. They have integrated conservation practices throughout the ranch and are dedicated to good stewardship. The Bonney Canyon still holds the same charm and mystery as it did when he was a child.